George Müller

A Narrative of some of the Lord's Dealings with George Müller

Part 3

George Müller

A Narrative of some of the Lord's Dealings with George Müller
Part 3

ISBN/EAN: 9783337353117

Printed in Europe, USA, Canada, Australia, Japan

Cover: Foto ©Andreas Hilbeck / pixelio.de

More available books at **www.hansebooks.com**

A NARRATIVE OF SOME

OF THE LORD'S DEALINGS WITH GEORGE MÜLLER

WRITTEN BY HIMSELF

THIRD PART

J. NISBET & CO., BERNERS STREET, LONDON.

PREFACE

TO THE

FIRST EDITION OF THE THIRD PART.

THE reasons which induced me to publish this third part of the Lords dealings with me are the same which led me to the publication of the second part, and which are stated in the preface to the first edition of the second part. In addition to those reasons it appeared to me desirable to give some account of my recent labours in Germany, and also to write on a few other points, which I considered of great importance to be made known.

GEORGE MÜLLER.

21, Paul Street, Kingsdown,

Bristol, June 18, 1845.

NARRATIVE,

&c. &c.

THIRD PART.

IN the deep consciousness of my entire natural inability for going through the work, which is before me, to the profit of the reader and to the glory of God, I am nevertheless of good cheer in beginning this service; for the Lord has enabled me often to bow my knees before Him, to seek His help respecting it; and I am now expecting His help. He delights in making His strength perfect in our weakness, and therefore will I also, though so weak, look for His strength. And if through this my feeble effort, to show forth the praises of the Lord, good be done (of which I have the fullest assurance, on account of the abundance of supplication which for many months past has been found in my spirit in reference to this service,) I do desire from my inmost soul to ascribe all the honour and glory to the Lord.

I purpose in writing this third part of my Narrative to adopt the same mode which I employed in the two former parts, namely that of giving extracts from my journal, and accompanying them with such remarks as it may be desirable to make for the profit of the reader. The second part carries on the Narrative up to the end of the year 1840, so far as it regards my own personal affairs; but only to Dec. 9, 1840, so far as it regards the Orphan-Houses, and other objects of the Scriptural Knowledge Institution, as on that day the accounts were closed. From this period, then, the Narrative is continued.

Dec. 10, 1840. When the accounts were closed last evening, the balance in hand was 15l. 0s. 6 1/4d., but as nearly 15l. of this sum had been put by for the rent of the Orphan-Houses, the sum really in hand for use was only 4s. 6 1/4d.

With this little sum we commenced the sixth year of this part of the work, while there are daily, as usual, more than a hundred persons to be provided for.

— A little boy brought half-a-crown to the Boys-Orphan-House, this morning, which is the first gift in this sixth year. Thus we had altogether 7s. 0 1/4d. for this day, which was enough to pay for the milk in the three houses, and to buy some bread in one of them. We have never before been so poor at the commencement of the year.

Dec. 11. Only 2s. 6d. more had come in since last evening. There was sufficient for dinner in the Girls and Infant-Orphan-Houses, but scarcely enough in the Boys-Orphan-House. This half-crown, therefore, supplied the remainder of the dinner in the Boys-Orphan-House. But now there was no money to take in milk, in any of the houses, for tea, or to buy any bread. However the Lord helped us through this day also. About one oclock some trinkets, which had been sent a few days since, were disposed of for 12s., by which the usual quantity of milk, and a little bread could be taken in. [I observe here that there is generally bread for two or three days in the houses, the children eating the bread on the third day after it is baked. When, therefore, we are unable to take in the usual quantity, for want of means, we procure stale bread afterwards.]

Dec. 12. Only 4s. had come in to meet this days necessities. Thus we should not have had sufficient means to provide for the dinner in the Girls-Orphan-House, had not 6s. come in this morning, just in time to help us through the difficulty. Still we had no means to buy bread, and a few other little things which were needed. In addition to all this it was Saturday, and therefore provisions for two days needed to be procured. About four oclock this afternoon, one of the sisters in the Orphan-Houses, to whom I had some days since sent a little money for her own personal necessities, gave 1l. Thus we were able to purchase sufficient provisions to last till breakfast on Monday morning. These last days have been very trying. The poverty has been greater than ever; the Lord, however, has not confounded us, but has, strengthened our faith, and always given us necessaries.

The School-Funds are also now again very low. There was only so much money in hand, as that two of the teachers, really in need, could be paid today. Truly, my dear fellow-labourers in the schools need to trust the Lord for their temporal supplies! [I notice here, that though the brethren and sisters have a certain remuneration, yet it is understood that, if the Lord should not be pleased to send in the means at the time when their salary is due, I am not considered their debtor. Should the Lord be pleased to send in means afterwards, the remainder of the salary is paid up, and also additional assistance is given in time of sickness or more than usual need, as the Lord may be pleased to grant the means. A brother or sister, in connection with this work, not looking for themselves to the Lord, would be truly uncomfortable; for the position of all of us is of such a character, that it brings heavy trials of faith, in addition to the many precious seasons of joy on account of answers to prayer.]

Dec. 13. Lords day. This morning I received 2l. 10s. Thus, before the last provisions are actually consumed in the Orphan-Houses, I have been able to give fresh supplies.

Dec. 14. Though 2l. 10s. had come in yesterday, there was still not sufficient this morning to buy coals in the Boys and Girls-Orphan-Houses. But the Lord kindly supplied us with means for that also; for there were given today six silver tea spoons, and a pair of silver sugar tongs. I received also 1l.

10s. which yesterday had been anonymously given for rent. Thus the Lord, in this particular also, again begins the year with blessings. [As during the two previous years 1l. 10s. a week was anonymously given to pay for the rent of the three Orphan-Houses, so during the whole of this year also, from Dec. 10, 1840, to Dec. 10, 1841, the donor continued the same contribution.] This evening was the first of our public meetings, at which I gave the account of the Lords dealings with us in regard to this work, during the last year. It was a good season. I felt much assisted by the Lord, and was, through grace, very happy, so that none of those who were present can have read in my countenance that I have nothing at all in hand towards the supply of the necessities of tomorrow. After the meeting this evening 2 1/2d. was left anonymously at my house.

Dec. 15. The day commenced with 2 1/2d. in hand. My eyes were directed to the living God. I was looking out for help. The greatness of our need led me to expect it. About eleven oclock I received from Barnstaple a 5l. note and half-a-sovereign. Thus the Lord in His faithful love delivered us. Half an hour afterwards I had the report from the Orphan-Houses about the state of things today, which will show how seasonably the money from Barnstaple came. Brother R. B., master at the Boys-Orphan~ House, wrote that last evening a sister gave 5s. and a cloak, but that there never was less bread in the Orphan-Houses at any time than this morning, and that both in the Boys and Infant-Orphan-Houses all bread had been, cut up for use. —We are now waiting on the Lord for means to enable us to have the Report printed. Till He provides, we will, by His help, do nothing in this matter. Though it seems to us important that the account of the Lords dealings with us in the work should be made known to the saints generally; yea, though this is the primary object of the work; nevertheless it appears to us a small matter for our kind and loving Father, who withholds nothing from His children that is really good for them, to give us the sum which we need for this purpose whenever His time shall have come. We do desire grace even in this thing to acknowledge Him; for His time may not yet have come for us to have the sweet privilege of sending forth far and wide the account of His goodness to us during the past year.

Dec. 16. To-night I received with Ecclesiastes ix. 10, 1l. 10s., and 12s. from another individual; also a Spanish dollar was sent. Thus we have something for the necessities of tomorrow.

Dec. 17. Today came in 3s., and from Bath 4l. 6s. 8d.; also 2l., the produce of the sale of ladies baskets.

Dec. 19. Only 11s. 2d. has come in since the day before yesterday. As I had to pay out today 6l. 10s., it being Saturday, we have now again only 5s. 9d. left, which is just enough to meet the expense of a parcel, the arrival of which has been announced. Thus we still have no means for printing the Report, The Lords time seems not yet to have come.

This afternoon came in from Exmouth 1l. 10s. 5d. for the other objects, so that, with what there was in hand, the teachers of the Day-Schools who were in need could be supplied.

Dec. 20. The Lord has again sent in rich supplies. He remembered that there was nothing in hand for the Orphans, and that we, who care for them, desire, through grace, not to be anxiously concerned about the morrow. There came in today altogether 6l. 17s.

Dec. 25. This morning there was 5l. given to me by a brother, to be used as most needed. As there is a little left for the Orphans, but about 5l. needed, tomorrow, for the schools, and there are only a few shillings in hand, I took this money for these funds.

Jan. 1, 1841. Since Dec. 20 has come in not only as much as was needed, but more. Of the donations which were given, I only notice: A sister brought the produce of her silver spoons, which she had sold, having had it laid on her heart to do so through the last public meetings. During this week we have daily met for prayer, for the especial purpose of asking the Lord to give us the means of having the last years Report printed. It is three weeks since it might have been sent to the press. We felt this now to be a matter of especial importance, as, if the Report were not soon printed, it would be known that it arose from want of means. By the donations which came in during these last days for the Orphans, and by 10l. which was given today for the other funds, we have the means of defraying the expenses of about two-thirds of the printing, and therefore a part of the manuscript was sent off, trusting that the Lord would be pleased to send in more means before two sheets are printed off; but if not, we should then stop till we have more. — Evening. There came in still further 5l.; and also 10s., and 3s.

Jan. 2. Today 18s. came in, and the following articles were sent anonymously to the Girls-Orphan-House: A smelling bottle, a metal chain and cross, a silver pencil case, a mother-of-pearl ring, a pebble, a necklace clasp, 2 pairs of studs, and 6 chimney ornaments. There were also sent anonymously, this evening, 2 pairs of skates. — There was needed today 1l. 1s. 6d. more than there was in hand, to pay the salaries of the teachers in the Day-Schools. About noon a sister brought three small donations, amounting to 9s.; and a sovereign came by post. Thus our need has been supplied.

Jan. 3. This morning a brooch was given to me, set with a brilliant and 10 small emeralds. The stones are to be sold for the benefit of the Orphans, and the gold is to be returned. I received also the following sums: From a sister in Bristol, 5l.; from the East Indies 2l.; from Devonshire 2l. 10s. and a silver vinaigrette; anonymously put into the boxes at Bethesda 2s., ditto by I. L. 3s. 6d., ditto for rent 1l. 10s.; and by sale of articles 1s. 6d. Thus the Lord has sent in today 11l. 7s., in answer to our united prayer during the last week.

Jan. 4. Today the following trinkets were given, to be disposed of for the benefit of the Orphans, or on behalf of the other objects. [They were taken for the latter, there being only about 7s. in hand.] Two chains and crosses of soap beads, an amber necklace, a bead necklace, a gold Maltese cross and chain, a Brazilian gold chain, a pearl hair brooch, a pearl cross, a mother-of-pearl buckle, 2 rings, a necklace snap, a moonstone brooch, a brooch of Ceylon stones, a pair of bracelet snaps, a gold brooch, a gilt vinaigrette, a pair of buckles, and a box. [The money which was obtained for the greater part of these trinkets, supplied our need on Saturday, January 9th.]

Jan. 11. Monday. During the last week the Lord not only supplied us richly with all we needed for the Orphans, but enabled us to put by several pounds towards printing the Report. On Saturday evening there was only 3s. 6d. left. On this account I was looking out for answers to my prayers for means, and the Lord did not disappoint me. There came in altogether yesterday 9l. 16s. 4d. We have now enough even for the last part of the Report. Thus the Lord has been pleased to answer our prayers in this respect also. This afternoon when there was again only 2s. 6d. in hand, came in by sale of articles 3l. 9s. 6d., and by a donation 5l.

Jan. 12. Today I have received a letter from a brother, in which he empowers me to draw upon his bankers, during this year to the amount of 1000l., for any brethren who have it in their hearts to give themselves to missionary Service in the East Indies, and whom I shall consider called for this service, as far as I am able to judge. [This power lasted only for that year; but no brethren who seemed to be suitable offered themselves for this service]

Jan. 13. This evening I was called to the house of a brother and sister who are in the deepest distress. The brother had become surety for the debts of his son, not in the least expecting that he ever should be called upon for the payment of them; but as his son has not discharged his debts, the father has been called upon to do so; and except the money is paid within a few days, he will be imprisoned.

How precious it is, even for this life, to act according to the word of God! This perfect revelation of His mind gives us directions for every thing, even the most minute affairs of this life. It commands us, "Be thou not one of them that strike hands, or of them that are sureties for debts." Prov. xxii. 26. The way in which Satan ensnares persons, to bring them into the net, and to bring trouble upon them by becoming sureties, is, that he seeks to represent the matter as if there were no danger connected with that particular case, and that one might be sure one should never be called upon to pay the money; but the Lord, the faithful Friend, tells us in His own word that the only way in such a matter "to be sure" is "to hate suretiship." Prov. xi. 15. The following points seem to me of solemn moment for consideration, if I were called upon to become surety for

10

another: 1. What obliges the person who wishes me to become surety for him, to need a surety? Is it really a good cause in which I am called upon to become surety? I do not remember ever to have met with a case in which in a plain, and godly, and in all respects Scriptural matter such a thing occurred. There was generally some sin or other connected with it. 2. If I become surety, notwithstanding what the Lord has said to me in His word, am I in such a position that no one will be injured by my being called upon to fulfill the engagements of the person for whom I am going to be surety? In most instances this alone ought to keep one from it. 3. If still I become surety, the amount of money, for which I become responsible, must be so in my power, that I am able to produce it whenever it is called for, in order that the name of the Lord may not be dishonoured. 4. But if there be the possibility of having to fulfill the engagements of the person in whose stead I have to stand, is it the will of the Lord, that I should spend my means in that way? Is it not rather His will that my means should be spent in another way? 5. How can I get over the plain word of the Lord, which is to the contrary, even if the first four points could be satisfactorily settled?

This morning (Jan. 13) I had again not one penny in hand for the Orphans, though there was enough for today at the Orphan-Houses, as I had sent yesterday sufficient for two days. The little stock being exhausted, I had been led to the Lord in prayer for fresh supplies, when soon afterwards a brother called on me, who stated, that, in considering the necessities of the poor, on account of the cold season, the Orphans had likewise been brought to his mind, and that he had brought me 15l. for them. This afternoon came in still further 1l. from two sisters, as a thank-offering for many mercies during the past year. Likewise 10l. "From a friend in Christ for the Orphans-House." Further: by sale of

11

articles 2l. 4s. 6d., by knitting 1l. 4s., by Reports 9d., and by four donations 13s. Thus the Lord has been pleased to send in this day altogether 30l. 2s. 3d., whilst, when the day commenced, I had nothing at all in hand.

Jan. 23. This day commenced without any thing in hand. In addition to this it was Saturday. About nine oclock Q. Q. called to see me, but, as I was in prayer with my family, she did not stay. About half an hour afterwards she called a second time, gave 5l. for the Orphans, and said, "I bring this because it is Saturday, and it may be needed." This sister was not deterred by not seeing me the first time, because our Father knew we had need of this money. There was likewise 5s. given me this afternoon, and when the sister gave it she said, "I bring this today, because it is Saturday."

Jan. 25. 2l. 19s. 10d. came in yesterday and this morning. When the necessities of the day had been supplied, and there was only 12s. 10d. left, I received a parcel from an unknown donor. It contained 1 lb. and 6 oz. of worsted and 4 sovereigns, with the following note: —"Your Father knoweth that ye have need of these things. All things whatsoever ye shall ask in prayer, believing, ye shall receive. An Orphan sends 3l. for the Orphans, and 1l. for Mr. G. Müllers own necessities, Jan. 23, 1841."

Feb. 1. Today we had not sufficient money for our own personal necessities, when we were helped in the following way. Some months ago several articles were sent to my dear wife from a distance of about 200 miles, which she did not at all need, and which therefore had been placed in the hands of a sister to be disposed of. This was only now done, and today, in this our need, the money was brought for them, being 1l.. 10s. 6d.

Feb. 4. Since Jan. 25, there has come in 10l. 14s. 11d. for the

Orphans. This morning a brother from Gloucestershire brought me a doubloon, (18 1/2 pennyweights of fine gold,) a Spanish dollar, 2 small Spanish coins, 4 old English crown pieces, 2 old English half-crown pieces, 3 old shillings, 2 old sixpences, and an old twopenny piece. He told me that he had purposed to come a day sooner, but that, though he was quite prepared for his journey, his business did not allow him to leave home, but that immediately, when these coins were given to him for the Orphans, he was able to leave. On his arrival in Bristol, this brother was asked by a gentleman, a fellow passenger, to go with him; but he replied he must go at once to me. On mentioning my name, the Gloucestershire brother was asked whether he did not believe that it was all chance work about the Orphan-Houses. He replied no, and showed him the handful of gold and silver coins, which he had received for the Orphan-Houses, and which he felt himself constrained at once to deliver. — There was also given this day a valuable gold lever watch. — Though these donations of today were not needed to supply the necessities of the children, yet they came very seasonably, and as the answer to many prayers which I had lately offered up to the Lord, to enable me to give 26l. to the labourers in the Orphan-Houses, for their own personal necessities.

Feb. 6. At the close of this week there is nothing at all in hand, either in the Orphan-Fund or in the other funds; but the Lord has enabled me to meet all the expences of the week, which only yesterday and today were above 30l.

Feb. 7. In answer to prayer, when we were without any money for the
Orphans, came in today altogether 2l. 18s.

Feb. 10. There came in yesterday and the day before several small donations; also by post, anonymously, a sovereign and a diamond ring from Leamington; but we are now again without means. May the Lord help us!

—Evening. There came in by sale of articles 10s., by sale of Reports 10s., and by a donation 1s. 6d. I also opened the box in my house, in which I found 1l. 0s. 6d. A sovereign had been put in by a brother from Stafford, who had already left my house, but felt himself constrained to return, in order to put in this money.

Feb. 12. Last evening there was left at my house, anonymously, a letter containing two sovereigns, in which was written, "For the Orphan-House 2l." This 2l. is exactly what is needed for today.

Feb. 13. Saturday morning. The Lord sent in yesterday 1l. 15s. which, though not enough for this day, was a little to commence with. Evening. Scarcely had I sent off this morning the 1l. 15s. to the Orphan-Houses, when I received from Clapham 9l. 6s. 6d. and 6 yds. of calico, for the Orphans, so that 1l. more, which was needed to meet this days demands, could be supplied. There came in also 14s. 6d.

We are very poor in reference to the funds for the other objects, and have now determined to meet daily for prayer, till the Lord may be pleased to send help.

There are now four sisters in the Lord staying at our house. This morning we had only 2s. left of our own money, when there was sent to us for ourselves from Clapham a sovereign and 2 lbs. of tea; and from Manchester 5 shillings worth of postages. Thus the Lord has kindly helped us for the present.

Feb. 14. The Lord has had pity, and helped us in some measure. A brother gave me 5l. for the first four objects of the Scriptural Knowledge Institution.

Feb. 22. Since the 14th there has come in still further for the first four objects 6s. 1d., 13s. 4d., 2s. 6d., 1l., and 5l., besides what has come in by the sale of Bibles, etc. Thus we have been able to meet all the expenses of this week.

March 4. From February 22 up to this day our necessities in the Day Schools were supplied by thirteen small donations, and by a donation of 8l. from Q. Q. Today I received the following letter

"Dear Brother,

I yesterday happened to meet with one of your Reports of the Orphan Institution for the last year, which I have read with much interest. I was not before at all aware how entirely you subsisted day by day on the good providence of the Lord, and it is very wonderful to see His constant care of such of His children as walk uprightly, and put their trust in Him. It must be very blessed thus to know and feel His care from day to day, in making bread and water sure. I am concerned to find that there was so much need at the time I saw you in

and that I did not assist you; but I will delay no longer, for there may be equal need now; and as I find many sums given with the text Ecclesiastes ix. 10, it reminds me, not to put off till tomorrow that which should be done today. Just before I fell in with your Report, I got a little portable money out of the bank, thinking it might be needed in some such way, so without delay I enclose it; the amount is 15l., and I hope that the Lord will direct my mind and incline my heart to help you again at the time of need. I perceive you have a list with the sums received, and the names of the donors open for inspection (though not published, which is well). Please to insert my donation, and any future ones I may give, under the initials A. B."

When this letter arrived, there was not one penny in hand for the Day Schools, whilst two days after about 7l. was needed. As the money was not given for any particular part of the work, it was put to this fund. There was also only 2l. in the Orphan fund. This money came from a considerable distance, and from a brother who never had assisted in this work before, whereby the Lord afresh shows how easily He can raise up new helpers.

March 11. From Feb. 13 to this day we have had comparative abundance for the Orphans, as 70 donations of 10l. and under have come in, also many pounds by sale of articles and Reports; but now, when we had again only 13s. 6d. in hand, not half of what is needed to meet the necessities of tomorrow, a sister at Plymouth sent 6l.

March 12. There came in still further today 5l. from "Friends to the
Orphan," besides 2s. 6d., 1s. 6d., 10s., and 8s. 6d.

March 18. Today I heard of the conversion of a gentleman, whose believing wife had prayed many years on behalf of her husband. He was a Roman Catholic and a great drunkard. But though he had been a Roman Catholic, he was truly made to rest upon the Lord Jesus alone for salvation; though he had been a great drunkard, the power of the Gospel was seen in his case, for he forsook his evil ways; and though his wife had had to continue to pray for him many years, yet at last the Lord answered the cries of his afflicted handmaid, and gave her the desire of her heart.

As I know it to be a fact, that many children of God are

16

greatly tried by having unconverted relatives, I relate here, for the encouragement of believers who are thus exercised, two precious facts, the truth of which I know, and by which the Lord manifested His power in converting, two of the most unlikely individuals, so far as natural appearance is concerned. Between forty and fifty years ago it pleased the Lord to convert the wife of a farmer at Ashburton in Devonshire, whose husband in consequence became her bitter opposer. This opposition was greatly increased when he had reason to believe that she was going to be baptized. The wife, however, thought that, on account of his great enmity, she would choose a time for being baptized when he was from home. A time was therefore chosen when he was to be absent at a fair in Exeter. The farmer went to the fair; but having learned on Thursday that his wife was to be baptized at eleven oclock the next morning, in haste to return he rose early on Friday morning, to put a stop to the proceeding. After he had rode several miles, he said to himself, "No, I will not go; let her do what she pleases, I will not care about her at all:" and he therefore rode back again towards Exeter. But after awhile he altered his mind again and said to himself, "Nay, I will go, she shall not have her way;" and he rode again towards Ashburton. He pursued his way, and then changed his mind a third time, and turned towards Exeter; but not long after this, a fourth time he had different thoughts, and determined to ride borne. Now, however, he remembered, that, on account of his having thus gone backwards and forwards, and that for several miles, he had wasted so much time, that he could not possibly be at Ashburton by eleven oclock, a distance of more than twenty miles from Exeter. Enraged by this thought, he dismounted from his horse on Haldon Common, between Exeter and Teignmouth, cut a large stick out of the hedge and determined to beat his wife with that stick, as long as a part of it remained. At last he reached his home, late in the afternoon, and found his wife had been baptized. In a great rage he now began to beat her, and continued to do so, till the stick in his hand was actually broken to pieces. Having thus most cruelly treated her, her body being full of bruises, he ordered her to bed. She meekly began to undress herself, and intended to go to bed, without saying a word. But when he saw her about to go, he said, "You shall not sleep in my bed any more. Go to the childrens bed." She obeyed. When now on the point of lying down on the childrens bed, he ran into the kitchen, fetched a piece of wood, threw her down on the bed, and was about to begin again to beat her, when suddenly he let the piece of wood fall, and went away without saying a word. The poor suffering wife saw no more of him that evening or night. On the next morning, Saturday, before she had risen, her husband left the house, and was absent all day till the evening. In the evening the wife gave him to understand when retiring for the night, that, according to his wish, she was again going to sleep in the childrens bed, when he meekly said to her, "Will you not sleep in your own bed?" She thought he meant to mock her, and would beat her again, if she did go into her own bed. As, however, he continued in a meek and kind way to desire her to lie down in her usual bed, she did so. All night from Saturday to the Lords day he lay groaning by her side, turning about in the bed, but having no sleep. On the Lords day morning he rose early. After awhile he came to her and said, "My dear, it is time to get up: if you will get up and make the breakfast, I will go with you to the meeting." Still the wife thought, he only meant to mock her, and that perhaps he would beat her again, when she was on the point of going to the meeting. Nevertheless she rose, prepared the breakfast, and at last, as he continued meek and kind as before, she made herself ready to go to the meeting. How great was the astonishment and surprise of the people in the small town, where the thing had become known almost to every one, when arm in arm he walked with his wife to the meeting and entered it himself, which he had never done before! After the meeting was over, he related before all persons present, what had passed in his mind between Exeter and Ashburton, how he had most cruelly beaten his wife, how he had ordered her to go to the childrens bed, how he had run into the kitchen to fetch a piece of wood to beat his wife a second time, how he had thrown her on the bed for that purpose, and how he had already lifted up his hand with the piece of wood in it, when there was like an audible voice saying to him: "Why persecutest thou me!" The piece of wood had then fallen out of his hand, and he had felt instantly that he was persecuting the Lord Jesus. From that moment his soul had become most distressed. He had been sleepless and miserable during the night from Friday to Saturday. On Saturday morning he had left the house early in the greatest agonies of soul, and had been roving about in the fields and neighbouring villages all the day. He had come home, and spent another sleepless night from Saturday to the Lords day. And then passed what has been related.

From this time this persecutor became a disciple of the Lord Jesus. He found peace through the blood of the Lord Jesus, by faith in His name, and walked about thirty years in peace and love with his wife, and adorned the gospel of the grace of God.

His wife outlived him. The husband died more than thirteen years ago. The aged sister told all the particulars of the case to a brother in the Lord, out of whose mouth I heard them; and I have related them faithfully to the best of my knowledge.

Surely the arm of the Lord is not shortened in our days! In

19

a moment He may turn the heart of the greatest persecutor. Think on Paul, think on Manasseh!

The other case of a remarkable conversion, which I am about to relate for the encouragement of the believing reader, occurred in my native country, the kingdom of Prussia, about the year 1820. I relate it as circumstantially as it was brought before me by a brother in the Lord. Baron von K. had been for many years a disciple of the Lord Jesus. Even about the commencement of this century, when there was almost universal darkness or even open infidelity spread over the whole continent of Europe, he knew the Lord Jesus; and when about the year 1806, there was the greatest distress in Silesia among many thousands of weavers, this blessed man of God took the following gracious step for his Lord and Master. As the weavers had no employment, the whole Continent almost being in an unsettled state on account of Napoleons career, it seemed to him the will of the Lord, that he should use his very considerable property to furnish these poor weavers with work, in order to save them from the greatest state of destitution, though in doing this there was not only no prospect of gain, but the certain prospect of immense loss. He therefore found employment for about six thousand weavers. But he was not content with this. Whilst he gave the bread which perishes, he also sought to minister to the souls of these weavers. To that end he sought to set believers as overseers over this immense weaving concern, and not only saw to it that the weavers were instructed in spiritual things, but he himself also set the truth before them. Thus it went on for a good while, till at last, on account of the loss of the chief part of his property, he was obliged to think about giving it up. But by this time this precious act of mercy had so commended itself to the government, that it was taken up by them, and carried on till the times altered. Baron von K. was, however,

appointed director of the whole concern as long as it existed.
—This dear man of God was not content with this. He
travelled through many countries to visit the prisons, for
the sake of improving the temporal and spiritual condition
of the prisoners, and among all the other things which he
sought to do for the Lord, was this also in particular: He
assisted poor students whilst at the University of Berlin,
(especially those who studied theology, as it is called,) in
order to get access to them, and to win them for the Lord.
One day a most talented young man, whose father lived at
Breslau, where there is likewise a university, heard of the
aged barons kindness to students, and he therefore wrote to
him, requesting him to assist him, as his own father could
not well afford to support him any longer, having other
children to provide for. A short time afterwards young T.
received a most kind reply from the baron, inviting him to
come to Berlin; but, before this letter arrived, the young
student had heard that Baron von K. was a pietist or mystic
(as true believers are contemptuously called in Germany;)
and as young was of a highly philosophical turn of mind,
reasoning about every thing, questioning the truth of
revelation, yea questioning most sceptically the existence of
God, he much disliked the prospect of going to the old
baron. Still, he thought he could but try, and if he did not
like it, he was not bound to remain in connexion with him.
He arrived in Berlin on a day when there was a great review
of the troops; and being full of this he began to speak about
it to the steward of the baron. The steward, however, being
a believer, turned the conversation, before the young
student was aware of it, to spiritual things; and yet he could
not say that it had been forced. He began another subject,
and a third, but still it always came presently again to
spiritual things. At last the baron came, who received
young T. in the most affectionate and familiar manner, as if
he had been his equal, and as if young T. bestowed a favour

21

on him, rather than that he was favoured by the baron. The baron offered him a room in his own house, and a place at his own table, while he should be studying in Berlin, which young T. accepted. He now sought in every way to treat the young student in the most kind and affectionate way, and as much as possible to serve him, and to show him the power of the Gospel in his own life, without arguing with him, yea without speaking to him directly about his soul. For, discovering in young T. a most reasoning and sceptical mind, he avoided in every possible way getting into any argument with him, while the young student again and again said to himself: "I wish I could get into an argument with this old fool, I would show him his folly." But the baron avoided it. When the young student used to come home in the evening, and the baron heard him come, he would himself go to meet him on entering the house, would light his candle, would assist and serve him in any way he could, even to the fetching the bootjack for him, and helping him to take off his boots. Thus this lowly aged disciple went on for some time, whilst the young student still sought an opportunity for arguing with him, but wondered nevertheless how the baron could thus serve him. One evening, on the return of young T. to the barons house, when the baron was making himself his servant as usual, he could refrain himself no longer, but burst out thus: "Baron, how can you do all this! You see I do not care about you, and how are you able to continue to be so kind to me, and thus to serve me!" The baron replied: "My dear young friend, I have learned it from the Lord Jesus. I wish you would read through the Gospel of John. Good night." The student now for the first time in his life sat down and read the word of God in a disposition of mind to be willing to learn, whilst up to that time he had never read the Holy Scriptures but with the view of wishing to find out arguments against them. It pleased God to bless him. From that time he became himself a follower of the Lord Jesus, and has been so ever since.

I continue now the extracts from my journal.

March 19, 1841. It is twelve years this day since I arrived in England. How exceedingly kind and gracious has the Lord been to me day by day ever since! And the Lord has crowned this day also with mercies. I have been for some time again very weak in body, on account of which it appeared to me desirable to change my sphere of labour for awhile, to which I was the more inclined as I purpose to write the second part of my Narrative, for which I need more time than I can well find in Bristol, along with my other engagements. Today I had fully determined to leave, as I am now exceedingly weak; but we had no means for it. This morning, after the exposition of the Scriptures to the Orphan and Day School children, there was given to me a check for 15l., of which 5l. is for brother Craik, 5l. for myself, and 5l. for the Orphans, Thus my way, even as to means, is made quite plain.

March 20. Nailsworth. I had purposed to take lodgings in the neighbourhood of Tetbury, passing only a night or so at Nailsworth. When I came here today, and heard about the state of the saints here and in the neighbourhood, I could not but think that the Lord had sent me to this place to labour for a season.

March 21. I ministered twice today among the brethren at Nailsworth, with much assistance from the Lord, and feel already much better from the change of air.

March 22. Truly God has sent me here! Certain matters which have been brought to light through my being here, prove it. May the Lord make it still more abundantly plain that He has sent me here! —There is a small house, which a brother left a few weeks since, but has to pay rent for at least three months longer. He will let me have it rent free, and he and brother—mean to put into it the needful furniture.—Thus the Lord has provided a lodging, not only for me, but also for all my family, who can now join me here.

A sister in the Lord in Ireland, who did not see her acceptance before God, and who was habitually without the assurance that she is a child of God, that she is born again, that her sins are forgiven, and that she shall be saved, in her distress of mind wrote to me about this time. As her case is by no means a solitary one, but as there are so many children of God who do not know that they are children of God; as there are so many whose sins are forgiven who do not know that they are forgiven; and as there are so many who will be saved, who do not know that they will be saved, and who are continually afraid of what would become of them, were they to be taken out of the world:—I have thought it well to say something here on this most important subject.

I. Question. How may I obtain the knowledge that I am a child of God, or that I am born again, or that my sins are forgiven, or that I shall not perish but have everlasting life?

Answer. Not by my feelings, not by a dream, not by my experience being like this or that ones, or unlike this or that ones; but this matter is to be settled, as all other spiritual matters, entirely by the revealed will of God, the written word of God, which is the only rule, the only standard for believers.

II. Question. By what passages, then, for instance, may I make out that I am a child of God, or born again?

Answer. 1. In 1 John v. 1, it is written: "Whosoever believeth that Jesus is the Christ is born of God." The meaning of these words is evidently this, that every one (whether young or old, male or female, one who has lived an outwardly moral or immoral life,) who believes that the poor, despised Jesus of Nazareth, of whom we read in the New Testament, was the promised Christ or Messiah, such a one is no longer in his natural state, but is born again, is born of God, is a child of God. The question therefore is, Do you believe that Jesus, who was born at Bethlehem, and crucified under Pontius Pilate, is the promised Saviour, the Messiah, the one for whom the Jews were to look? If so, you are a child of God, else you would not believe it. It is given unto you to believe it. Millions may SAY that Jesus is the Saviour, the Messiah, but none BELIEVE it except the children of God. It proves me to be a child of God that I believe it; to none besides is it given to believe it, though millions might say so.

Perhaps you say, I do not feel that I am born again, born of God, and
I have therefore no enjoyment.

Answer. In order that you may have the enjoyment, which is the result of the knowledge that you are a child of God, that you are born of God, or born again, you must receive Gods testimony. He is a faithful witness, He speaks nothing but the truth, and His declaration is, That every one who believes that Jesus is the Christ is born of God. If you receive this testimony of God, you, to whom by grace it is given to believe that Jesus is the Christ, cannot but be happy, from the fact that God Himself says, that you are His child. But if you will wait till you feel that you are a child of God, you may have to wait long; and even if you felt it, yet your feelings would be worth nothing; for either it might be a false feeling, or, though it were real, it might be lost the next hour. Feelings change; but the word of God remains unalterably the same. You have, then, without having had a dream about it, without having had a portion of the word in a more than usual way impressed upon your mind concerning the subject, without having heard something like a voice from heaven about it, to say to yourself: If I believe that Jesus is the promised Messiah, I am a child of God. And then, from a belief of what God declares in this passage concerning you who believe that Jesus is the Christ, even that you are His child, spring peace and joy in the Holy Ghost.

Answer 2. In Galatians iii. 26, it is written: "Ye are all the children of God by faith in Christ Jesus." The question here again is: Do I believe in the Lord Jesus? Do I depend upon Him alone for the salvation of my soul? If so, I am a child of God, whether I feel it or not.

Answer 3. In John i. 1113, it is written of the Lord Jesus: "He came unto His own, and His own received Him not. But as many as received Him, to them gave He power (or the right or the privilege) to become the sons of God, even to them that believe on His name: which were born, not of blood, nor of the will of the flesh, nor of the will of man, but of God." The question here again is simply this, Have I received the Lord Jesus, i.e., Do I believe in His name? If so, I am born of God, I am a child of God, else I should never have believed in the Lord Jesus; for none but the children of God do believe in Him.

III. Question. How may I know that my sins are forgiven? Have I to wait till I feel that they are forgiven, before I may take comfort concerning this matter? Or, must I wait till I have in some powerful way a portion of the word of God applied to my mind, to assure me of it?

26

Answer. This point is again only to be settled by the word of God. We have not to wait till we feel that our sins are forgiven. —I myself have now been a believer for more than nineteen years (i.e. in the year 1845). How long it is, since I have had no doubt whatever about the forgiveness of my sins, I cannot tell with certainty; but this I am quite sure of, that ever since I have been in England, which is now about sixteen years (in 1845), I have never once had a single moments doubt that my sins are all forgiven; and yet I do not remember that I even once have felt that they were forgiven. To know that they are forgiven, and to feel that they are forgiven, are two different things. —The way to settle, whether our sins are forgiven, is, to refer to the word of God alone with reference to it. In Acts x. 43, it is written concerning the Lord Jesus, "To him give all the prophets witness, that through His name whosoever believeth in Him shall receive remission of sins." All the prophets speaking under the immediate power of the Holy Spirit, bore testimony, that through the obedience and sufferings of the Lord Jesus, whereby He becomes our Saviour or is our Jesus, all who believe in Him for salvation, who depend upon Him and not upon themselves, who receive Him to be the one whom God declares Him to be, should receive the forgiveness of their sins. The questions therefore to be put to ourselves are simply these: Do I walk in utter carelessness? Do I trust in my own exertions for salvation? Do I expect forgiveness for my sins on account of living a better life in future? Or, do I depend only upon this, that Jesus died upon the cross to save sinners—and that Jesus fulfilled the law of God to make sinners righteous? If the latter is the case, my sins are forgiven, whether I feel it or not. I have already forgiveness. I shall not have it merely when I die, or when the Lord Jesus comes again; but I have it now, and that for all my sins. I must not wait to feel that my sins are forgiven, in order to be at peace, and in order to be happy; but I must take God at His word, I must believe that what He says in true, and He says, "That whosoever believeth in the Lord Jesus should receive remission of sins;" and when I believe what God says, peace and joy will be the result.

Again, in Acts xv. 8, 9, it is written with reference to us Gentile sinners: "And God which knoweth the hearts, bare them witness, giving them the Holy Ghost, even as He did unto us; and put no difference between us and them, purifying their hearts by faith." Here we see how the guilt is to be removed from the heart, how we can get a clean heart, obtain the forgiveness of our sins,—even by faith in the Lord Jesus. Depending upon the sufferings of the Lord Jesus in the room of sinners, and depending upon His obedience in fulfilling the law of God, His sufferings are considered as endured by us, His obedience as if found in ourselves: in Him (if we believe on Him) we are considered to have hung on the cross, and therefore were punished in Him, on account of which God, though perfectly holy and just, can forgive us our sins for Jesus sake, as well as reckon us righteous, through faith in the Lord Jesus, who in the room of those who believe on Him fulfilled the law of God.

I would here by the way especially warn against one error, which is, that persons say, I can believe that Jesus is the Christ, the Saviour, that through Him alone the forgiveness of sins is to be obtained, and I do depend on Him alone for forgiveness, but I desire to know that He is my Christ, my Saviour, and because I am not sure about that, I can have no peace. Now, the Gospel which is preached in the New Testament is not, you must believe that Jesus of Nazareth is your Christ, your Saviour, but that He is the Christ, the Saviour; and if you believe that, you have a right to look upon Him as your Saviour.

IV. Question. How may I know that I shall be saved?

Answer. "If thou shalt confess with thy mouth the Lord Jesus, and shalt believe in thy heart that God hath raised Him from the dead, thou shalt be saved." Rom. x. 9. The point is simply this: Do I confess with my mouth the Lord Jesus? Do I own Him by the confession of my mouth before men, and do I believe in my heart that Jesus of Nazareth who was crucified was not left in the grave, but was raised again by God on the third day? If so, I shall be saved. For while there may be the confession of the Lord Jesus with the month, without the person being finally saved, there does not go along with this the believing in the heart that God has raised Him from the dead, without the person, in whom both are found, being finally saved; for in none but the children of God are these two points found united together. We have here particularly to observe, that it is not written: If thou shalt say that God has raised Him from the dead; but if thou shalt believe in thine heart that God has raised Him from the dead, thou shalt be saved. I have, then, to take God at His word. If I do confess the Lord Jesus with my mouth, and do believe in my heart that God has raised Him from the dead, I shall be saved, though I do not feel it, though I am utterly unworthy of salvation, yea, though I am altogether deserving condemnation. I must not wait till I feel that I shall be saved before I take comfort; but I must believe what God says in this verse, and, out of that, peace and comfort will flow into my soul. Should, however, one or the other of the children of God, believe in his heart the resurrection of the Lord Jesus, if at the same time he has never made confession of the Lord Jesus with his mouth, he cannot be surprised that the assurance about his salvation is wanting to him; yet if both be found in you, my dear reader, God has been gracious to you, you are His child, you shall be saved.

Further, in John iii. 16, it is written: "God so loved the world that He gave His only begotten Son, that whosoever believeth in Him should not perish, but have everlasting life." Notice here in particular: 1. It matters not how great a sinner I am. 2. The promise is positive concerning my salvation, if I believe in the Lord Jesus. 3. I have only to believe in the Lord Jesus. No matter how it may have been with me hitherto; if only now I trust in and depend upon the Lord Jesus for salvation, I shall have everlasting life.

Further, in Acts xvi. 30, 31, it is written: "Sirs, what must I do to be saved? And they said, Believe on the Lord Jesus Christ, and thou shalt be saved."

Further, in John iii. 36, it is written: "He that believeth on the Son hath everlasting life; and He that believeth not the Son shall not see life; but the wrath of God abideth on him." As assuredly as I depend upon and trust in the Lord Jesus for the salvation of my soul, I shall be saved, I have already everlasting life; for He died, to deliver those who believe on Him from the wrath of God, under which all men are in their natural state; but if I do not believe in the Lord Jesus, the wrath of God, which rests upon all men in their natural state, will finally destroy me, if I remain without faith in the Lord Jesus; for then I reject the one only remedy, in refusing to take Jesus as my substitute, who bore the punishment that He might deliver the sinner from it, and who fulfilled the law of God that He might make the sinner who believes on Him a just one before God.

V. Question. How may I know that I am one of the elect? I often read in the Scriptures about election, and I often hear about election, how may I know that I am a chosen one, that I am predestinated to be conformed to the image of the Son of God?

Answer. It is written: "As many as were ordained, (i.e. appointed) to eternal life believed." Acts xiii. 48. The question therefore simply is this: Do I believe in the Lord Jesus? Do I take Him to be the one whom God declares Him to be, i. e. His beloved Son in whom He is well pleased? If so, I am a believer, and I should never have believed, except I had been appointed by God to eternal life—except I had been made by God to be a vessel of mercy. Therefore the matter is a very simple one: if I believe in the Lord Jesus, I am a chosen one,—I have been appointed to eternal life.

Again, in Rom. viii. 29, 30, it is written: "For whom He did foreknow, He also did predestinate to be conformed to the image of His Son, that He might be the first-born among many brethren. Moreover, whom He did predestinate, them He also called: and whom he called, them He also justified; and whom He justified, them He also glorified." How are we justified, or constituted just ones, before God? By faith in the Lord Jesus. Rom. iii. 2026. Therefore if I believe in the Lord Jesus, it follows (on account of the inseparable connection of all the precious things spoken of in these two verses), that I have been foreknown by God, that I have been predestinated by Him to be conformed to the image of His Son, that I have been called, that I have been justified, and that, in the sight of God, I am already as good as glorified, though I am not as yet in the actual possession and enjoyment of the glory.

The reason why persons who renounce confidence in their own goodness for salvation, and who only trust in the merits and sufferings of the Lord Jesus, do not know that they are the children of God, that their sins are forgiven, and that they shall be saved, generally arises from one of these things: 1. They do not know the simplicity of the Gospel; or, 2. They seek to settle it by their feeling; or, 3.

31

They wait for some powerful impulse, or a dream, or something like a voice from Heaven to assure them of it, or for some passage being in a powerful way applied to their mind to assure them of it; or, 4. Because they are living in sin. Should the last be the case, then, however correctly we may understand the Gospel; however much we may desire by the Holy Scriptures alone to settle these questions; yea, however much in former times we may have enjoyed the assurance of the forgiveness of our sins, or of our being the children of God, or that we shall be saved: in such a state of heart all peace would be gone, and would not return as long as we live in sin. There may be found much weakness and many infirmities even in the believer who has assurance about these points; but the Holy Ghost does not comfort us, and will not comfort us, if we habitually indulge in those things which we know to be contrary to the mind of God. An upright, honest heart, is of the utmost importance in all divine things; and especially with reference to the assurance about our standing before God.

April 15. From March 12th up to this day we had always a little money in hand for the Orphans, so that there was comparatively no trial of faith. Of the many donations which came in during this period I only mention two, as rather deserving to be noticed, to show what various ways the Lord uses to send us supplies. On March 16th I received from the neighbourhood of London 5l., respecting which the brother who sent it writes, that he was in the habit of giving this sum to his wife, a sister, on her birth days, to lay it out in buying any little thing she liked, and that she this time preferred giving it to the Orphans. On April 3rd a sister gave 5l., which came in most seasonably. She had lost a sum of money, which was afterwards found again, and she felt constrained to give 5l. of it to the Orphans. Now today,

April 15, when all was again spent, 3l. came in from Wales.

On Friday, April 30, while I was at Nailsworth, in Gloucestershire, I received the following letter from brother R. B., Master at the Boys-Orphan-House:

"My dear Brother,

"When I wrote last, on Tuesday evening, there was not one penny in hand. But since then the Lord has most graciously dealt with us. Only 1s. 6d. came in on Wednesday morning; but as there were enough provisions in the house for the day, the sisters experienced no difficulty: it was only necessary to refuse to take in what there was not money to pay for. About six I went out for a walk with the boys, and returned after eight, when I found a letter in which was enclosed 5l., with these words; "From the Lord, for the present necessities of the Orphans." It was indeed for the present necessities. Etc.

"Your Brother,

R. B."

This letter came after a previous one, in which brother R. B. informed me about the need in the Orphan-Houses, which led me to prayer. When this letter came from brother B., I received at the same time another from Birmingham, in which was enclosed 10l., from a brother, who had sold some of his books. It was from a most unexpected quarter, as that brother is himself, as a servant of the Lord, depending upon Him for temporal supplies. The same post brought me also information of 1l. 4s, 6d., having been sent from Dublin. The sister in Ireland writes that she sends the money now, as we may be in want of even so small a sum. With regard to the above-mentioned 5l., I mention still further that I know from the handwriting who the donor is; and it is remarkable that he had not given or sent the money to me, as he not only knew I was not in Bristol at the time, but that I was in the neighbourhood where he lives. But this was not only of the Lords ordering, but it was a direct answer to prayer; for knowing the need at the Orphan-Houses, I had been especially led to ask the Lord not to allow the money to be first sent to me in letters or parcels, but to cause it to be directly sent to brother B. How truly precious it is that every one, who rests alone upon the Lord Jesus for salvation, has in the living God a father, to whom he may fully unbosom himself concerning the most minute affairs of his life, and concerning every thing that lies upon his heart! Dear reader, do you know the living God? Is He, in Jesus, your Father? Be assured that Christianity is something more than forms and creeds, and ceremonies: there is life, and power, and reality, in our holy faith. If you never yet have known this, then come and taste for yourself. I beseech you affectionately to meditate and pray over the following verses: John iii. 16, Rom. x. 9, 10, Acts x. 43, I John v. 1.

May 2. A sister who lives near Lutterworth sent me yesterday 5l., which was given for the Orphans by a friend of hers. This 5l. supplies our need today, it being Saturday, for there was only 1l. in hand when this money came.

From March 20th, to May 7th, I spent at Nailsworth, where I prepared the second part of my Narrative for the press, and laboured in the Word. These seven weeks were on the whole, by the help of God, profitably spent in the service of the Lord, and to the benefit of my own soul. There was much love shown to me and my family by the dear saints among whom I was labouring, and I know that my service among them has not been in vain.

Today, May 7, I returned with my family to Bristol.

While I was staying at Nailsworth, it pleased the Lord to teach me a truth, irrespective of human instrumentality, as far as I know, the benefit of which I have not lost, though now, while preparing the eighth edition for the press, more than forty years have since passed away. The point is this; I saw more clearly than ever, that the first great and primary business to which I ought to attend every day was, to have my soul happy in the Lord. The first thing to be concerned about was not, how much I might serve the Lord, how I might glorify the Lord; but how I might get my soul into a happy state, and how my inner man might be nourished. For I might seek to set the truth before the unconverted, I might seek to benefit believers, I might seek to relieve the distressed, I might in other ways seek to behave myself as it becomes a child of God in this world; and yet, not being happy in the Lord, and not being nourished and strengthened in my inner man day by day, all this might not be attended to in a right spirit. Before this time my practice had been, at least for ten years previously, as an habitual thing, to give myself to prayer, after having dressed myself in the morning. Now I saw, that the most important thing I had to do was, to give myself to the reading of the word of God and to meditation on it, that thus my heart might be comforted, encouraged, warned, reproved, instructed; and that thus, by means of the word of God, whilst meditating on it, my heart might be brought into experimental communion with the Lord. I began therefore to meditate on the New Testament from the beginning early in the morning. The first thing I did, after having asked in a few words the Lords blessing upon His precious word, was, to begin to meditate on the word of God, searching, as it were, into every verse, to get blessing out of it; not for the sake of the public ministry of the Word; not for the sake of preaching on what I had meditated upon; but for the sake of obtaining food for my own soul. The result I have found to be almost invariably this, that after a very few minutes my soul has been led to confession, or to thanksgiving, or to intercession, or to supplication; so that, though I did not, as it were, give myself to prayer, but to meditation, yet it turned almost immediately more or less into prayer. When thus I have been for awhile making confession, or intercession, or supplication, or have given thanks, I go on to the next words or verse, turning all, as I go on, into prayer for myself or others, as the Word may lead to it; but still continually keeping before me, that food for my own soul is the object of my meditation. The result of this is, that there is always a good deal of confession, thanksgiving, supplication, or intercession mingled with my meditation, and that my inner man almost invariably is even sensibly nourished and strengthened, and that by breakfast time, with rare exceptions, I am in a peaceful if not happy state of heart. Thus also the Lord is pleased to communicate unto me that, which either very soon after, or at a later time, I have found to become food for other believers, though it was not for the sake of the public ministry of the Word that I gave myself to meditation, but for the profit of my own inner man. With this mode I have likewise combined the being out in the open air for an hour, an hour and a half, or two hours before breakfast, walking about in the fields, and in the summer sitting for a little on the stiles, if I find it too much to walk all the time.7 I find it very beneficial to my health to walk thus for meditation before breakfast, and am now so in the habit of using the time for that purpose, that when I get into the open air, I generally take out a new Testament of good sized type, which I carry with me for that purpose, besides my Bible: and I find that I can profitably spend my time in the open air; which formerly was not the case, for want of habit I used to consider the time spent in walking a loss, but now I find it very profitable, not only to my body, but also to my soul. The walking out before breakfast is of course not necessarily connected with this matter, and every one has to judge according to his strength and other circumstances. —The difference then between my former practice and my present one is this. Formerly, when I rose, I began to pray as soon as possible, and generally spent all my time till breakfast in prayer, or almost all the time. At all events I almost invariably began with prayer, except when I felt my soul to be more than usually barren, in which case I read the word of God for food, or for refreshment, or for a revival and renewal of my inner man, before I gave myself to prayer. But what was the result? I often spent a quarter of an hour, or half an hour, or even an hour on my knees, before being conscious to myself of having derived comfort, encouragement, humbling of soul, &c.; and often, after having suffered much from wandering of mind for the first ten minutes, or a quarter of an hour, or even half an hour, I only then began realty to pray. I scarcely ever suffer now in this way. For my heart being nourished by the truth, being brought into experimental fellowship with God, I speak to my Father, and to my Friend (vile though I am, and unworthy of it!) about the things that He has brought before me in His precious word. It often now astonishes me that I did not sooner see this point. In no book did I ever read about it. No public ministry ever brought the matter before me. No private intercourse with a brother stirred me up to this matter. And yet now, since God has taught me this point, it is as plain to me as any thing, that the first thing the child of God has to do morning by morning is, to obtain food for his inner man. As the outward man is not fit for work for any length of time, except we take food; and as this is one of the first

things we do in the morning; so it should be with the inner
man. We should take food for that, as every one must allow.
Now what is the food for the inner man? Not prayer, but
the word of God; and here again not the simple reading of
the word of God, so that it only passes through our minds,
just as water runs through a pipe, but considering what we
read, pondering over it, and applying it to our hearts. When
we pray, we speak to God. Now, prayer, in order to be
continued for any length of time in any other than a formal
manner, requires, generally speaking, a measure of strength
or godly desire, and the season, therefore, when this exercise
of the soul can be most effectually performed, is, after the
inner man has been nourished by meditation on the word
of God, where we find our Father speaking to us, to
encourage us, to comfort us, to instruct us, to humble us, to
reprove us. We may therefore profitably meditate, with Gods
blessing, though we are ever so weak spiritually; nay, the
weaker we are, the more we need meditation for the
strengthening of our inner man. There is thus far less to be
feared from wandering of mind, than if we give ourselves to
prayer without having had previously time for meditation.
—I dwell so particularly on this point because of the
immense spiritual profit and refreshment I am conscious of
having derived from it myself, and I affectionately and
solemnly beseech all my fellow-believers to ponder this
matter. By the blessing of God I ascribe to this mode the
help and strength which I have had from God to pass in
peace through deeper trials in various ways, than I had ever
had before; and after having now above forty years tried
this way, I can most fully, in the fear of God, commend it. In
addition to this, I generally read after family prayer larger
portions of the word of God, when I still pursue my practice
of reading regularly onward in the Holy Scriptures,
sometimes in the New Testament and sometimes in the Old,
and for more than fifty-two years I have proved the

blessedness of it. I take also either then or at other parts of the day, time more especially for prayer.

How different, when the soul is refreshed and made happy early in the morning, from what it is when, without spiritual preparation, the service, the trials, arid the temptations of the day come upon one!

May 29. Today I received from the East Indies 100l.—Notice here, that without any solicitation, simply in answer to prayer, the Lord is pleased to send us from time to time even large sums, and that from such a distance as the East Indies.

June 4. Two or three weeks since, a brother at a distance requested me to let him know the names of my bankers, and the names of their agents in London, in order that he might by means of his bankers send me some money. One day after another passed away, and I heard no more about it. Today I received the following letter

"My dear Brother,

"I have delayed writing to you under the expectation of seeing you at Bristol; but I am not yet suffered to leave ****. I have, by this post, written to ***** of London, desiring them to pay over to Messrs. Robarts, Curtis & Co., in favour of Messrs. Stuckey & Co. of Bristol, to the credit of George Müller, the sum of fifty pounds. This apply, dear brother, as the Lord gives you wisdom. I am not concerned at my having been prevented for so many days from sending this money: I am confident it has not been needed."

This last sentence is remarkable. It is now nearly three years since our funds were for the first time exhausted, and only at this period, since then, could it have been said in truth, as far as I remember, that a donation of 50l. was not needed. From the beginning of July, 1838, till now, there never had been a period when we so abounded as when this donation of 50l. came; for there was then in the Orphan-Fund and the other funds between two and three hundred pounds. The words of this brother are so much the more remarkable, as, on four former occasions, when he likewise gave considerable donations, we were always in need, yea, great need, which he afterwards knew from the printed accounts.

On the same day came in still further from Hackney 10l., besides several small donations.

July 7, 1841. For some time past brother Craik and I have questioned whether, under our present circumstances, the mode of receiving the free-will offerings of the saints among whom we labour, by means of boxes over which our names were fixed, together with the explanation of the object of the boxes, was any longer the more excellent way. We have at last been quite decided about it, and put today the following short statement into the press.

To the Saints in Christ Jesus assembling at Bethesda Chapel, Bristol.

"Dear Brethren,

"It has seemed well to us to remove, from the chapel, the boxes appropriated for the reception of the free-will offerings towards our temporal support. In order to prevent misapprehension or misrepresentation, we desire affectionately to lay before you the following statement of our reasons for taking this step.

Upon our first coming to Bristol we declined accepting anything in the shape of regular salary, or by means of seat-rents, from the brethren among whom we were labouring. We did not act thus because we thought it wrong that those who were ministered unto in spiritual things should minister unto us in temporal things; but 1. because we would not have the liberality of the brethren to be a matter of constraint, but willingly; 2. because on the ground of James ii. 1-6, we objected to seat-rents. Boxes were put up for the sake of those into whose hearts God might put it to desire to act according to that word, "Let him that is taught in the Word communicate unto him that teacheth in all good things." Gal. vi. 6.

When the boxes were first put up, we were the only brethren that seemed called to labour in the Word and doctrine. Since then, however, circumstances have considerably altered; and, partly from the change in circumstances, and, partly from increased light in reference to the position of those who minister the Word, we have for some time past felt that it might be well, for certain reasons, that the present mode of receiving the offerings of the saints should be discontinued. At the same time we are very desirous of having it clearly understood, that, in the great principles which led to the adoption of the boxes, in the first instance, we are unchanged: or rather we are more strengthened, by the experience of more than ten years, in the propriety of rejecting seat-rents and fixed salaries.

1. As long as the boxes are there, it ought to be understood for what purpose the money, which is put into them, is applied. This necessity requires that our names should be given, as those who labour in the Word and doctrine. This again has the appearance of elevating ourselves above all the

41

other brethren, and of assuming office to ourselves, instead of just seeking to fill the place which the Holy Ghost may have given us in the body.

2. It may please the Lord increasingly to call and qualify other brethren for the work of ruling and teaching in the church; but still, as long as we are looked upon as we have been hitherto, in consequence of our names being affixed to the boxes, unnecessary difficulties may probably be put in the way of any others being fully recognised by the saints generally as occupying, equally with ourselves, the place in which the Lord may set them.

3. The question may be asked even now, "Are these the only labourers?" and the reply would be that there are others who also labour, but who are not supported in the same way. This fact is fitted to give the impression to those who do not know us, that we were seeking to keep our place in the church by some outward title, rather than just filling it up in obedience to the Lord, and quietly leaving it with His Spirit to produce subjection unto us on the part of the saints.

4. Lastly, from the manner in which our names appear in public, we have reason to believe that some of the saints look upon us as exclusively the "ministers," and thus that some may have felt themselves neglected because not visited personally by us. The notion that two individuals should be able to exercise pastoral inspection over about five hundred and fifty believers, we consider to be very unsound; but for ourselves we feel that it is a responsibility which we dare not take. According to our gift and strength we desire to rule, teach, and feed the sheep of Christ; but we dare not undertake the personal inspection of all who are already gathered, or may be gathered, simply as believers in the Lord Jesus, in this city.

Thus we have endeavoured very briefly to state our reasons for declining any longer to receive your offerings through boxes publicly put up, and having our names appended to them. We desire grace to serve you more faithfully than ever, and cast ourselves, as we have done hitherto, upon Him who hath said, "If any man serve me him will my Father honour."

HENRY CRAIK, GEORGE MÜLLERMüller

Bristol, July 7, 1841. .

When this alteration was made, I had another proof of the many blessings which are connected with the life of faith. Under other circumstances the question would have naturally arisen in my mind, And what will you do for support, if the boxes are removed? How will the offerings come in? Will any come in? But none of these things troubled me even for a moment. I said to myself, somehow or other the Lord will provide for me. If not through the instrumentality of the saints in Bristol, He will send help by means of those who live elsewhere. All I have to do in this matter is, to serve the Lord and to trust in Him, and He will surely take care of my temporal necessities. And thus it has been since July 1841 also, even as before. The reader may desire to know, how the Lord has since that time provided for my temporal necessities, seeing that the boxes, which were put up in the two chapels for the reception of the free-will offerings, were removed. I therefore state it. 1, I have received, as at former times, some presents in provisions, clothes, etc., from the saints among whom I labour and from other saints. 2, Some of the brethren and sisters among whom I labour have either habitually or from time to time put up some money in paper, and directed it to brother Craik or to me, or to both of us, and have put these little money parcels into one of the boxes for the reception of the offerings of the poor saints, or into the boxes into which the free-will contributions for the rent and expenses of the chapels are put. These little packets have been handed over to us by the deacons, and as they were directed so they have been appropriated, Those which are directed to brother Craik only, are handed over to brother Craik; those which are directed to me only, I appropriate for myself; and those which are directed to both of us, the contents are divided between us. 3, In a few cases, brethren and sisters in communion with us have also given me presents in money. 4, The Lord has also continued to incline the hearts of some of His children, not living in Bristol, to send me presents in money, and again and again even those whom I have never seen, and whose names, sometimes, I do not even know.

The only thing that was a real difficulty in my mind in making this alteration was, not that I should be a loser, and much less that the Lord would not care for my temporal necessities; but lest some of the children of God should find, in the removal of the boxes for the reception of the offerings for brother Craik and me, an excuse for doing nothing at all for our temporal necessities; and lest especially the poor, because they might have only pence or halfpence to give, should be deterred from doing so, and thereby both classes should rob themselves of blessing. It was not, because I feared to lose the gifts of some; for, I can, by the grace of God, say in some measure at least with the apostle Paul, "Not because I desire a gift: but I desire fruit that may abound to your account." Philip iv. 17. My aim also is, by the help of God, to be brought into that state of heart in which the apostle Paul was when he said, "I will very gladly spend and be spent for you; though the more abundantly I love you the less I be loved." 2 Cor. xii. 15. But yet with this desire on my part, I knew that the dear children of God among whom I labour would rob themselves and not me of a blessing, if they did not contribute towards my temporal necessities and I feared, lest this alteration should be used by Satan as an instrument to their injury.

But the mind of God seemed to us, after all, on account of the reasons before stated, that the alteration ought to be made, notwithstanding any possible evils which might result from it.

We are thus in such a position, that there is free room for the Holy Ghost to commend all the various labourers among us, according to the measure of grace and gift given to them, to the consciences of the brethren, not only with reference to their spiritual position in the body, butt also with reference to their temporal need.

Aug. 7. Today we had one sixpence left for our own personal necessities. We needed some money to buy eggs and cocoa for a brother who is come to stay with us, when this brother gave me four shillings, which he had brought

45

for me from the place whence he comes. Thus we are helped for the present.

Aug. 26. After a season of comparative poverty with reference to myself, though always having what was really needful in the way of nourishing food, etc., a brother sent me today 17l. 18s. from a considerable distance, of which half is for the Orphans, and half for my own temporal necessities.

Sept. 2. During the last four months we have had more in hand for the Orphans than we needed. Since July 1838, when for the first time the funds were exhausted, we have had at no period so much money in hand. There was as it were, during these four months, one continual even running of the river of Gods bounty, both by presents in money and articles. Of the donations which were received during this period, I mention only the following:—On May 12th I received from Florence, in Italy, the following donations:—3 silver pins and 4 dollars; 3 dollars and a sixpence; 2 Pauls (Italian coins); 5l.; 3 pincushions, 6 penwipers, and a little shawl How abundantly do these donations from Florence prove how easily the Lord is able to provide us with means for His work, even from the most unexpected quarters!—As we had now for several months abounded in a greater degree than at any previous time of the same length during the past three years and three months, so it pleased the Lord after this period to try our faith more severely than during any time since the work first commenced. Indeed, so sharp were the trials of our faith for more than six months after this;—so long the seasons when, day after day, only daily supplies were granted to us, and when even from meal to meal we had to look to the Lord;—so long had we to continue in prayer, and yet help seemed to fail;—that it can be only ascribed to the especial mercy of God, that the faith of those who were engaged in this work did not altogether fail, and that they did not entirely grow weary of this way of carrying on the Lords work, and go, in despair of help from God, back again to the habits and maxims of this evil world. How my fellow-labourers have felt during all this time, I am, of course, unable to state; but, if I may speak of myself, I joyfully state, to the praise of the Lord, that during all the following months my faith was sustained without wavering, but still so greatly was it tried, that often I had no other petition, but that the Lord would be pleased to continue it, and that He would pity me as a father pitieth his children. In the midst of the trial I was fully assured that the Lord would lighten His hand in His own good time, and that, whilst it lasted, it was only in order that in a small measure, for the benefit of the church of Christ generally, that word might be fulfilled in us—"Whether we be afflicted it is for your consolation." I now give an account of the commencement and progress of our trial of faith during the months which succeeded the time of abundance.

Sept. 3. The money in hand had come to 3l. 5s. I therefore asked the Lord this morning for fresh supplies, and very soon after came a post-office order from Glasgow for 3l.

Sept. 7. 5l. 9s. more had come in since September 3rd, but this morning the last money had been given out. After the great abundance during the last months, now not a farthing was left. I gave myself therefore to prayer, and in the afternoon I received a post-office order from a brother at Plymouth for 3l. In the evening was left at my house a bonnet box from G. T. I., which contained 5s., 4 shirts and 4 handkerchiefs.

Sept. 8. Today came in 4s. from the neighbourhood of Wolverhampton, 2s. 6d. from Bath, and 1l. was given by a brother, who had just arrived from Ceylon.

Sept. 9. This morning 5l. was sent by a brother, a student in the University of Cambridge, who had read my Narrative; also 13s. 6d. came in besides.

Sept. 18. From the 9th to this day we were comfortably supplied with what we needed. Today, when 3l. was needed, and there was only 1l. 9s. 2d. in hand, 12l. came in from the neighbourhood of Wolverhampton, and 3s. by knitting.

Sept. 25. Saturday. Since the 18th was received, by donations and sale of articles, 5l. 19s. 8d., which enabled us, together with the 12l. 3s. which came in on the 18th, to meet all the expenses. But when I had sent off yesterday what was needed to meet the days need, nothing at all was left in hand for this day, whilst I knew that above 3l. would be required. The Lord, therefore, in His faithful love sent in yesterday afternoon 11s. 0 1/2d.; this morning 5l. from Plymouth; and 1l. 1s. with several articles of clothing for the Orphans from Clapham. Thus we had about twice as much as was required for this day.

Sept. 26. 2l. 11s. came in today.

Sept. 28. As 2l. was needed for the supplies of this day, and only 1l. 13s. 0 1/2d. was in hand, the boxes in the Orphan-Houses were opened, in which was found 10s. 2d.

Sept. 29, When there was again only 3s. 2 1/2d. in hand towards the need of today, a brother, a commercial traveller, having returned last night to Bristol, brought me two sovereigns, which had been given him for the Orphans by a lady at Marlborough, who had read one of the Reports. There came in still further today 2l. 8s. 6d.

Oct. 1. When I had again not one penny in hand for the

necessities of this day, there was brought to me this morning 10s. for the Orphans, which had been sent from Kensington. In the paper, which contained the money, was written: "Your Heavenly Father knoweth that ye have need of these things." "Trust in the Lord." This word of our Lord is to me of more value than many bank notes. About five minutes later I received from an Irish sister 10l., through her banker in London. At the same time I received information from Tetbury that three boxes, containing articles to be disposed of for the benefit of the Orphans, were on the way, and two hours after, 14 small donations were given to me, amounting to 1l. 7s. 4d. —I mention here, as a point particularly to be noticed, that after the season of comparative abundance had come to an end in September, the Lord did not at once allow us to be so sharply tried as we were afterwards. He dealt in the same gentle way with us three years before, when the trials of faith in this part of the work first commenced.

Oct. 6. As only 4l. more had been received for the Orphans since Oct. 1; the last money had now again been given out to supply this days necessities, when 2l. 15s. came in, being the produce of some of the articles which had been sent from Tetbury. This evening I also received from a brother a sovereign, which his believing wife, on her dying bed, had requested him to give after her decease. There came in likewise this evening by a donation 10s., and by sale of articles 2l. 10s. 5d.

During the last five months we have had comparatively an abundance of means for the other objects of the Scriptural Knowledge Institution also; but now we are again very poor. Just now, in this our great need, a brother, who has learned to esteem the Holy Scriptures above every other book, sent me a box of books, the produce of which supplies

49

our present need for the Day Schools.

Oct. 9. No more than 1l. 2s. 11d, having been received for the Orphans since the 6th, there was only 2l. 3s. 9d. in hand, whilst 4l. was needed, it being Saturday. In the course of the morning 2l. came in for stockings, from a sister who resides five or six miles from Bristol; and in the afternoon another sister sent 1s., and a third brought 5l. The latter had it particularly laid on her heart not to delay till tomorrow the giving of this money, as it might be needed today. Thus the Lord has not only given us enough for today, but also a little to begin the next week with.

Oct. 10. Today we received still further 5l. 9s. 11d. for the Orphans.

Oct. 11. When today again money was needed for the Day Schools, there arrived from Marlborough a box of books, containing 110 volumes and several pamphlets. The produce of the books, together with 1l. 9s. 4d., which came in at the same time, supplied again our present necessities.

Oct. 16. More than 10l. had come in since the 10th for the Orphans; but today there was again only 10s. 11 1/2d. in hand, whilst about 3l. was required. The boxes at the Orphan-Houses were therefore opened, which contained 1l. 1s. In the course of the day also 5s. 5d. was paid for stockings. About seven oclock this evening sister E. C. brought several small donations, amounting to 1l. 17s. 4d., for the Orphans, and 9s. 8d. for the other funds. Thus we had even for this day 3l. 14s. 4 1/4d.

Oct. 21. As only between 9l. and 10l. had come in since the 16th for the Orphans, we were this day again, as is often the case, without anything in hand, when 12s. 2d. was sent from Exmouth, and 8s. 8d. came in by sale of stockings.

There arrived also a box and a basket from Ilfracombe, the contents of which are to be sold for the benefit of the Orphans. Moreover 15s. 6d. was taken out of the boxes in the Orphan-Houses.

Oct. 22. By the money which was yesterday taken out of the boxes, and by 1l. 3s. which came in by disposing of some of the articles sent from Ilfracombe, we were comfortably supplied today.

Oct. 23. We had only 5s. 6d., which I found in the box in my house, 8s. 9d. for stockings, and 9s. which came in morning, besides a few shillings in the hands of the matrons, to help us through the day.

Oct. 24. Today, when we had not enough to pay the salaries of the teachers in the Day Schools, I received 5l. from a sister at Topsham, which supplied our need.

Oct. 25. Yesterday and today was given 2l. 17s. for the Orphans.

Oct. 26. This afternoon I had only one penny left, when two Orphans arrived from Bath, with whom 5l. 15s. 6d. was brought. At the very moment, while I was receiving this money, I was called on for money from the Girls-Orphan-House, which I was thus able to send. It has often been so ordered by the Lord, that, whilst we require nothing at all to be paid at the admission of the children, nevertheless that which has been brought with them has been the means of supplying the need, in which we were at the time when they were sent. There came in still further today 1l.

Oct. 29. Today we were again very poor; for not only had I nothing at all in hand, but the provision stores were much reduced. About twelve oclock a sister gave me 3s. 2d., also from a distance was sent 9d. In the afternoon we were able to dispose of some articles for 3l., which had been sent a long time ago. Three shillings came in for needlework, and 2s. 6d. as a donation. Thus we had 3l. 9s. 5d.—The day before yesterday I had asked the Lord that He would be pleased to send us some potatoes, as we have no means to lay in a stock. This morning I was informed that the same brother who had sent 20 sacks last year, had again ordered 20 sacks to be sent, and 6 sacks have also been given by another individual.

Oct. 30. As this is Saturday, the money which came in yesterday was not quite enough for today. But this mornings post brought, in answer to prayer, from Clapham 10s. and anonymously from Plymouth 10s.

Nov. 1. Yesterday was received altogether 2l. 10s. 3d.

Nov. 2. At a time of the greatest poverty 1l. was sent by a lady from Birmingham. About half an hour afterwards I received 10l. from a brother who had saved up 150l. and put it into a savings bank, but who now sees that, to devote this money to the promotion of the work of God tends more to the glory of the name of Jesus, than to retain it in a savings bank upon interest for a time of sickness or old age; for he is assured that should such times come, the same Lord, who has hitherto cared for him whilst in health and strength, and able to work, will also care for him then. The same brother gave me 3l. a fortnight since. This 10l. came in very seasonably; for though we had been able to provide for the absolute necessities of today, yet there was want in many respects, especially as a boy is just going out as an apprentice, who needs tools and an outfit.

Nov. 3. This afternoon two little boys were received, with whom three little girls sent 13s. 6d.

Nov. 4 and 5. 2l. 5s. ld. more was given.

Nov. 7. When there was now again nothing at all in hand, there came in 2l., being the profit of the sale of ladies baskets; and also 3l. 1s. 10d.

Nov. 8-11. 4l. 9s. 4d. was received during these four days.

Nov. 12. This morning after the exposition of the Scriptures to the children, 10s. was given to me, at a time when there was not only nothing at all in hand, but when without some help we should not have had every thing that was really needed for today.

Nov. 13. Saturday. This morning I took 1s. out of the box in my house. This one shilling was all there was towards the need of today.—Pause, dear reader, for a few moments! Consider that there are more than a hundred persons to be provided with every thing they require; consider that there is no money in hand; and consider also that this is the case not once nor twice in the course of the year but very frequently. Is it not precious, under such circumstances, to have the living God as a father to go to, who is ever able and ever willing to help as it may be really needed? And to this privilege every one has a title who believes in the Lord Jesus, being as such a child of God. Galatians iii. 26. For though all believers in the Lord Jesus are not called upon to establish Orphan-Houses, Schools for poor children, etc., and trust in God for means; yet all believers, according to the will of God concerning them in Christ Jesus, may cast, and ought to cast, all their care upon Him who careth for them, and need not be anxiously concerned about any thing, as is plainly to be seen from 1 Peter v. 7, Philippians iv. 6, Matthew vi. 25-34. Under these circumstances of need, a silver watch, which only yesterday afternoon had become the property of the Orphan-Fund, was disposed of, whereby we were helped through the expenses of today. The coals are almost gone in each of the houses. Every article of provision, etc., is likewise much reduced. Truly, we are exceedingly poor; nevertheless there are the necessary provisions till Monday morning, and thus we were brought to the close of another week. This afternoon all the labourers met for prayer.

Nov. 14. When we met again this afternoon for prayer, we had reason to praise, for the Lord had sent in means. This morning was given to me 5l., and 6s. had come in by sale of articles. There came also by post a small parcel from Wales, containing a few little articles, which are not to be mentioned, and 2s. 6d.

Nov. 15. Last Friday brother Craik and I had a meeting for inquirers and candidates for fellowship. We saw eight and had to send away ten whom we could not see, our strength being quite gone after we had seen the eight, one after another. This evening we saw seven and had to send away three.

Nov. 16. The last four days we have daily met for prayer, there being no means to pay the teachers in the Day Schools. Besides this, we need a stove in one of the school rooms; also some Bibles and Tracts. Today I received 2l. from a brother at Exmouth.

As only 2s. had been given yesterday for the Orphans, there was this morning again only 4s. 6d., in hand, which between ten and eleven oclock I was on the point of sending to the Orphan-Houses, having been called on for money. While I was writing the note to that effect, I received a post-office order for 3l. from a brother at Barnstaple, which was again a most precious deliverance, as our stores had been in every way so much reduced. About two hours later I received 4l. more from a brother at Exmouth, the half of which was for the Orphans, and the other half for the other objects. Through the same brother also was sent with Luke xxii. 32. 1l. for the Orphans. There came in still further today 2l. for stockings, which were bought by two ladies who visited the Orphan-Houses. They also gave 3s. 9d. Also an individual who had removed at four different times the furniture of the Orphan-Houses to and from Westbury, where the children had been, in turn, from Aug. 10 to Nov. 12, while the houses were coloured down and painted inside, charged only 1l. 1s. 10 1/2d., instead of 4l. 2s. 10 1/2d., which would have been the regular charge, and stated that he had long wished to do something for the Orphans, and that he should not have charged even this 1l. 1s. 10 1/2d. had he not had to lay it out in money. Thus the Lord in various ways helps us, and all without our asking any human being, but only in simplicity telling Him day by day our need.

Nov. 18. To day we had again a meeting with inquirers, and saw seven.

Nov. 21. Only 1l. 11s. 4d. came in since the 16th for the Orphans, on account of which there was today again no money at all in hand, and the stores were very much exhausted. How kind, therefore, of the Lord to send in again at this time 2l. 10s.

Nov. 23. Yesterday came in 5s. for stockings, which provided today the means for the breakfast in the Boys-Orphan-House. A sister sent also a gammon and some peas. Now we are very poor indeed. One of the labourers was able to provide a dinner in the Girls-Orphan-House out of his own means. In this our great need came in 17s. 6d. by sale of Reports, which money had been expected for some months past, but which the Lord sent just now most seasonably.

Besides this, 2s. 6d. was also received for the childrens needlework. Thus we were provided for this day also. In the afternoon the Lord gave us a still further proof of the continuance of His loving care over us, now that we are so poor; for a box arrived from Plymouth, containing clothes, trinkets, etc.

Nov. 24. We have been daily meeting for prayer the last twelve days. Today, just before I was going to the meeting, one of the articles, which came in the box from Plymouth yesterday afternoon, was sold for 2l. 2s., which sum supplies us with means for this day. The donors may not have thought, perhaps, that their bounty would so soon be needed. —When I came to the prayer-meeting, I heard of a little circumstance which is worthy of notice. The Infant Orphans took a walk this morning with their teacher. A poor woman came to her, whilst they were walking, and gave her two pence for the benefit of the Orphans, adding "It is but a trifle, but I must give it you." Now, one of these two pence had been needed, by the time I came, to make up the little sum which was required for the bread. —This afternoon was received still further 9d., and also 12s. by the sale of some of the articles which came from Plymouth.

Nov. 25. With 12s. 1d. we began the day, which was not sufficient for all that was required. In the afternoon came in 11s. for knitting. Thus we had enough for this day also.

Nov. 26. One of the labourers gave 5s.; 11s. came in by sale of articles, and 6d. was taken out of the box in my house. Little as this was, yet we were able to procure with it all that was really needful; but now our provision stock is very much reduced.

Nov. 27. This is Saturday, and nothing at all was in hand when the day commenced. My especial prayer had been, that the Lord would, be pleased early in the morning to send us supplies, as otherwise there would not be sufficient for dinner. Accordingly, about 10 oclock, a parcel came from Clapham, containing 11s. and the following articles: 12 yards of calico, a frock, a chemise, 2 petticoats, a flannel ditto, 2 handkerchiefs, 2 pinafores, a furnished workbag, an old silver thimble, and half a franc. Thus the Lord kindly provided us with means for the dinner, and we took it as a token for good that He would send what else might be needed this day. There came in still further in the course of the afternoon, by sale of an article, given by one of the labourers, 5s.; by sale of some lithographic sketches, given by one of the labourers, 4s. 6d.; by sale of articles given some time since, 16s.; by sale of stockings, 2s. 9d.; and by a donation, 2s. Thus the Lord was pleased to give us in the course of this day 2l. 1s. 3d., while we were in the greatest need in the morning, and without any natural prospect of having the means which were required for the day.

Nov. 29. The Lord has kindly sent in supplies. Yesterday was given altogether 5l. 19s. 7d. These two weeks we have been likewise in the greatest poverty in reference to the Day Schools; but the Lord has almost daily sent in a little to supply the absolute necessities of the brethren and sisters, who are engaged in that part of the work.

Nov. 30. Though 5l. 19s. 7d. had been given, yet, as the stores had been previously so reduced, there was again some more money needed today. 5s. came in by sale of articles, and one of the labourers gave some money of his own. In this time of great need there arrived a parcel, sent anonymously, which contained the following articles: 3 combs, 6 shells, 5 pairs of gilt bracelets, 4 single bracelets, a pair of ditto, a gilt chain, a gilt necklace, a cornelian ditto, a bead ditto, a brooch, a buckle, 2 pairs of earrings, 3 rings, 3 pairs of drops, and a single ear-ring.

Dec. 1. Again there were many shillings needed for this day.
At the Boys-Orphan-House matters stood so in the
morning, that, with an addition of eight pence, the dinner
could be provided; but there was only seven pence in hand.
Brother B. having heard that something had been put last
evening into the box at the Girls-Orphan-House, went, and
it was found to be one penny, which an aged sister had put
in, whereby the present need was supplied. Even the gift of
this one penny was thus evidently under the ordering of
our kind Father, who not in anger, but for the trial of our
faith, keeps us so poor. About ten oclock this morning was
sent by post, half a sovereign. In the letter was written:
"From the wife of a clergyman, for the Orphan-Houses, Nov.
30 1841." This donation was truly sweet, as coming from
our faithful Lord, though it was not nearly enough. But He
had pity on us, and sent in still further today by the sale of
stockings 5s., and by the sale of other articles 12s.

Dec. 2. In the course of this morning was sold a part of the
trinkets which came on Nov. 30th, for 1l. 4s. 10d. Besides
this came in by sale of articles 1s. 6d. Thus was our present
need supplied in the afternoon 3l. was sent by a sister from
Plymouth, and by a sister in Bristol was given to me 2s.

Dec. 3 and 4. 1l. 10s. 6d. has been received during these two
days.

Dec. 6. Yesterday the Lord again, in His faithful love, sent in
means for the need of today. A gentleman from Devonshire
came to me after the meeting, introduced himself as a
brother, and gave me 5l. for the work of the Lord, as it
might be needed. I had pleasant brotherly communion with
him, but he preferred not to give me his name. Besides this,
came in 18s. 11 1/2d. by sale of articles. As this 18s. 11 1/2d.

was not enough for the supply of the Orphans for this day, there being nothing at all in hand besides, and 1l. more needed, I took 1l. of the 5l. for the Orphans, and 4l. for the other objects. Through the same stranger I received also 2s. 6d. from a sister. There came in this evening 1l. 3s. besides.

By the 4l. which I took of the 5l. given by the gentleman from
Devonshire, the most pressing need with regard to the teachers in the
Day Schools is relieved. This stranger gave me also 1l. for Missionary purposes.

Dec. 7. Three weeks and three days we have now been daily meeting for prayer, on account of the state of the funds, and to ask the Lords blessing upon the work. We have been daily asking Him to supply us with means for the School-Bible-Missionary-and Tract Fund. Now, today, in this our great poverty, was sent by a sister from one of the Northern counties, whom I have never seen, the sum of 50l. of which, according to her wish, 10l. is to be applied to each of these objects, and 10l. for the Orphans. Thus the Lord has been pleased to send us a little help, which is greatly needed for all the objects: for the teachers have had only as much as was absolutely needful, the Bible stock is almost entirely exhausted, the Tract stock is quite exhausted, and to some Missionary brethren we greatly desired to send help, but were unable to do so. Nevertheless, even now we are waiting upon the Lord for further supplies.

When this money came, there was none at all in hand for the Orphans, though for many reasons fresh supplies were much needed. By this 10l., then, the Lord has again helped us for the present. There was likewise sent anonymously by post, 1l.

Dec. 9. Today came in for the Orphans by the sale of stockings 10s. 10d. — We are now brought to the close of the sixth year of this part of the work, having only in hand the money which has been put by for the rent; but during the whole of this year we have been supplied with all that was needed.

During the last three years we had closed the accounts on this day, and had, a few days after, some public meetings at which for the benefit of the hearers, we stated how the Lord had dealt with us during the year, and the substance of what had been stated at these meetings was afterwards printed for the benefit of the church at large. This time, however, it appeared to us better to delay for awhile both the public meetings and the publishing of the Report Through grace we had learned to lean upon the Lord only, being assured, that, if we never were to speak or write one single word more about this work, yet should we be supplied with means, as long as He should enable us to depend on Himself alone. But whilst we neither had had those public meetings for the purpose of exposing our necessity, nor had had the account of the Lords dealings with us published for the sake of working thereby upon the feelings of the readers, and thus inducing them to give money, but only that we might by our experience benefit other saints; yet it might have appeared to some that in making known our circumstances we were actuated by some such motives. What better proof, therefore, could we give of our depending upon the living God alone, and not upon public meetings or printed Reports, than that, in the midst of our deep poverty, instead of being glad for the time to have come when we could make known our circumstances, we still went on quietly for some time longer, without saying any thing. We therefore determined, as we sought and still seek in this work to act for the profit of the saints generally, to delay both the public meetings and the Report for a few months. Naturally we should have been, of course, as glad as any one to have exposed our poverty at that time; but spiritually we were enabled to delight even then in the prospect of the increased benefit that might be derived by the church at large from our acting as we did.—I now proceed where I left off.

Dec. 11. Since the day before yesterday the following sums came in for the Orphans, whereby the need of yesterday and today has been supplied. A brother gave 2l. A little boy and girl brought the produce of their savings banks, amounting to 19s. 5d. By the sale of stockings came in 15s. 1d., and by six donations 10s. 6d.

Dec. 13. Yesterday came in 1l. 11s. 6d., and today 10s. By this 2l. 1s. 6d. this days need has been met. There was also, very seasonably, half a ton of coals sent to each of the three Orphan-Houses.

Dec. 14. Yesterday afternoon a lady sent a sovereign for the Orphans. There came in 15s. 6d. besides. Thus we had enough for this day likewise.

Dec. 15. Having now again nothing in hand for the Orphans, the boxes were opened, in which 4s. 4d. was found. This, with a little which one of the labourers was able to add of his own, helped us through the day.

From Nov. 12 up to this day, my fellow-labourers in the Church and I have seen thirty inquirers and candidates for fellowship, and some of them we have seen repeatedly. How can we sufficiently praise the Lord for still continuing to use us in His service.

Dec. 16. Nothing at all had come in for the Orphans; but as

one of the labourers had last evening, most unexpectedly, received some money from a distance of about two hundred miles, and as the Lord inclined his heart to give of it for the present need, we were supplied for today also.

Dec. 17. In like manner we are helped today.

Dec. 18. Saturday morning. There is now the greatest need, and only 4d. in hand, which I found in the box at my house; yet I fully believe the Lord will supply us this day also with all that is required.—Pause a few moments, dear reader! Observe two things! We acted for God in delaying the public meetings and the publishing of the Report; but Gods way leads always into trial, so far as sight and sense are concerned. Nature always will be tried in Gods ways. The Lord was saying by this poverty, "I will now see whether you truly lean upon me, and whether you truly look to me." Of all the seasons that I had ever passed through since I had been living in this way, up to that time, I never knew any period in which my faith was tried so sharply, as during the four months from Dec. 12, 1841, to April 12, 1842. But observe further: We might even now have altered our minds with respect to the public meetings and publishing the Report; for no one knew our determination, at this time, concerning the point. Nay, on the contrary, we knew with what delight very many children of God were looking forward to receive further accounts. But the Lord kept us steadfast to the conclusion, at which we had arrived under His guidance.—Now to return to Saturday, Dec. 18th. Evening. The Lord has been very kind to us this day. In the course of the morning 6s. came in. We had thus, with what provisions there were in hand, all that was needed for the dinner, but no means to provide for the next meal in the afternoon. A few minutes after the labourers had met together for prayer this morning, there was given to one of them a sovereign for himself. By means of this, all that was needed for tea could be procured. Another labourer gave 3s. 6d. and two books, which were sold for 4s. There came in still further in the course of the afternoon and evening:—by sale of stockings, 8s. 8d.; by needlework, 8d.; and by sale of articles, 5s. Thus, when we again met in the evening for prayer, we found that the supplies had amounted to 2l. 8s. 2d., enough for all that was required today. But one thing more is to be noticed respecting this day. I was informed that three more of the Orphans have been recently brought to the knowledge of the truth. We have now been meeting daily for prayer during the last five weeks, and thus the Lord has not merely heard our prayers respecting the funds, but has also blessed these children.

Dec. 20. The Lord has again kindly sent fresh supplies. A sister gave 1l.; a servant sent 1l.; another servant, 2s 6d. by sale of articles 13s. 1d. This morning, just before was going to the prayer-meeting, a lady brought 3l.; and 5s. more I received this evening.

Dec. 21. Though 6s. 0s. 7d. had been received yesterday and the day before, there was only 5s. remaining towards the supply of the necessities of today. At one oclock three little boys gave me the produce of their Orphan-box, which was 4s. 7d. When I came home, I found that 18l. had come in, being a legacy left for the Orphans by a lady who died at the commencement of the year. This money comes in most seasonably, not merely for the supply of the wants of the children, but also as enabling me to give to some of the labourers in the Orphan-Houses supplies for themselves.

Dec. 23. This is now the sixth week that the labourers in the Day-Schools and Orphan-Houses have daily met for prayer. Several precious answers we have already received since we began to meet, as it regards pecuniary supplies, fresh instances of conversion among the children, etc. One of our petitions has been that the Lord would be pleased to furnish us with means for a stove at Callowhill Street School-room. But though we had often mentioned this matter before the Lord, he seemed not to regard our request. Yesterday afternoon, while walking in my little garden, and meditating and praying, I had an unusual assurance that the time was now come when the Lord would answer our request, which arose partly from my being able to believe that He would send the means, and partly from the fact that the answer could no longer be delayed, without prayer having failed in this matter, as we could not assemble the children again, after the Christmas vacation, without there being a stove put up. And now, dear reader, observe: —This morning I received from A. B. 20l., and we have thus much more than is required for a stove.

Dec. 24. On the 22nd and 23rd 2l. 0s. 5d. came in for the Orphans. The need of today was 3l. 10s., but only 3l. was in hand. This afternoon, however, 1l. was sent from Kensington and 1l. from Plymouth. This evening we received still further anonymously 4s., and by knitting 2l. 10s.

Dec. 25. By sale of articles was received 14s. 2d.

Dec. 26. This afternoon I was walking in my little garden, meditating on and turning into prayer Rom. viii. 28-32. When I came to verse 32, the necessity of the Orphans came to my mind, as tomorrow we shall again need more money than there is in hand, and I therefore asked the Lord that He would be pleased to give me a fresh proof that He will "freely give us all things," by supplying our present need. This evening I spoke on the above-mentioned passage, and after the meeting a sister gave to my wife 12l., of which 10l.

was for the Orphans, and 2l. for my own necessities. There came in 5s. besides.

Dec. 31. As only 1l. 15s. had been received since the 26th, there was again nothing in hand towards the need of this day. About an hour before the money was sent for from the Orphan-Houses, an individual who lives in Redcliff Parish, Bristol, sent 5l. By sale of stockings came in likewise 3s. 6d.

REVIEW OF THE YEAR 1841.

I. In reading over my journal, I find that the Lord has given me during this year many precious answers to prayer, in addition to those which have been recorded in the previous part of the Narrative. I mention the following for the encouragement of the reader: 1, One of the Orphan-Boys needed to be apprenticed. I knew of no suitable believing master, who would take an in-door apprentice. I gave myself to prayer, and brought the matter daily before the Lord. I marked it down among the subjects for which I would daily ask the Lord; and at last, though from May 21 to September I had to pray about the matter, the Lord granted my request; for in September I found a suitable place for him. 2, On May 23rd I began to ask the Lord that He would be pleased to deliver a certain sister in the Lord from the great spiritual depression under which she was suffering, and after three days the Lord granted me my request. 3, On June 15th I began to ask the Lord to deliver a brother at a distance from the great spiritual nervousness in which he found himself shut up, which not only distressed him exceedingly, and in a great measure hindered him in his service towards the world and the church; but which, in consequence, was also a trial to the saints who knew and valued this dear brother. This petition I brought many times before the Lord. The year passed away, and it was not granted. But yet at last this request also has been granted to me and to the many dear saints who, I know, prayed for this dear brother; for though he was for some years in this state, it is now [in 1845] two years and more since he has been quite restored. 4, On June 15th I also began to ask the Lord daily, in His mercy to keep a sister in the Lord from insanity, who was then apparently on the very border of it; and I have now [in 1845] to record to His praise, after nearly four years have passed away, that the Lord has kept her from it. 5, During this year I was informed about the conversion of one of the very greatest sinners, that I ever heard of in all my service for the Lord. Repeatedly I fell on my knees with his wife, and asked the Lord for his conversion, when she came to me in the deepest distress of soul, on account of the most barbarous and cruel treatment that she received from him, in his bitter enmity against her for the Lords sake, and because he could not provoke her to be in a passion, and she would not strike him again, and the like. At the time when it was at its worst I pleaded especially on his behalf the promise in Matthew xviii. 19: "Again I say unto you, that if two of you shall agree on earth as touching any thing that they shall ask, it shall be done for them of my Father which is in heaven." And now this awful persecutor is converted. 6, On May 25th I began to ask the Lord for greater real spiritual prosperity among the saints, among whom I labour in Bristol, than there ever yet had been among them; and now I have to record to the praise of the Lord that truly He has answered this request; for, considering all things, at no period has there been more manifestation of grace and truth, and spiritual power among us, than there is now while I am writing this for the press (1845). Not that we have attained to what we might;

we are far, very far from it; but the Lord has been very, very good to us, and we have most abundant cause for thanksgiving.

II. The state of the church with reference to numbers, etc.

68 brethren and sisters brother Craik and I found in communion, when we came to Bristol.

775 have been admitted into communion since we came to Bristol.

843 would be, therefore, the total number of those in communion with us, had there been no changes. But,

101 have left Bristol.

55 have left us, but are still in Bristol

48 are under church discipline.

67 have fallen asleep.

271 are therefore to be deducted from 843, so that there are only 572 at present in communion.

88 have been added during the past year, of whom 30 have been brought to the knowledge of the Lord among us.

III. The Lords goodness as to my temporal supplies during this year.

1. The Lord has been pleased to give me by means of the anonymous freewill offerings of the saints, put into the boxes at our meeting places £116 2s. 4 3/4d.

2. By presents in money from the brethren among whom I labour in Bristol £43 9s. 9d.

3. By presents in money from children of God not living in Bristol £53 19s. 0d.

4. By presents in provisions, clothes, furniture, etc., from the saints among whom I labour, worth to us at least £15 0s. 0d.

5. By presents in clothes, &c., from believers not living in Bristol, worth to us at least £10 0s. 0d.

Altogether £238 11s. 1 3/4d.

Thus during this year also, without asking any one but the Lord for help, with regard to ray temporal necessities, I have been richly supplied with all I needed; yea, I have had much more than I needed.

January 1, 1842. Last night we had our usual prayer-meeting at the close of the year, which this time lasted from seven in the evening till half-past twelve.

Jan. 3. This evening we had a most precious public prayer-meeting. When the usual time for closing the meeting came, it appeared to me that there was a desire to continue to wait upon the Lord. I therefore proposed to the brethren that those who had bodily strength, time, and a desire for waiting still longer upon the Lord, would do so. At least thirty remained, and we continued till after ten in prayer, whilst several brethren prayed. I never knew prayer more really in the Spirit. I experienced for myself unusual nearness to the Lord, and was enabled to ask in faith, nothing doubting.

On the 1st of January came in for the Orphans 1l.7s. 6d.; on the 2nd 10l. 13s. 7d.; and today came in from Plymouth 6l., from Exmouth 5l., from a sister in Bristol 5l., and from the East Indies 2l. I have by this 30l. 1s. 1d. been enabled, as it had been my prayer, to give some money to the other five sisters who labour in the Orphan Houses, for their own personal necessities.

Jan. 4. As we have often found it to be the case, so it is now. After a season of more than usual poverty, comes a time of more than usual abundance. Today the same brother, who has been spoken of under November 2nd, and who has drawn his money out of the Savings-bank to spend it for the Lord, sent 20l. more of it. There came in also from Guernsey 1l., and 1l. 7s. besides. I am now able to order oatmeal from Scotland, buy materials for the boys clothes, order shoes, etc. Thus the Lord has been pleased to answer all our requests with respect to the pecuniary necessities of the Orphans, which we have brought before Him in our prayer meetings during the last seven weeks. We have thus had of late an abundance, but the expenses have been great also; for within the last twenty-five days I have paid out above 100l.

Jan. 22. As only little above 32l. had been received since the 4th, there was today again only 1l. 8s. 0 1/2d. in hand, whilst 31, 8s. was needed, it being Saturday. However, as the Lord has helped us very many Saturdays, when we had still less at the commencement of the day, so it was today also. About an hour before the money was called for, I received from the neighbourhood of Crediton 4l., which came with the especial recommendation of a gentleman and lady to introduce the use of oatmeal in the Orphan-Houses, if we had not done so, and this money was sent towards the first supply. We have, however, used oatmeal now for many months, and have found it decidedly of great benefit to the children As about a fortnight since I had ordered 10l. worth from Glasgow, this money came in most seasonably to supply the other necessities of this day.

Jan. 24. Yesterday the Lord sent in 3l. 5s. 7d., to supply the need of this day.

Jan. 25. There was now again this morning nothing in hand for the Orphans. About ten oclock there was sent to me, as the produce of an Orphan box, a small necklace, an old sixpence, and 5s. 8d. There came in also by sale of stockings 3s. 9d. As this 9s. 5d. was not enough, the boxes in the Orphan-Houses were opened, which contained 17s. 2d., and thus we were again supplied.

Perhaps, dear reader, you have said in your heart before you have read thus far: "How would it be, suppose the funds for the Orphans were reduced to nothing, and those who are engaged in the work had nothing of their own to give, and a meal time were to come, and you had no food for the children." Thus indeed it may be, for our hearts are desperately wicked. If ever we should be so left to ourselves, as that either we depend no more upon the living God, or that "we regard iniquity in our hearts," then such a state of things, we have reason to believe, would occur. But so long as we shall be enabled to trust in the living God, and so long as, though falling short in every way of what we might be, and ought to be, we are at least kept from living in sin, such a state of things cannot occur. Therefore, dear reader, if you yourself walk with God, and if, on that account, His glory is dear to you, I affectionately and earnestly entreat you to beseech Him to uphold us; for how awful would be the disgrace brought upon His holy name, if we, who have so publicly made our boast in Him, and have spoken well of Him, should be left to disgrace Him, either by unbelief in the hour of trial, or by a life of sin in other respects.

Jan. 26. Again there was nothing in hand when the day commenced. In the course of the morning a gentleman from Yorkshire came to the Orphan-Houses. He bought two Reports, and one copy of the "Improved Renderings," put 2s. 6d. into the box at the Boys-Orphan-House, and 3s. into the box at the Infant-Orphan-House. There was also one penny found in the box at the Girls-Orphan-House. This 6s. 10d. would have provided the absolute necessities for today, but it was desirable to have more means. I therefore opened the box in my house, in which I found a sovereign and a shilling. We were thus comfortably provided.

Jan. 27. Last evening came in 4s. This morning a parcel arrived from E. P., containing 3s., and the following articles: 7 books, a Bible, 6 pairs of socks, 4 pairs of babies shoes, a purse, a ladys comb, a ladys bag, a pair of knitted over-shoes, and 2 pairs of muffetees. Yesterday afternoon a gentleman came to see the Orphan-Houses, and put a sovereign into the box at the Boys-Orphan-House, which our need has brought out. We have thus 1l. 7s. for this day. —Evening. This afternoon came in still further 2l. from a lady at Kensington, on whose heart the Lord seems to have particularly laid the work.

Jan. 29. The two sovereigns, which came in on the 27th, supplied our need yesterday. When I had again nothing in hand, to meet todays necessities, a sister came last evening, who brought me 1l. 6s., a sovereign from another sister, and 6s. from herself. She said: "I do not know whether the Orphans have a dinner for tomorrow or not, but I had no rest in delaying to bring this money." I had but just then come home from a meeting, and had on the way to my house been lifting up my heart to the Lord, that He would be pleased to remember our need. — This morning was sent from Clapham 1l. 2s. 6d., with 3 frocks, a petticoat, 4 handkerchiefs, and 2 pinafores.

My dear reader, do you indeed recognise the hand of God in all these instances I have given instance upon instance, I have brought before you not this particular case, nor another particular case; but I have purposely shown you how we have fared day after day in our poverty, in order that you may adore the Lord for His goodness to us, and that you yourself may be led to depend upon Him for every thing, should you not have done so before. I affectionately beseech you, not to take these instances as a matter of course. Say not in your heart, This is a charitable Institution; persons know that the maintenance of these many Orphans, and the support of these Day Schools, etc., costs much money; and therefore they will contribute. Nor suffer Satan to rob you of the blessing which the account of the Lords faithfulness to us, and His readiness to listen to our supplications is calculated with Gods blessing, to communicate to you, by allowing him to whisper into your ears, that, because the Report are read by many, donations will of course be coming in, and that not all at once, but gradually, and that this is the way in which we are supplied. Dear reader, it is not thus. Suppose, we have been for some time on the whole bountifully supplied. Suppose, now all is gone. Suppose, the expenses are great, but very little comparatively is coming in. What shall we do now? If we took goods on credit, or if we made known our necessities at such times to the liberal Christians who have means, and who are interested in the work in our hands, then, humanly speaking, there might be little difficulty; but we neither take goods on credit, nor do we speak to any one about our need, but we wait upon God. Now, suppose our expenses are week after week, 30l., 40l., 50l., or 60l.? How are the means to come? Persons might still give; yea, many persons might still give, but it might just happen so, that all the donations that are received at the time when our expenses are most heavy are very small donations; how shall we do then? Sometimes the outgoings have been so great, that if I had sold every thing I possessed, I could not thereby have met the expenses of two weeks. What then is to be done? We wait upon God, and he always helps us, and has done so now [i. e. in 1881] for more than forty-five years with reference to the Orphans, and for more than forty-seven with reference to the other parts of the work.

Feb. 5. Saturday. As only 10l. 10s. 6d. had been received since January 29th, i. e. only so much as day by day was needed to provide necessaries for the Orphans, there is again the greatest need. It is now twelve oclock, and there are no means as yet to meet the expenses of today. The words in the prayer of Jehoshaphat, "Neither know we what to do, but our eyes are upon Thee," are at this moment the language of my heart. I likewise know not what to do, but my eyes are upon the Lord, and I am sure that He will help this day also. Our kind Father still gives us proofs that He is mindful of our need; for last evening were anonymously sent to my house, 2 waistcoats, a shawl, a net collar, 3 3/4 yards of print, 2 decanters, and Clarendons History of England. And just now, a small silver book, a pepper box with silver top, and some muslin work have arrived from Birmingham. — Evening. In the course of the morning came in, by sale of articles, 12s. We were able likewise to dispose of one of the articles, which were sent last evening, for 5s. This afternoon one of the labourers gave me 10s., and 3s. came in for needle-work. By means of this 1l. 10s. we were able to supply all that was needed.

Feb. 7. Yesterday was received 1l. 13s. 5d., and today 5s. 6d.

Feb. 8. By what came in yesterday, and the day before, the need of yesterday was supplied, and there is enough in all the houses for the meals of today; but in none of the houses have we been able to take in any bread; and as yesterday also but little could be taken in, there will not remain any for tomorrow; nor is there money enough to take in milk tomorrow morning. There are likewise coals needed in two houses. Indeed, so far as I know, these three years and seven months, since first the funds were exhausted, we were never in greater poverty; and if the Lord were not to send means before nine oclock tomorrow morning, His name would be dishonoured. But I am fully assured that He will not leave us.—Evening. The Lord has not yet been pleased to send us what is needed for tomorrow, but He has given us a fresh proof that He is mindful of us. Between four and five oclock this afternoon were sent nine plum cakes, which a sister had ordered to be baked as a treat for the Orphans. These cakes were an encouragement to me to continue to look out for further supplies. There was also found in the boxes at the Orphan-Houses, 2s. 1 1/2d., and 1s. 4d. came in for stockings. These little donations are most precious, but they are not enough to meet the need of tomorrow; yea, before nine oclock tomorrow morning we need more money to be able to take in the milk. Truly, we are poorer than ever; but, through grace, my eyes look not at the empty stores and the empty purse, but to the riches of the Lord only.

Feb. 9. This morning I went between seven and eight o clock to the Orphan-Houses, to see whether the Lord had sent in any thing. When I arrived there, He had just two or three minutes before sent help.—A brother, in going to his house of business this morning, had gone already about half a mile, when the Lord was pleased to lay the Orphans upon his heart. He said, however, to himself, I cannot well return now, but will take something this evening; and thus he walked on. Nevertheless he could not go any further, but felt himself constrained to go back, and to take to brother R. B., at the Boys-Orphan-House, three sovereigns. [The donor himself stated this to me afterwards.]—Thus the Lord in His faithfulness helped us. Help was never more truly needed, for our poverty was never greater; nor did the help of the Lord ever come more manifestly from Himself; for the brother was gone on a good distance, it was between seven and eight oclock in the morning, and it was so short a time before money was needed. Consider this, beloved reader, and with us praise the Lord. Praise Him particularly, that He enabled us to trust in Him in this trying hour. There came in besides, today, 7s. 6d.

Feb. 11. The 3l. 11s. 6d. supplied our need the last two days. Today again a few shillings more were needed, which one of the labourers was able to give of his own; but this was only enough to take in the usual quantity of milk, and some bread.

Feb. 12. Saturday. Never since the funds were for the first time exhausted, had there come in less during any week, than during this. We were only able to supply the absolute necessities; but this we were enabled to do. When the meal times came, the Lord always provided what was needful, and, considering the great distress there is now almost everywhere, our dear Orphans are very well provided for. Now this day began not only without there being any thing in hand, but our stores were greatly reduced, and we had to procure provisions for two days. One of the labourers gave 5s. in the morning, to provide the means to take in the milk. I collected together some pamphlets, which had been given for sale, to dispose of them, and they were

75

sold about eleven oclock for 4s. There came in also by sale of stockings 3s., and 12s. was paid on behalf of one of the Orphans. Thus we were provided with means to procure a dinner, and had a little towards purchasing bread, but by no means enough. All the labourers were together in prayer from half-past eleven till one, and me separated comfortably, with the purpose of meeting again in the evening. When I came home, there was given to me an old broken silver pencil case, which, though worth very little, I took as a fresh proof that our Father was mindful of our need. When we met again this evening, we found that 3s. 6d. had come in by sale of stockings, and 6d. for two Reports. As all this was not enough, a few old and needless articles were disposed of for 4s., also the broken pencil ease for 6d. I say needless articles, for other articles it did not seem right to us to dispose of, in order that the Lords own deliverance might be manifest. A labourer was also still further able to give 7s. of his own. To one of the labourers 2s. had been owed by a certain individual for more than a twelvemonth, which being paid just now, and given by him for the Orphans, came in most seasonably. Thus we had 1l. 18s. 6d., as much as was needful to procure provisions till after breakfast on Monday morning. However, the Lord helped still further. Between eight and nine this evening, after we had been together for prayer, and had now separated, some money was given to one of the labourers for himself, by which means he was able to give 9s., so that altogether 2l. 7s. 6d. had come in this day. This has been of all the weeks, during the last three years and seven months, one of the most trying, so far as it regards the trial of faith. Thanks to the Lord, who has helped us this day also! Thanks to Him for enabling us already this morning, when we met for prayer, to praise Him for the deliverance, which we were sure He would work!

Feb. 14. Yesterday came in from Wolverhampton 1l. 2s. 6d. and a necklace. There was also given to me 1l. 0s. 6d., which had come in by sale of articles, and 6d. for Reports. In the course of this day came in still further 3l. 2s. 4d.

Feb. 15. By needlework came in 4s. 9d.

Feb. 16. This morning there was now again only sufficient money in hand to take in milk at two of the houses; but as a labourer was able to give 6s. 6d., we had sufficient for the milk, and had also enough, with the provisions that were in the houses, to provide for the dinner. Nothing more came in in the course of the morning, nor was I able to make inquiries how matters stood. In the afternoon between three and four oclock, having once more besought the Lord to send us help, I sat peacefully down to give myself to meditation over the Word, considering that that was now my service, though I knew not whether there was a morsel of bread for tea in any one of the houses, but being assured that the Lord would provide. For, through grace, my mind is so fully assured of the faithfulness of the Lord, that, in the midst of the greatest need, I am enabled in peace to go about my other work. Indeed, did not the Lord give me this, which is the result of trusting in Him, I should scarcely be able to work at all; for it is now comparatively a rare thing that a day comes, when I am not in need for one or the other part of the work. Scarcely had I sat down to meditate, when a note was sent to me from the Orphan-Houses, in which brother R. B., master of the Orphan Boys, had written thus: "On visiting the sisters in the Infant and Girls-Orphan-Houses, I found them in the greatest need. There was not bread in one of the houses for tea this evening, and the 6s. 6d. was scarcely enough to supply what was needed for the dinner. I therefore opened the box in the Boys-Orphan-House, and most unexpectedly found 1l. in it.

Thus, through the kindness of the Lord, we were again abundantly supplied as it regards present necessities."—In the evening the Lord, in His love and faithfulness, stretched out His hand still farther. I had expounded at the meeting a part of John xi. The last words of which I spoke were: "Said I not unto thee, that, if thou wouldest believe, thou shouldest see the glory of God?" When the meeting was over, as a fresh proof of the truth of this word, a note was given to me, in which a sick sister sent me 5l. for the Orphans.

Feb. 17 and 18. These two days came in 8s. 2d.

Feb. 19. Saturday. Our means were now again completely spent. Our provision stores, were, perhaps, even more exhausted than on any previous Saturday. There was not the least human likelihood of obtaining menus for sufficient provisions for this one day, and much less for two days. When I went before breakfast to the Orphan-Houses, I found a letter from Nottingham, containing 1s., which had arrived last evening. This was not only a sweet proof that our Father remembered our need, but it was also like an earnest that He would supply us this day also with all we required. In the course of the morning came in by sale of stockings 4s. 11d. In the box at my house I found 1s. One of the labourers gave 4s. 10d. Thus we were provided with those things which were absolutely needed for this day. We met between eleven and twelve oclock for prayer. When we met again in the evening, a second letter had arrived from Nottingham, with another shilling. This was a further sweet proof of our Fathers loving remembrance of our need; but with all this we were still without any means to provide bread for tomorrow, the Lords day. At eight oclock I separated from my fellow-labourers, as I expected brother R. C. to arrive a little after eight at my house. I therefore requested one of the brethren to go with me, in order to take back to the Orphan-Houses what the Lord might send in by post or in any other way. It was now half-past eight in the evening, and there was no bread yet in any one of the three houses for tomorrow. A few moments after, brother C. arrived, and he had not been more than about five minutes in my house when he gave me half a sovereign, which he brought for the Orphans. I soon found an opportunity to leave the room for a little, gave the 10s. to the brother whom I had brought with me from the Orphan Houses, and who was waiting in another room; and thus, between nine and ten oclock, sufficient bread could be bought. Observe! For the trial of our faith the Lord had allowed us to be kept waiting so long. When, however, brother C. had arrived, having money for the Orphans, he could not delay giving it at once, a matter most worthy of notice. This has been a week full of trials of faith, but also full of deliverances.

Feb. 21. Since Saturday evening came in 1l. 8s. 11d. There was also sent from Plymouth, a piece of blond, a piece of quilling net, and eleven pairs of childrens stockings, for sale. Thus we were supplied with means for that which was requisite for the beginning of this day; but as our stores had been so reduced at the end of last week, there was not enough for tea this afternoon. Four oclock had now come, one hour before the usual tea time, when a brother from Somersetshire came to see the Orphan-Houses, and put a sovereign into each of the boxes. Our great need soon brought out the money, and thus we were supplied. [Observe! The brother (as he himself told me a few days after in the course of conversation), had but little time, and therefore rather hastily went over the houses. Had he stayed long and conversed much, as might have been the case, his donations would not have been in time for the tea.] There

79

came in 1s. besides, by needlework done by the children.

Feb. 22. This morning a parcel arrived from the neighbourhood of Manchester, containing 4 old silver thimbles, 1 seal, 2 gold pins, 10 cent (an American coin), a buckle, a watch key, a broken seal, some pamphlets and 549 sheets of Hintwafers.

Feb. 23. We were again in want of means. A few of the articles which had come from Manchester were disposed of, and one of the labourers was able to give enough for what remained to be supplied. —The narrative of time events of these days is most imperfect. The way in which the Lord stretched out His hand day by day, and from meal to meal, cannot be accurately described. To enter fully into it, one need be a witness to His inspecting the stores, so to speak, from meal to meal, and giving us those things which we needed.

Feb. 24. Yesterday the following clothes were sent: 3 pairs of boys trousers, 2 boys dresses, 2 frocks, a spencer, 5 pairs of childrens stays, a pair of boots, and a few other little articles. The clothes were all much worn, and in other respects not fit for the Orphans; but the Lord used them to supply us with the means for the dinner, as they were disposed of this morning. In the afternoon we again met for prayer. On my way to the Orphan-Houses, between four and five, when I knew that there would not be any bread, at least in one of the houses, for tea, I felt quite peaceful, being fully assured that for this meal also the Lord would provide. On inquiry I found that there was bread enough in the Girls-Orphan-House, none at all in the Boys-Orphan-House, but enough in the Infant-Orphan-House both for the Infants and Boys. Therefore we were at this time supplied by the bread which was not needed at the Infant-Orphan-House. We have thus this day also what is absolutely needful. But now there is no bread in any of the houses, nor scarcely any thing else in the way of provisions.

Feb. 25. Greater than now our need had never been. Our trials of faith have never been so sharp as during this week. Indeed, so much so, that most of the labourers felt today considerably tried. Yet neither this day has the Lord suffered us to be confounded. Through a remarkable circumstance one of the labourers obtained some money this morning, so that all the need of today could be amply met. In the afternoon a physician of this city kindly sent 1l. for the Orphans, which was a sweet proof to us, when we met for prayer, that our kind Father had not forgotten us. Also on my way to the prayer-meeting at the Orphan-Houses I received 9s.

Feb. 26. My prayer this morning was in particular, that the Lord would be pleased now to look in pity upon us, and take off His hand. Indeed, for several days my prayer has been that He would enable us to continue to trust in Him, and not lay more upon us than He would enable us to bear. This is now again Saturday. There having been given yesterday a rich supply to the matrons, I knew that not so much as usual would be required this Saturday; still I thought that 1l. 10s. would be needed. Between ten and eleven oclock this morning a parcel came from Clapham, containing 2l. 2s., with 2 frocks, 2 petticoats, 2 chemises, 2 pinafores, and 6 handkerchiefs (all new.) Thus we were richly supplied for today, for only 1l. 10s. was needed. There was moreover half-a-sovereign put into the box at my house this day by a little boy, and 2s. 6d. came in by sale of articles. Thus we were brought to the close of a week in which more than at any previous time the Lord has been pleased to try our faith. To Him most manifestly we owe it that our faith has not failed completely.

Feb. 28. Yesterday Q. Q. gave me an order for 8l. As it was left to me to lay out the money as I thought well, I put 4l. of it to the School-Fund, and 4l. to the Orphan-Fund. Thus both parts of the work have been again most seasonably helped, as today the teachers in the Day-Schools greatly needed some money for themselves. Today 13s. was received for the Orphans.

March 2. Yesterday I found a sovereign in the Orphan-box at my house; received 9s. 2 3/4d. from three little boys, being the produce of their Orphan-box; 2s. 6d. for Reports; and 1l. 10s., being the profit of the sale of ladies baskets. Thus we were again supplied for yesterday and today. This evening were also sent, by order of an Irish sister, 33 1/2 lbs. of woollen yarn. Respecting this donation it is to be remarked, that last Saturday we had asked the Lord in our prayer-meeting, that He would be pleased to send us means to purchase worsted, in order that the boys might go on with their knitting.

March 3. Yesterday 5s. came in, and this evening a sovereign, when there was now again great need, there being no money in hand.

March 5. Saturday. It was not a small deliverance, that the Lord sent this morning, between ten and eleven oclock, 2l. 10s. from Edinburgh, when there were no means in hand to meet this days necessities, nay, not even the means to procure a dinner, as only 4s. had come in yesterday.— Evening. About eight oclock a gentleman called on me. He said "I come at a late hour, but I trust not the less acceptable on that account. I bring you a little money for the Orphans." He then gave me two sovereigns. When I requested him to give me his name, he told me, that if the giving of his name would be of any benefit he would do so, but as it would not, I might simply put down in the Report

"Sent," for he was sure that the Lord had sent him. —I believe it, for the help came most seasonably and in answer to prayer. There was likewise taken out of the box in my house half-a-sovereign.

March 9. At a time of the greatest need, both with regard to the Day-Schools and the Orphans, so much so that we could not have gone on any longer without help, I received this day 10l. from a brother who lives near Dublin. The money was divided between the Day-Schools and the Orphan-Houses. The following little circumstance is to be noticed respecting this donation:—As our need was so great, and my soul was, through grace, truly waiting upon the Lord, I looked out for supplies in the course of this morning. The post, however, was out, and no supplies had come. This did not in the least discourage me. I said to myself, the Lord can send means without the post, or even now, though the post is out, by this very delivery of letters He may have sent means, though the money is not yet in my hands. It was not long after I had thus spoken to myself, when, according to my hope in God, we were helped; for the brother who sent us the 10l., had this time directed his letter to the Boys-Orphan-House, whence it was sent to me.

March 11. Yesterday a box arrived from one of the Northern Counties, respecting which the donor had requested that neither the articles which it contained, nor the name of the place whence it came, should be mentioned in the public account. I, therefore, only state here that thus the Lord has again most seasonably helped us, besides giving us a fresh proof, in raising up this new and anonymous donor, that He does not cease to care for us. It is intended to apply the produce of the articles contained in the box partly for the Orphans, and partly for the other objects. Though the box arrived only yesterday, we are even this day helped through means of it; for we disposed today of some of the articles to the amount of 9l. 6s. 6d. Of this sum 7l. 6s. 6d. was divided among the teachers, who much needed it; and 2l. was taken for the Orphan-Fund, without which the need of this day could not have been supplied in the Orphan-Houses.

March 17. From the 12th to the 16th had come in 4l. 5s. 11 1/2d. for the Orphans. This morning our poverty, which now has lasted more or less for several months, had become exceedingly great. I left my house a few minutes after seven to go to the Orphan-Houses, to see whether there was money enough to take in the milk, which is brought about eight oclock. On my way it was especially my request, that the Lord would be pleased to pity us, even as a father pitieth his children, and that He would not lay more upon us than He would enable us to bear. I especially entreated him that He would now be pleased to refresh our hearts by sending us help. I likewise reminded Him of the consequences that would result, both in reference to believers and unbelievers, if we should have to give up the work because of want of means, and that He therefore would not permit its coming to nought. I moreover again confessed before the Lord that I deserved not that He should continue to use me in this work any longer. While I was thus in prayer, about two minutes walk from the Orphan-Houses, I met a brother who was going at this early hour to his business. After having exchanged a few words with him, I went on; but he presently ran after me, and gave me 1l. for the Orphans. Thus the Lord speedily answered my prayer. Truly, it is worth being poor and greatly tried in faith, for the sake of having day by day such precious proofs of the loving interest which our kind Father takes in every thing that concerns us. And how should our Father do otherwise? He that has given us the greatest possible proof of His love which He could have done, in giving us His own Son, surely He will with Him also freely give us all things. It is worth also being poor and greatly tried in faith, if but thereby the hearts of the children of God may be comforted and their faith strengthened; and if but those who do not know God, and who may read or hear of His dealings with us, should be led thereby to see, that faith in God is more than a mere notion, and that there is indeed reality in Christianity. In the course of this day there came in still further 13s.

March 19. Saturday. As it has often been the case on Saturdays, so it was this day in particular. We began the day in very great poverty, as only 7s. had come in since the day before yesterday. There was not one ray of light as to natural prospects. The heart would be overwhelmed, at such seasons, were there not an abundance of repose to be found by trusting in God. The trial having continued so long, and our poverty having now come to such a degree, that it was necessary we should have help, in order that the name of the Lord might not be dishonoured, I had proposed to my fellow-labourers that we should set apart this day especially for prayer. We met accordingly at half-past ten in the morning. By that time had come in 4s. 6d., 7s. 6d., and 10s. In the afternoon we met again at three, when 10s. came in. In the evening at seven we met once more, there being yet about three shillings needed, to provide all that was required. This also we received, and even 3s. more than was actually needed came in, just when we were about to separate.

Today we were also very poor with reference to our own personal necessities. In the morning we had only 2 1/2d. left, when a sister in the Lord, who knew nothing about our need, gave us the contents of her purse, being 1l. 7s.

March 23. This afternoon, when we had no money at all of our own, a brother gave us 3s. for ourselves.

March 25. During the last four days we received 6l. 12s. 2d. for the Orphans. This morning, when we were now again without any thing, a parcel arrived from Clapham, containing 1l. 10s., with a frock, a chemise, 2 petticoats, 2 pinafores, and 2 handkerchiefs (all new). About the same time was sent a post-office order from Bath for 2l. This is no small deliverance. The need has been so great during this week that the matrons, in order that there might be no lack in the way of provisions for the children, have been unable to order even half-a-ton of coals at once, and have been obliged to buy them in very small quantities.

When again we had only 6d. Left for our own personal necessities, I received 9s.

March 26. We are helped to the close of one more week with reference to our own personal necessities. During this week we have had several times not one single penny for ourselves; yet during this week also we have had all that was needed in the way of nourishing food, etc., and we have 3d. left.

March 30. From the 25th up to this day we were poor, with reference to the Orphans but the Lord helped us. This morning a brother from Devonshire came to stay for a few days with me. He gave me two sovereigns for the Orphans, and told me the following facts in connexion with them. Last year he portioned out a piece of ground, for the benefit of the Orphans. Having done so, all the members of the family were gathered together, and he asked with them the Lords blessing upon the crop that was to be planted. This prayer was often repeated afterwards, while the crop was known to belong to the Orphans; and the ground yielded a good crop. The potatoes were to have been sent, but it was considered better to sell them for the benefit of the Orphans, and now this brother brought the produce. These two sovereigns came in most seasonably, as they were only just in time to supply the dinner and other necessaries of this day; for when I came with the brother from the railway station to my house, I found an Orphan boy waiting for money, and I had nothing in hand. This evening I received still further from a sister 1l. 1s. 5 1/2d.

This morning we had not one single halfpenny left for our own necessities, when two brethren arrived to stay with us for some days, the one from Somersetshire and the other from the North of Devon. The brother from the North of Devon brought 12s. for my own use from Barnstaple, and also gave 1l. to my dear wife this afternoon for our own need. Thus we were again supplied. My mind has been quite in peace on account of our own need, and the only inconvenience that we had in this case was, that our dinner was about half an hour later than usual. Such a thing, as far as I remember, scarcely ever occurred before, and has never occurred since; but suppose it had, it is well, in some little measure, to know from ones own experience the meaning of that word, "I know both how to be abased, and I know how to abound: everywhere and in all things I am instructed both to be full and to be hungry, both to abound and to suffer need." Philip iv. 12.

March 31. This afternoon 5s. came in from Bath, and from a sister in the Lord in one of the Northern counties 5l. for the Orphans and 15l. for the other objects; and through the same donor 12s. This money arrived when there was again only 5s. in hand for the Orphans, which had come in this afternoon, and when there was particular need of means, as many pairs of shoes needed to be mended, and other extra expenses were to be met. When this money came, there was also great need of fresh supplies for the Day-Schools, on account of which this donation was a precious help from the Lord.

April 2. We received 1l. 19s. 6d. for the Orphans.

April 4. When again our little stock had been exhausted, the Lord was pleased to send in yesterday 5l. through a sister of Bristol; also by sale of articles 10s., and by Reports 5s. Today came in from Kensington 1l.

April 6. As only 3s. more had come in yesterday, the money was now again all gone, when this evening was sent from a distance a post office order for 2l.

April 8. This afternoon, when again much money was needed, we received from Plymouth 1l., and from a donor in Bristol 1l.

April 9. Saturday. Only 1s. 6d. had come in since yesterday afternoon. We needed more money than there was in hand, especially as it was Saturday, but the Lord was pleased particularly to try our faith. In the course of the morning came from some sisters in Dublin, 18 yards of calico, 34 yards of print, 43 balls of cotton, and a pair of worn ladys boots. This donation came most seasonably, as we had been mentioning repeatedly the need of calico and print in our prayers; and the sewing cotton and the pair of boots came at once into use. Moreover, this donation was a sweet encouragement to me to continue waiting upon the Lord. Evening was now approaching, and no money had yet come in for provisions, etc., which would be needed on the Lords day. About six oclock, I gave myself once more to prayer with my wife, and requested the Lord in my prayer that if the sister, who in love to Him has taken upon her the service of disposing of the articles which are given for sale, had any money in hand, He would be pleased to incline her heart to bring or send the money this evening. After this I sat down peacefully to read the Scriptures, being assured that this time also the Lord would stretch out His hand on our behalf. About half-past seven oclock the sister to whom reference has just now been made, came and brought 1l. 10s. 4d., for articles which she had sold, stating that though she was unwell, yet she felt herself constrained not to delay bringing this money. Thus we had all that was needed, and 6s. more. When I arrived with the money at the Infant-

Orphan-House, about eight oclock, I found my fellow labourers in prayer, and while we still continued in prayer a sister sent a large basket of stale bread, being five brown loaves, seven bread cakes, and five French loaves.

April 11. It is this day six years since the first children were taken in, and, as usual, we are poor this day also; for only 13s. 10 1/2d. has come in since Saturday evening.

April 12. We were never in greater need than today, perhaps never in so much, when I received this morning 100l. from the East Indies. It is impossible to describe the real joy in God it gave me. My prayer had been again this morning particularly, that our Father would pity us, and now at last send larger sums. I was not in the least surprised or excited when this donation came, for I took it as that which came in answer to prayer, and had been long looked for. As it was left to me to use the money as might be most needed, I took one half of it for the Orphan Fund, and the other half for the other funds. We have thus also an answer to our prayer for oatmeal, new shoes, and for means to enable us to have the old shoes mended, means for replenishing somewhat our stores, money for some articles of clothing for the children, and also a little money for the sisters who labour in the Orphan-Houses. How precious to look to the Lord! I was always sure that He would at last send larger sums, therefore had my heart been kept in peace, though my faith had never been more tried than during the last months.

April 14. There was half-a-sovereign taken out of the box at the Boys-Orphan-House this morning. This afternoon three individuals called on me. One of them gave 6l., 3 collars, and 2 veils, and brought likewise 3 gold rings. Another of them gave me 2s. 6d. After they had left I found in my room on the mantelpiece in a paper 2 sovereigns for my own personal expenses, and in three papers 3 sovereigns for the three

Orphan-Houses, and also a fourpenny piece on the floor.

April 30. As since the 14th only little more than 16l. had come in, there was again this day not quite enough in hand to supply all that was needed. However, the Lord sent from Clapham a parcel which contained 10s., 2 frocks, 2 pinafores, 2 handkerchiefs, 2 nightcaps, and 2 pieces of list.

May 1. Today was given by a brother a gold watch with a small gold chain and key. The gift was accompanied by the following note to me:

"Beloved Brother,

"A pilgrim does not want such a watch as this to make him happy; one of an inferior kind will do to show him how swiftly his time flies, and how fast he is hastening on to that Canaan where time will be no more: so that it is for you to do with this what seemeth good to you. It is the last relic of earthly vanity, and, while I am in the body, may I be kept from all idolatry.

"Your affectionate brother,

*****"

May 2. There was now again no money in hand, not even the few shillings which were required to take in the milk tomorrow morning, when a sister gave a sovereign to brother R. B. for the Orphans, whereby we are helped.

May 6. Only 3l. 10s. 2 1/2d. had been received since the 2nd, on which account there would have been only enough means in hand to provide for the breakfast tomorrow morning, when in this our fresh need 80l. was sent by the same brother who has been spoken of under "June 4, 1841," in the details respecting the other funds; and also 6l. from Great Malvern. The half of this 80l. was put to the Orphan Fund, and the other half to the other funds: the donation from Great Malvern was put to the fund for the other objects. There arrived at the same time from the East Indies by post a small parcel, containing 2 pairs of gold ear-rings, a brooch, and 2 rupees. These donations came especially in season, as they enable me to give supplies to the brethren and sisters who labour in the Day Schools and Orphan-Houses for their own personal necessities, besides meeting the wants in other respects.

May 10. 6l. 15s. 10d. more has come in since the 6th. Today, in closing the accounts, we have left at the end of this period of seventeen months, in which we have been so often penniless, the sum of 16l. 18s. 10 1/2d. for the Orphans, and 48l. 12s. 5 1/4d. for the other objects of the Scriptural Knowledge Institution.

The time now seemed to us to have come, when, for the profit of the church at large, the Lords dealings with us, with reference to the various objects of the Scriptural Knowledge Institution, should be made known by publishing another Report. For, whilst we, on purpose, had delayed it at this time five months longer than during the previous years, and that during a period when we were in deeper poverty than during any previous time; yet, as from the commencement it had appeared to me important, from time to time to make known the Lords dealings with us, so I judged it profitable still, to seek to comfort, to encourage, to exhort, to instruct, and to warn the dear children of God by the printed accounts of the Lords goodness to us.

The following are a few additional remarks with reference to the period of the seventeen months previous to May 10, 1842.

1. Though our trials of faith during these seventeen months lasted longer, and were sharper than during any previous period, yet during all this time the Orphans had every thing that was needful in the way of nourishing food, the necessary articles of clothing, etc. Indeed I should rather at once send the children back to their relations than keep them without sufficient maintenance.

2. I desire that all the children of God who may read these details may thereby be led to increased and more simple confidence in God for every thing which they may need under any circumstances, and that these many answers to prayer may encourage them to pray, particularly as it regards the conversion of their friends and relations, their own progress in grace and knowledge, the state of the saints whom they may know personally, the state of the church of Christ at large, and the success of the preaching of the Gospel. Especially I affectionately warn them against being led away by the device of Satan, to think that these things are peculiar to me, and cannot be enjoyed by all the children of God; for though, as has been stated before, every believer is not called upon to establish Orphan-Houses, Charity Schools, etc., and trust in the Lord for means, yet all believers are called upon, in the simple confidence of faith, to cast all their burdens upon Him, to trust in him for every thing, and not only to make every thing a subject of prayer, but to expect answers to their petitions which they have asked according to His will, and in the name of the Lord Jesus. — Think not, dear reader, that I have the gift of faith, that is, that gift of which we read in 1 Cor. xii. 9, and which is mentioned along with "the gifts of healing," "the working of miracles," "prophecy," and that on that account I am able

to trust in the Lord. It is true that the faith, which I am enabled to exercise, is altogether Gods own gift; it is true that He alone supports it, and that He alone can increase it; it is true that, moment by moment, I depend upon Him for it, and that, if I were only one moment left to myself, my faith would utterly fail; but it is not true that my faith is that gift of faith which is spoken of in 1 Cor. xii. 9, for the following reasons.

1, The faith which I am enabled to exercise with reference to the Orphan-Houses and my own temporal necessities, is not that "faith" of which it is said in 1 Cor. xiii. 2 (evidently in allusion to the faith spoken of in 1 Cor. xii. 9), "Though I have all faith, so that I could remove mountains, and have not charity (love), I am nothing"; but it is the self-same faith which is found in every believer, and the growth of which I am most sensible of to myself; for, by little and little, it has been increasing for the last fifty-six years.

2, This faith which is exercised respecting the Orphan-Houses and my own temporal necessities, shows itself in the same measure, for instance, concerning the following points: I have never been permitted to doubt during the last fifty-six years that my sins are forgiven, that I am a child of God, that I am beloved of God, and that I shall be finally saved; because I am enabled, by the grace of God, to exercise faith upon the word of God, and believe what God says in those passages which settle these matters (1 John v. 1-Gal. iii. 26-Acts x. 43-Romans x. 9, 10-John iii. 16, etc.)—Further, at the time when I thought I should be insane (though there was not the least ground for thinking so), as recorded on pages 209, 210, and 223, I was in peace, quite in peace; because my soul believed the truth of that word, "We know that all things work together for good to them that love God." Rom. viii. 28.—Further, When my brother in the flesh, and my dear aged father died, and when concerning both of them I had no evidence whatever that they were saved (though I dare not say that they are lost, for I know it not); yet my soul was at peace, perfectly at peace, under this great trial, this exceedingly great trial, this trial which is one of the greatest perhaps which can befall a believer. And what was it that gave me peace? My soul laid hold on that word, "Shall not the judge of all the earth do right!" This word, together with the whole character of God, as He has revealed Himself in His holy word, settled all questionings. I believed what He has said concerning Himself, and I was at peace, and have been at peace ever since, concerning this matter. —Further, When the Lord took from me a beloved infant, my soul was at peace, perfectly at peace; I could only weep tears of joy when I did weep. And why? Because my soul laid hold in faith on that word: "Of such is the kingdom of Heaven." Matthew xix. 14. Believing, therefore, as I did, upon the ground of this word, my soul rejoiced, instead of mourning, that my beloved infant was far happier with the Lord, than with me. —Further, When sometimes all has been dark, exceedingly dark, with reference to my service among the saints, judging from natural appearances yea, when I should have been overwhelmed indeed in grief and despair, had I looked at things after the outward appearance: at such times I have sought to encourage myself in God, by laying hold in faith on His mighty power, His unchangeable love, and His infinite wisdom, and I have said to myself: God is able and willing to deliver me, if it be good for me; for it is written: "He that spared not His own Son, but delivered Him up for us all, how shall He not with Him also freely give us all things?" Rom. viii. 32. This, this it was which, being believed by me through grace, kept my soul in peace. —Further, When in connection with the Orphan-Houses, Day Schools, etc., trials have come upon me which were far heavier than the want of means, when lying reports were spread that the Orphans had not enough to eat, or that they were cruelly treated in other respects, and the like; or when other trials, still greater, but which I cannot mention, have befallen me in connexion with this work, and that at a time when I was nearly a thousand miles absent from Bristol, and had to remain absent week after week: at such times my soul was stayed upon God; I believed His word of promise which was applicable to such cases; I poured out my soul before God, and arose from my knees in peace, because the trouble that was in the soul was in believing prayer cast upon God, and thus I was kept in peace, though I saw it to be the will of God to remain far away from the work.

—Further, When I needed houses, fellow-labourers, masters and mistresses for the Orphans or for the Day Schools, I have been enabled to look for all to the Lord, and trust in Him for help.—Dear reader, I may seem to boast; but, by the Grace of God, I do not boast in thus speaking. From my inmost soul I do ascribe it to God alone that He has enabled me to trust in Him, and that hitherto He has not suffered my confidence in Him to fail. But I thought it needful to make these remarks, lest any one should think that my depending upon God was a particular gift given to me, which other saints have no right to look for; or lest it should be thought that this my depending upon Him had only to do with the obtaining of MONEY by prayer and faith. By the grace of God I desire that my faith in God should extend towards EVERY thing, the smallest of my own temporal and spiritual concerns, and the smallest of the temporal and spiritual concerns of my family, towards the saints among whom I labour, the church at large, everything that has to do with the temporal and spiritual prosperity of the Scriptural Knowledge Institution, etc. Dear reader, do not think that I have attained in faith (and how much less in other respects!) to that degree to which I might and ought to attain; but thank God for the faith which He has given me, and ask Him to uphold and increase it. And lastly, once more, let not Satan deceive you in making you think that you could not have the same faith, but that it is only for persons who are situated as I am. When I lose such a thing as a key, I ask the Lord to direct me to it, and I look for an answer to my prayer; when a person with whom I have made an appointment does not come, according to the fixed time, and I begin to be inconvenienced by it, I ask the Lord to be pleased to hasten him to me, and I look for an answer; when I do not understand a passage of the word of God, I lift up my heart to the Lord, that He would be pleased, by His holy Spirit, to instruct me, and I expect to be taught, though I do not fix the time when, and the manner how it should be; when I am going to minister in the Word, I seek help from the Lord, and while I in the consciousness of natural inability as well as utter unworthiness, begin this His service, I am not cast down, but of good cheer, because I look for His assistance, and believe that He, for His dear Sons sake, will help me. And thus in other of my temporal and spiritual concerns I pray to the Lord, and expect an answer to my requests; and may not you do the same, dear believing reader? Oh! I beseech you, do not think me an extraordinary believer, having privileges above other of Gods dear children, which they cannot have; nor look on my way of acting as something that would not do for other believers. Make but trial! Do but stand still in the hour of trial, and you will see the help of God, if you trust in Him. But there is so often a forsaking the ways of the Lord in the hour of trial, and thus the food of faith, the means whereby our faith may be increased, is lost. This leads me to the following important point. You ask, How may I, a true believer, have my faith strengthened? The answer is this

I. "Every good gift and every perfect gift is from above, and cometh down from the Father of lights, with whom is no variableness, neither shadow of turning." James i. 17. As the increase of faith is a good gift, it must come from God, and therefore He ought to be asked for this blessing.

II. The following means, however, ought to be used: 1, The careful reading of the word of God, combined with meditation on it. Through reading of the word of God, and especially through meditation on the word of God, the believer becomes more and more acquainted with the nature and character of God, and thus sees more and more, besides His holiness and justice, what a kind, loving, gracious, merciful, mighty, wise, and faithful Being He is, and, therefore, in poverty, affliction of body, bereavement in his family, difficulty in his service, want of a situation or employment, he will repose upon the ability of God to help him, because he has not only learned from His word that He is of almighty power and infinite wisdom, but he has also seen instance upon instance in the Holy Scriptures in which His almighty power and infinite wisdom have been actually exercised in helping and delivering His people; and he will repose upon the willingness of God to help him, because he has not only learned from the Scriptures what a kind, good, merciful, gracious, and faithful being God is, but because he has also seen in the word of God, how in a great variety of instances He has proved Himself to be so. And the consideration of this, if God has become known to us through prayer and meditation on His own word, will lead us, in general at least, with a measure of confidence to rely upon Him: and thus the reading of the word of God, together with meditation on it, will be one especial means to strengthen our faith. 2, As with reference to the growth of every grace of the Spirit, it is of the utmost importance that we seek to maintain an upright heart and a good conscience, and, therefore, do not knowingly and habitually indulge in those things which are contrary to the mind of God, so it is also particularly the case with reference to the growth in faith. How can I possibly continue to act faith upon God, concerning any thing, if I am habitually grieving Him, and seek to detract from the glory and honour of Him in whom I profess to trust, upon whom I profess to depend? All my confidence towards God, all my leaning upon Him in the hour of trial will be gone, if I have a guilty conscience, and do not seek to put away this guilty conscience, but still continue to do things which are contrary to the mind of God. And if, in any particular instance, I cannot trust in God, because of the guilty conscience, then my faith is weakened by that instance of distrust; for faith with every fresh trial of it either increases by trusting God, and thus getting help, or it decreases by not trusting Him; and then there is less and less power of looking simply and directly to Him, and a habit of self-dependence is begotten or encouraged. One or other of these will always be the case in each particular instance. Either we trust in God, and in that case we neither trust in ourselves, nor in our fellowmen, nor in circumstances, nor in any thing besides; or we no trust in one or more of these, and in that case do NOT trust in God. 3, If we, indeed, desire our faith to be strengthened, we should not shrink from opportunities where our faith may be tried, and, therefore, through the trial, be strengthened. In our natural state we dislike dealing with God alone. Through our natural alienation from God we shrink from Him, and from eternal realities. This cleaves to us more or less, even after our regeneration. Hence it is, that, more or less, even as believers, we have the same shrinking from standing with God alone,—from depending upon Him alone,—from looking to Him alone:—and yet this is the very position in which we ought to be, if we wish our faith to be strengthened. The more I am in a position to be tried in faith with reference to my body, my family, my service for the Lord, my business, etc., the more shall I have opportunity of seeing Gods help and deliverance; and every fresh instance, in which He helps and delivers me, will tend towards the increase of my faith. On this account, therefore, the believer should not shrink from situations, positions, circumstances, in which his faith may be tried; but should cheerfully embrace them as opportunities where he may see the hand of God stretched out on his behalf, to help and deliver him, and whereby he may thus have his faith strengthened. 4, The last important point for the strengthening of our faith is, That we let God work for us, when the hour of the trial of oar faith comes, and do not work a deliverance of our own. Wherever God has given faith, it is given, among other reasons, for the very purpose of being tried. Yea, however weak our faith may be, God will try it; only with this restriction, that as, in every way, He leads on gently, gradually, patiently, so also with reference to the trial of our faith. At first our faith will be tried very little in comparison with what it may be afterwards; for God never lays more upon us than He is willing to enable us to bear. Now when the trial of faith comes, we are naturally inclined to distrust God, and to trust rather in ourselves, or in our friends, or in circumstances. We will rather work a deliverance of our own somehow or other, than simply look to God and wait for His help. But if we do not patiently wait for Gods help, if we work a deliverance of our own, then at the next trial of our faith it will be thus again, we shall be again inclined to deliver ourselves; and thus with every fresh instance of that kind, our faith will decrease; whilst, on the contrary, were we to stand still in order to see the salvation of God, to see His hand stretched out on our behalf, trusting in Him alone, then our faith would be increased, and with every fresh case in which the hand of

100

God is stretched out on our behalf in the hour of the trial of our faith, our faith would be increased yet more. Would the believer, therefore, have his faith strengthened, he must especially, give time to God, who tries his faith in order to prove to His child, in the end, how willing he is to help and deliver him, the moment it is good for him.

I now return, dear reader, to the Narrative, giving you some further information with reference to the 17 months, from December 10, 1840, to May 18, 1842, as it respects the Orphan-Houses, and other objects of the Scriptural Knowledge Institution for Home and Abroad, besides the facts of which mention has been already made.

During this period also—1, Two Sunday Schools were entirely supported by the funds of the Institution. 2, There were two adult schools, one for females, and one for males, entirely supported during these 17 months, in which on two evenings of the week the males, and on two evenings the females were instructed, quite gratuitously, in reading and writing, and were furnished with books and writing materials gratuitously. There were, during these 17 months, 344 adults taught in these two schools, and on May 10, 1842, the number under instruction amounted to 110. The chief object of these adult schools is, to teach grown up persons to read, in order that they may themselves be able to read the Holy Scriptures; but, at the same time, those who teach them take opportunity to point out the way of salvation to them, and, while the word of God is read, they seek to make remarks on the portions which are read.—3, There were, during these 17 months, also six Day Schools entirely supported by the funds of the Institution, three for boys and three for girls. These schools are principally intended to enable persons of the poorer classes of the inhabitants of Bristol, to send their children to school,

101

either entirely free, or on paying only the fifth or sixth part of the expenses connected with the instruction which the children receive; they are also, especially, intended to keep believing parents, who have not much means, from the necessity of sending their children to unbelievers for instruction. On May 10, 1842, the number of the children, who attended these Day Schools, was 363; and the total number, who from the formation of the Institution on. March 5, 1834, up to May 10, 1842, had been instructed in the Day Schools, which are supported by the funds of the Institution, amounts to 2616.—4, During these 17 months, 798 copies of the Holy Scriptures were circulated, and from the commencement of the Institution, up to May 10, 1842, 6,842 copies. 5, During these 17 months was spent for Missionary purposes, the sum of 126l. 15s. 3d. of the funds of the Institution, whereby assistance was rendered to the work of God in Jamaica, in Australia, in Canada, and in the East Indies. 6, At the commencement of these 17 months, i.e. on December 10, 1840, a new object was begun., the circulation of such publications as may be instrumental, with the blessing of God, to benefit both unbelievers and believers. We laid out for this object, during these 17 months, from December 10, 1840, to May 10, 1842, the sum of 62l. 17s. 4d., for which twenty-two thousand one hundred and ninety such little publications were purchased, and of which number nineteen thousand six hundred and nine were actually given away.—7, There were received into the three Orphan-Houses, from Dec. 10, 1840, to May 10, 1842, 15 Orphans, who, together with those who were in the houses on Dec. 10, 1840, make up 106 in all. Of these, five girls were sent out to service, two boys and one girl were apprenticed, one girl was removed by a lady who had placed her for a time under our care, and one was sent back to his relations, as he was injurious to the other children.

There were on May 10, 1842, 96 Orphans in the three houses, i.e. 30 in the Girls-Orphan-House, 37 in the Infant-Orphan-House, and 29 in the Boys-Orphan-House. Besides this, three apprentices were supported by the funds of the Institution, so that the total number was 99. The number of Orphans who were under our care from April, 1836, to May 10, 1842, amounts to 144.

I notice further the following points in connexion with the Orphan-Houses.

Without any one having been asked for any thing by me, the sum of 5,276l. 14s. 8d. was given to me from the beginning of the work up to May 16, 1842, as the result of prayer to God. Besides this, also, many articles of clothing, furniture, provisions, &c.—During these 17 months we had very little sickness in the three houses, and not one of the children died. I desire publicly to state this, and in it to acknowledge the hand of God.

The total of the expenditure for the various objects of the Institution, exclusive of the Orphan-Houses, during these 17 months, amounted to 710l. 11s. 5d.; the total of the income amounted to 746l. 1s. 0 1/2d. The total of the expenditure for the three Orphan-Houses, from December 10, 1840, to May 10, 1842, amounted to 1,337l. 15s. 2 3/4d.; the total of the income amounted to 1,339l. 13s. 7d.

May 11, 1842. When the accounts were closed last evening, the balance in hand for the Orphans was 16l. 18s. 10 1/2d., though the actual amount for use at present is only 6l. 8s. 10 1/2d. as 10l. 10s. is put by for the rent.—With this 6l. 8s. 10 1/2d. therefore we had to begin again the work, whilst there were 107 persons to be provided for with all they required.

From May 11 to May 27, we were always so provided for by the Lord, that we received fresh donations before the last money was spent, for there came in 28l. 15s. 8 1/2d.; but now we should not have had sufficient for the need of tomorrow, May 28th, when today there arrived a parcel from Kendal, containing 6 frocks, 5 tippets, 6 pinafores, 6 chemises, 2 shirts, 3 aprons, and the following donations in money: with Ps. xxvii., 10s.; Proverbs iii. 5, 6, 2s. 6d.; from a sister who earns her own, bread by her daily exertions, 10s.; from another individual 10s. There came in also by sale of articles, given for that purpose, 2l. 1s.

May 28. There came in still further today 3l. 4s. 4d., so that we are richly provided, with all we need, and have more than enough.

June 3. For several days past I had not been particularly led to pray for means for the Orphans. Last evening, however, I did so, as we had now again no money in hand, there having come in only 10l. 2s. 2d. during the last five days; and in answer to my request 2l. 19s. 6d. came in this morning.

June 6. Monday. There was now no money at all in hand. I had therefore asked the Lord for fresh supplies, and since Saturday afternoon the following sums have come in: By sale of articles 1l. 4s., FROM AN AGED SERVANT, ILL IN A MORTAL DISEASE, 4l.; anonymously put into the boxes at Bethesda yesterday, in a small parcel, 11s., a gold ring, 3 small Spanish silver coins, and a small American silver coin; ditto 4d.; by a sister was given 6d., and by another sister 5s.; anonymously put into the box at Callow-hill Street Chapel 2s.

This morning I received from A. B. 50l., to be laid out as it might be most useful. I took the whole of this sum for the other objects, as the disposal of it was left to me, whereby I am enabled to order a fresh supply of tracts, some Bibles and Testaments, and to give something to the brethren and sisters who labour in the Day Schools, who are much in need of some supply. The stock of Bibles, as far as I remember, has never been smaller than it is now, for several years; there is likewise only a small quantity of tracts left, and the demand for them is great on the part of brethren who gratuitously circulate them. How kind therefore of the Lord to give us this supply! If our work be His work, He is sure to provide the means for it!

June 9. On the 7th came in 3s. for the Orphans, —on the 8th 2l. 6s. 2d. Today was sent anonymously from Bath 5l., with the words "Jehovah Jireh." These words are very appropriate; for the money came after I had asked the Lord for some, and is required for our need tomorrow.

June 11. Saturday afternoon. As only 6s. 10d. had come in since the 9th for the Orphans, there remains no money in hand for Monday. —Saturday evening. The Lord has already sent a little towards the need of next week, as an earnest, that during the coming week also He will be mindful of us for this evening came in by sale of articles, 1l. 8s. 7d., and a little boy gave 3s. 7 1/4d.

June 12. There came in further today 7s. 6d.; anonymously 10s.; ditto 2l.; and with Ecclesiastes ix. 10, was given. 10s.

June 15. As since the 12th only 1l. 13s. 6d. had come in, there was now again no money in hand for the need of to-morrow. I gave myself therefore to prayer. Immediately after I had risen from my knees, I was told that some money had been put into the box at my house. I opened the box, and found it to be a sovereign.

June 16. The sovereign which yesterday had been put into the box at my house was not enough. On my morning walk I asked the Lord, therefore, for more means, and when I came home I found that 1l. 16s. had been sent for articles given for sale, There came in still further by sale of articles, 1l. 1s. 6d., and by a donation from Leeds, 2l. 10s. 3d.

June 17. 1l. 18s. 9d. came in today.

June 18. Having had to meet the expenses of the funeral of a dear Orphan boy, who, after having been two years in fellowship with the saints, and walked consistently, had fallen asleep, all means were now again gone, when an Irish lady sent this morning 10l., of which 8l. is to be used for the Orphans, and 2l. for my own personal necessities. Thus we are again supplied for the-present.

June 25. As, besides the 8l. which came in on the 18th, only 9l. 14s. 10 1/2d. had been received since, there was now not sufficient in hand for the expenses of the day; but the Lord, as usual, made it manifest, that He is mindful of our need, and that He hears our prayers. For there was sent today from Clapham a parcel, containing a frock, a pinafore, and 13s. 4d. Also, through the same donors, in the same parcel, were sent from Brighton, 8 frocks, 6 pinafores, 6 handkerchiefs, 3 chemises, 2 petticoats, and 10s. Likewise a Christian lady sent a sovereign; and 1s. 6d. came in by sale of Reports, and 1l. 18s. 0 1/2d. by sale of articles. Thus we were abundantly supplied for the need of today.

July 1. All our money was again spent, as only 8l. 15s. 4d. had come in since the 25th, when last evening an Orphan arrived from Barnstaple, with whom there was sent 2l. 5s. 10d. The Lord has repeatedly ordered it so, that when Orphans have been brought, money has been sent with them, whereby our present necessities have been supplied.—

I add here, that we do not require any money to be sent with them, nor is there any interest required to get the children admitted, and much less is the Institution of a sectarian spirit, so that only persons of certain religious views could succeed in making application for the admission of Orphans; but without respect of persons, from all parts of the kingdom, so long as there is room, needy children, bereaved of both parents, may be admitted. —I received today still further 10l. And likewise, by six other donations, came in 1l. 10s. 2d. We are now again for a few days supplied.

July 6, On July 2nd came in 10s.; on the 3rd 2l. 2s. 9d.; on the 4th 1l. 18s.; on the 5th came in four donations from Hackney, amounting to 3l. 6s.; a donation of 2l. from Plymouth; a donation of 4s. from a brother in Bristol; by sale of Reports 5s. 3d.; anonymously was sent from Fairford 3l.; a Christian lady gave 1l., and the following articles were sent from Tottenham: a two-guinea piece, a quarter-guinea piece, a half doubloon, (a Portuguese gold coin), a gold coin of James I., and two gold chains. Likewise this evening came in with Ecclesiastes ix. 10, 3l. 1s. 6d., and 3s. 6d. by sale of stockings. By the donations of yesterday and today I am enabled to meet many needful expenses, such as ordering oatmeal from Scotland, buying peas, rice, Scotch barley, materials for boys clothes, &c.

July 9. On July 7, 8, 9, had only come in 3l. 11s., so that now today, Saturday, after I had supplied the matrons with what they needed for today and for tomorrow, all the money was again spent; yet we had been, by the good hand of the Lord, brought through another week, and nothing, that had been needed during the week, had been lacking.

July 11. Monday. Yesterday and today came in 3l. 9s. 6d. This money was quite enough for the need of today; and when now again, after this days need had been met, scarcely any thing was left, the boxes in the Orphan-Houses were opened, which contained 2l. 3s. 4 1/2d.

July 12. 13s. 9d. came in today.

July 13. When our purse was now again empty, the Lord kindly sent 5l. this morning from Glasgow.

From July 13th to 19th the Lord sent in 22l. 5s. 10d., and on July 19th I left Bristol for a season, being able, through grace, to leave the work in His hands, and feeling assured, that He would provide while I was absent from Bristol; and truly the Lord did not suffer me to be disappointed. For during the time of my absence, from July 19th to Sept. 10th, whilst I was labouring at Barnstaple, and in the neighbourhood of Bideford, the Lord richly furnished us with means, though twice during that period we were quite poor.

From July 19th to Aug. 10th had come in, during my absence, 51l. 3s. 7 1/2d.; but now on Wednesday, Aug. 10th, all the money, except ONE PENNY, was spent in the three Orphan-Houses. Between 9 and 10 oclock in the evening brother M. brought 7l. to the Boys-Orphan-House. 5l. of this he had received from Q. Q., 1l. with Ecclesiastes ix. 10, and 1l. from a sister who had received this money from Weymouth. When the latter told brother M. that the money might be applied as most needed, he replied to her, that he would give it to the Orphans, as he believed them to be in need. When brother M. brought the money, he said, that when in prayer in the morning for the Orphans, who had been particularly laid on his heart, he felt assured, that we were in need. Thus this brother not knowing any thing about our circumstances, was led by God to help us with his intercessions.

The whole sum which came in from the 10th to the 26th was 25l. 5s. 3d. On the 26th of August there was now again need of a fresh manifestation of the loving care of our Heavenly Father, as on the coming day, being a Saturday, much was needed, and there were only a few pence in hand. And truly, the Lord did appear on our behalf; for this evening came in 10l. with Eccles. ix. 10.—Behold, you who do not know the Lord, what a precious thing it is, even for this life, to walk with God! Behold also you, dear brethren, who tremble to lean fully and solely upon. Him, that those who trust in Him, according to His word, shall not be confounded!

From Aug. 26th to Sept. 10th came in 22l. 6s. 8 1/2d.

Besides the 98l. 15s. 7d. which had come in, in money, during my absence, many articles of clothes, books, provisions, &c. were given for the benefit of the Orphans; but especially a great quantity of trinkets was sent, to be disposed of for the benefit of the Orphans. When I had all these precious spoils before me, which the power of the love of Jesus had won, I found there were no less in my possession than 31 brooches, 2 gold clasps, a pair of gold bracelets, 33 gold rings, a silver gilt vinaigrette, 16 pairs of gold earrings, 2 gold crosses, a gold chain, a gold thimble, 8 gold seals, a gold watch key, a gold watch, 3 lockets, 2 watch hooks, 2 ornamental ladies combs, 3 ornamental gold hair pins, 2 silver cups, above 30 necklaces, and many other ornaments; also above 60 old silver coins. I cannot describe how great the joy is, which I have, when I see the Lord Jesus, by means of this Institution, bringing forth one needless article after the other, to be disposed of for the benefit of the Orphans.

From Sept. 10th to 28th the Lord supplied our need richly. There came in altogether during these 18 days 92l. 19s. 4d,

Though so large a sum had come in, in so short a time, yet as our expenses also had been great, there was again this day, Sept. 28th, not enough to meet this days need, when, A FEW MINUTES before I was called on for money, 2l. 10s. was sent from Birmingham.

Sept. 29. There came in by knitting 2s. 6d., and by two donations 7s. 6d. with these words: "J. W. from the Lord" 5s., and "From the Lord" 2s. 6d.

Sept. 30. There was again only 16s. 5 1/2d. left towards the necessities of today, when yesterday afternoon a donor left at my house a good silver watch, which, being disposed of for 6l., supplies us not only for today, but leaves something towards the need of tomorrow.

Oct 1. Yesterday afternoon. 1l. came in from Kensington, and this morning by sale of articles 2s. 6d., and 5s. was put into the box at my house. Thus we had, with what was left, something towards the necessities of this day, but not enough, as this is Saturday. As the Lord, however, had given me both yesterday and this morning prayer and faith with reference to the need, I was looking out for help, when at half past ten this morning a small parcel was anonymously left at my house, which contained a 5l. note, a gold chain, and an old 5s. piece, to be used for the Orphans. The Lord be praised who disposed the heart of the unknown donor at so seasonable an hour to send this donation! Half an hour, after I had received the little parcel, I was called upon for money, and was thus able to supply the need of today, and have something left towards the beginning of the week. —There came in still further today 4l. 1s.; for this afternoon a sister in the Lord sent two half sovereigns, which had been sent to her by two donors in Wales, and which she would not delay sending at once, "as it was Saturday." In the evening about eight oclock an individual residing in the parish of St. Philip, Bristol, brought a sovereign for the Orphans, and after eight oclock 2l. 1s. came in by the sale of articles: so that, whilst the day commenced, without there being enough to meet its expenses, we received several pounds more than was needed.

Oct. 8. As since Oct. 2 there had come in by sale of the gold chain, the old 5s. piece, and donations, only the sum of 12l. 16s. 6d., there was (after I had sent yesterday morning the money which was requisite for the day), again only 1s. 6 1/2d. left, towards the need of today, being Saturday. But the Lord, in whom I had particularly again made my boast this morning before four German musicians, was mindful of our need; for, besides half a sovereign coming in from Hereford, the boxes in the Orphan-Houses were opened, in which there was found 2l. 3s. 6d. Thus we have already in the morning the greater part of what is needed for today, waiting upon the Lord for the rest. —Evening. This evening came in still further 1l. 5s. 2d., so that we have all that is needed for today.

Oct. 10. Yesterday were put into the chapel boxes three papers, one with Eccles. ix. 10, containing 1l., and two containing 1s. each. There came in also this morning by the knitting of the Orphan Boys 6s. 6d. Thus we have, with a little that was left on Saturday, all that is required for today, and 3s. 5d. over.

Oct. 11. The Lord has again kindly multiplied the 3s. 5d., which was left after the necessities of yesterday were met. A brother in the Lord from Bath called yesterday at one of the Orphan-Houses and gave 5l. as a donation, besides 8s. 3d. for reports. Also by a clergyman near Cirencester was sent 5s., and this morning came a post office order for 10s. from Crediton, and 6d, was given by a sister in Bristol. My dear Reader, pause and admire the hand of the Lord! Day after

111

day He helps us! His help never fails, nor is it ever too late! We may be poor, very poor; but when the help is really needed, the Lord opens His bountiful hand and supplies our need! The help may come in a variety of ways, but it is certain! It may be that He allows us to wait long on Him, and pray very often, whilst He appears not to be mindful of us; yet in the end, in His own appointed and best time, the help comes. Dear Reader, if you know the Lord, and you have not a similar experience, be it known to you, that you may have the same in your sphere of labour or service, though you may not be called by the Lord to establish Orphan-Houses, or Day Schools, or Adult Schools, or Sunday Schools, or circulate Bibles and Tracts in an extensive way. Make but trial of this way, and you will see how truly precious it is to wait upon the Lord for every thing, even for the bread which perishes. Should you, dear Reader, not be reconciled with God through faith in the Lord Jesus, then you may know, that this precious privilege belongs to him who becomes a child of God by faith in the Lord Jesus, that he may come to his Heavenly Father for everything, and that his Father delights in giving him all he can need, while here in the world.

On. Oct. 12th came in 2l. 7s., and Oct. 13th 6s.

Oct. 15. Saturday. Yesterday arrived from Gloucestershire the following letter:—Oct. 13, 1842.

"My dear Brother,

As I have no doubt on my own mind, but the Orphans are in present need, the enclosed 5l. is sent by the constraining power of the Lord through me.

Yours affectionately,

*****"

The money came indeed in a time of need; for though we had about enough for yesterdays necessities, there was nothing for todays demands, which are 5l. 5s. There came in besides, yesterday afternoon, from a brother in. Bristol 1l., and from an individual in his employment 10s. Thus we could meet both yesterdays and todays need, and are brought to the close of another week. Evening. There came in still further this evening, by sale of articles 2l. 11s. 8d., from Ledbury 1s., and from two sisters in. Bristol 11s. Thus we have something towards the need of another week.

Oct. 19. Wednesday. As only 1l. 2s. had come in since Saturday evening, there was now again not sufficient money in hand for the need of today. I therefore opened an Orphan box in my house, in which I found two sovereigns. The Lord was pleased to send still further, in the course of the day, from the neighbourhood of Droitwich, 8s.; by profit from the sale of ladies bags, made by a sister for the benefit of the Orphans, 10s.; by a donation 2l. 10s.; by Reports 1s. 3d.; and by another donation, from two ladies, three-pence. These ladies, sisters in the Lord, had it much in their hearts to give considerable sums, and had given in former times gold chains, a brilliant, and many other valuable articles for the benefit of the Orphans, besides money; but now, having no means, through particular family circumstances, they were not ashamed to offer these three-pence. I doubt not that I have their prayers, and I value them more than gold; and I know, that if they had gold for the Orphans, they would give that also. The child of God ought to consider that word for his comfort: "If there be first a willing mind, it is accepted, according to that a man hath, and not according to that he hath not." 2 Cor. viii. 12.

On October 21st came in 1l. 9s. 8 1/2d.

Oct. 24. Monday. The necessities of the 22nd, being Saturday, called for all the money that was left, about 3l. Not one farthing was then remaining in my hands. And now observe, dear Reader, how the Lord helped, and praise Him with me, that He always causes the stream to flow again, when there is need. On the same day on which the last money was given out, the day before yesterday, there was handed over to me 1l. 2s. 9d. for sale of articles. Yesterday I received through a sister, from an Indian gentleman and lady, two sovereigns, and one from herself, being the produce of a piece of work, which she had done for the benefit of the Orphans. A poor brother also gave me 3s. Today I received the following anonymous note: —Oct. 22, 1842.

"Beloved Brother,

The enclosed 35l. was given to the Lord some time since. It was received for service done according to Eph. vi. 7; and believing that laying up treasures for myself upon earth (having enough for my own necessities without it) would be disobedience to Matthew vi. 19, I put it into your hands. You will kindly dispose of it as the Lord may direct you.

Yours in the Lord Jesus.

You will oblige me by receiving 10l. of the enclosed for your own need, or that of your family."

This money came indeed most seasonably; for though, by the donations of yesterday, todays need had been supplied, nevertheless as about 100 yards of flannel and materials for the boys clothes are needed, and as many other expenses require to be met, besides the regular daily expenses; we are thus in some measure provided. Half of this money I took for the Orphans and half for the other objects, as they also were in great need. There was likewise yesterday put anonymously into the boxes at Bethesda 1s. and 1l. Still further came in, through the boxes in the Orphan-Houses, 6s. 5 1/2d., from a poor widow 2s. 6d., from another individual 1l., in eight donations through a brother 10s. 3d., and a box of worn clothes.

Oct. 29. The need of today is 5l. 5s. We should not have had enough, humanly speaking, had there not been sent yesterday afternoon 5l. from Hull, as on the 26th and 28th only 3l. 5s. 5d. had come in.; so that there was only 3l. 0s. 6 1/2d. in hand, when this 5l. came. There came in still further today 1l. 12s. 4d. How kindly does the Lord, as it were, day by day inspect our stores! He, in general, does not supply our need for many months at once; in order both that He Himself may often have the Joy of our calling upon Him for the supplies we need; and that He may give unto us the joy of obtaining our supplies day by day in answer to prayer; and that thus also other children of God might be encouraged, to wait upon Him for all they may need.

On Oct. 30 was given 11s.

Nov. 1. There would have been again nothing in hand, for the need of this day, had not the Lord kindly sent in yesterday afternoon three donations of 1l., 2l., and 2s. Besides this there came in by sale of stockings 3s. 7d.

Nov. 2. After the demands of yesterday had been met, there remained only 16s. 9 1/2d. in hand, I therefore again besought the Lord, that He would be pleased to send in fresh supplies. Accordingly, about one oclock, a brother left a note at my house, containing a cheque for 7l., of which 1l. was for the Orphans, 1l. for the other objects, and 5l. for my own necessities. Between two and three oclock I met another brother in my walk in Redland Fields, who gave me a sovereign for the Orphans; and at four oclock a sister sent a sovereign for the Orphans. Thus our need for today is supplied and something left.

Nov. 7. Monday. Since the afternoon of the 2nd I received 8l. 9s. 10d. After the necessities of Saturday, the 6th, had been supplied, amounting to between 3l. and 4l., there was once more nothing at all left in my hands, which led me afresh to the Lord in prayer. On the same evening I received, as the answer to my prayers, from a sister 10s., and by sale of articles 1l. 16s. 10d., and this morning there came in still further, by several donations, 2l. 15s. 7 1/2d.

Nov. 9. Again all our money was spent after the expenses of today had been met, when this evening there came in 4l. 1s. by sale of articles, 7s. 9d. by sale of Reports, and 3d. as a donation. A parcel was also given to me this evening, sent by two sisters in the Lord, in Bath, containing the following articles: 5 gold rings, a locket, a gold seal, 15 brooches, a pair of ear-rings, a gold pin, a small telescope, an ornamental comb, 4 pairs of clasps, 2 head brooches, some ornaments of mock pearls, 9 necklaces, 11 bracelets, 4 waist buckles, and a few other articles.

Nov. 15, Yesterday came in from W. D. B. 1l. 1s., from a sister 2s., and through an Orphan box 4s. This 1l. 7s. was all there was in hand, and with out it we should not have been able to provide for the need of today.

Nov. 16. After the need of yesterday had been provided for, and I now again had nothing in hand, I received for Reports 1s., and from a believing clergyman 1l. —When, this morning, after I had been asking the Lord for means, the post brought none, I fell again on my knees, further beseeching Him to supply me with fresh means, as for several days little had come in. I especially also told Him, that, though the post was now out, yet He could in various ways send help. It was ONLY A FEW MINUTES AFTER, when brother C. B. brought me 1l. 3s. which just then had been given to him for the Orphans. About an hour afterwards two brethren called on me, the one from Wiltshire, the other from Essex, who stayed with me some time, and on leaving gave me 2l. 10s. for the Orphans. In the evening I saw still further that the Lord had not only not disregarded my prayers in the morning, but also that He was not confined to sending means by the post. A sister called on me, and brought me, for several purposes, twelve sovereigns, of which six are to be applied for the benefit of the Orphans. This was not all. A brother brought me 9 silver forks and a silver butter knife, the produce of which I might use as most needed. This also, therefore, might have been applied for the Orphans, but I put it to the funds for the other objects as being more in need. In the evening was still further given to me with Eccles. ix. 10, 4s., and as the profit from the sale of ladies baskets, 1l.; so that a rich supply has been received this day from the hand of our loving Father.

Nov. 20. When we were now again in very great need on account of means for the other objects, there came in this day from a sister in the Lord, a servant in Dorsetshire, 10l., which sum being left at my disposal, to use in any way I thought best, I took it for the School-Bible-Missionary and Tract-Fund.

Nov. 26. Saturday. Only 7l. 16s. 11 1/2d. had come in since the 16th for the Orphans. The day began without any thing in hand. In the course of the morning came in by sale of stockings, 6s. 4d., and through the box at the Boys-Orphan-House 8d. At two oclock in the afternoon a believing clergyman sent to two of the labourers in the work 2 sovereigns, of which the one was able to give half the sovereign, and the other the whole sovereign. By this means we were supplied with what was needed today.

Nov. 28. Monday. Yesterday came in from Cheltenham 5s.; with Eccles. ix. 10, 5s.; anonymously was left at the Girls-Orphan-House a paper, containing the letters E.V. with a crown piece; and anonymously was put into the boxes at Bethesda 1s. There was sent also from Bath, a coral necklace and a gold necklace clasp. By these donations we were supplied today.

Nov. 29. This morning I took a shilling out of an Orphan-box at my house, which was all we had wherewith to commence the day. JUST AT THE MOMENT when the letter bag was sent to me from the Orphan-Houses, with the statement of what would be required for this day, I received a post-office order from Barnstaple for 1l. Thus the Lord, in His faithful love, has sent a little, for which I had been waiting upon Him. Through His grace my heart is looking out for more, for I am sure He will never forsake us.

Nov. 30. Nothing at all has come in since yesterday. But as one of the labourers was able to give 17s., we were supplied with bread and a few other little things, which were needed.

Dec. 1. Nothing had come in, except 5s. for needlework of the Orphans. The labourers had nothing to give of their own, except one of them 1s. 6d.; yet this little supplied the absolute need, which was only milk. We were unable to take in the usual quantity of bread. (The bread is eaten by the children on the third day after it is baked. If we are unable to take in the usual daily quantity of bread, for want of means, we afterwards seek to procure stale bread.) Should it be said that the not taking in the usual quantity of bread would at once prove to the bakers that we are poor; my reply is, that that does not follow, because bread has often been sent as a present, as may be seen in the list of articles, given for the Orphans, at the end of the printed Reports. But perhaps it may be stated: Why do you not take the bread on credit? What does it matter, whether you pay immediately for it, or at the end of the month, or the quarter, or the half-year? Seeing that the Orphan-Houses are the work of the Lord, may you not trust in Him, that He will supply you with means, to pay the bills which you contract with the butcher, baker, grocer, &c., as the things which you purchase are needful? My reply is this: 1, If the work in which we are engaged is indeed the work of God, then He, whose work it is, is surely able and willing to provide the means for it. 2, But not only so, He will also provide the means at the time when they are needed. I do not mean that He will provide them, when we think that they are needed; but yet, that, when there is real need, such as the necessaries of life being required, He will give them; and on the same ground on which we suppose we do trust in God to help us to pay the debt which we now contract, we may and ought to trust in the Lord to supply us with what we require at present, so that there may be no need for going in debt. 3, It is true, I might have goods on credit, and to a very considerable amount; but, then, the result would be, that the next time we were again in straits, the mind would involuntarily be turned to further credit which I might have, instead of being turned to the Lord, and thus faith, which is kept up and strengthened only by being EXERCISED, would become weaker and weaker, till at last, according to all human probability, I should find myself deeply in debt, and have no prospect of getting out of it. 4, Faith has to do with the word of God,—rests upon the written word of God; but there is no promise that He will pay our debts,—the word says rather: "Owe no man any thing;" whilst there is the promise given to His children.: "I will never leave thee, nor forsake thee," and "Whosoever believeth on. Him shall not be confounded." On this account we could not say upon the ground of the Holy Scriptures: Why do you not trust in God that He will supply you with means to pay your debts, which you contract in His service for the necessaries of the Orphans? 5, The last reason why we do not take goods on credit is this: The chief and primary object of the work was not the temporal welfare of the children, nor even their spiritual welfare (blessed and glorious as it is, and much as, through grace, we seek after it and pray for it); but the first and primary object of the work was: To show before the whole world and the whole church of Christ, that even in these last evil days the living God is ready to prove Himself as the living God, by being ever willing to help, succour, comfort, and answer the prayers of those who trust in Him: so that we need not go away from Him to our fellow-men, or to the ways of the world, seeing that He is both able and willing to supply us with all we can need in His service. From the beginning, when God put this service into my heart, I had anticipated trials and straits; but knowing, as I did, the heart of God, through the experience of several years previously, I also knew that He would listen to the prayers of His child who trusts in Him, and that He would not leave him in the hour of need, but listen to his prayers, and deliver him out of the difficulty, and that then, this being made known in print for the benefit of both believers and unbelievers, others would be led to trust in the Lord. Thus it has now been for more than nine years (i.e. in. 1845, when the third part was first published). These accounts have been greatly owned by the Lord. We discern, therefore, more and more clearly, that it is for the churchs benefit that we are put into these straits; and if, therefore, in the hour of need, we were to take goods on credit, the first and primary object of the work would be completely frustrated, and no heart would be further strengthened to trust in God, nor would there be any longer that manifestation of the special and particular providence of God, which has hitherto been so abundantly shown through this work, even in the eyes of unbelievers, whereby they have been led to see that there is, after all, reality in the things of God, and many, through these printed accounts, have been truly converted. For these reasons, then, we consider it our precious privilege, as heretofore, to continue to wait upon the Lord only, instead of taking goods on credit, or borrowing money from some kind friends, when we are in need. Nay, we purpose, as God shall give us grace, to look to Him only, though morning after morning we should have nothing in hand for the work—yea, though from meal to meal we should have to look to Him; being fully assured that He, who is now (1845) in the tenth year feeding these many Orphans, and who has never suffered them to want, and that He who is now (1845) in the twelfth year carrying on the other parts of the work, without any branch of it having had to be stopped for want of means, will do so for the future also. And here I do desire, in the deep consciousness of my natural helplessness and dependence upon the Lord, to confess that through the grace of God my soul has been in peace, though day after day we have had to wait for our daily provisions upon the Lord; yea, though even from meal to meal we have been required to do this.—I now go on with extracts from my journal.

Dec. 2, 1842. By the produce of six old silver coins, which I received last evening, and by 9s. 6d. which came in besides, we were able to meet the expenses of today; but now there were before us the heavy expenses of tomorrow, Saturday, which I knew would be particularly great, and there was nothing at all in hand to meet them. In this our need there came in this evening from Lutterworth and its neighbourhood two donations, one of 5l., and the other of 1l. The 1l. was for the Orphans, and the 5l. was left to my disposal, as it might be most needed. I took of it 3l. 12s. 3d. for the Orphans, and 1l. 7s. 9d. for the Day Schools. This afternoon a gentleman passed the Girls-Orphan-House. The house door being opened, he rolled half a crown into the house. This half crown came in when there was nothing at all in hand. There came in also by knitting of the Infants 6d., by knitting of the Boys 6d., from a poor believing widow 6d., and by sale of a Report 3d. Thus we have 4l. 15s. for the necessities of the Orphans tomorrow (the other little sums have been spent today).

Dec. 5. Monday. On Saturday, Dec. 3, 10s. came in from Brighton., and yesterday 1l. with Eccles. ix. 10, and by a sister from Nailsworth 10s. Also by sale of articles 11s, 6d. Thus we had 2l. 11s. 6d., which was nearly but not quite enough for the necessities of today, as it would be desirable to have a few shillings more. I went, therefore, to see whether there was any money in the two boxes at my house, and I found a sovereign. Thus we had more than sufficient for the need of today, which is 3l. This evening I received 1l. 10s. for articles which had been sold.

Dec. 8. A few little donations which came in on the 6th, together with the little there was in hand, supplied our need on the 7th. On the 6th a shilling was anonymously left on the mantel piece in the Infant-Orphan-House; and one of the Orphans, formerly under our care, but now in service, gave 2s. 6d. These two small donations were most seasonable towards the supply of our need on the 7th. Now this day commenced without our having anything in hand. Just while the Orphan-Boy, who had been sent to my house for money, was waiting, I received from the neighbourhood of Droitwich 10s. This, with 3s. 9d. for Reports, and 6d. for knitting of the Infant-Orphans, and 4s. 6d. which one of the labourers was able to give of his own, helped us through this day.

Dec. 9. There was again nothing at all in hand this morning to meet the expenses of the day. A little after ten oclock an Orphan arrived from Northam, with whom there was sent for my own personal necessities 10s., and 2l. 2s. 4d. besides. As about this latter sum nothing had been written, I put it to the Orphan-Fund, whereby we are supplied for today, and have a little left towards the need of tomorrow. There was also 6d. in the boxes at my house.

Dec. 10. 1l. was left, after the need of yesterday had been met. This morning, Saturday, when I knew that again several pounds would be needed, and I had therefore been waiting on the Lord, I received about nine oclock 1l. from a brother, who, on his return from Spain to Devonshire, had been intrusted with it for the Orphans, by a sister in the Lord who lives in London. A few minutes after I had received this sovereign, I had to pay on behalf of one of the apprentices 2l., which took exactly all the money I had, so that there was still nothing to meet the ordinary housekeeping expenses of this day, which I knew would be at least 3l. I gave myself therefore still further to prayer, being fully assured, by grace, that my loving faithful Father would this day also provide me His child with everything I needed. Scarcely was I risen from my knees, when I received a bank post bill from Torquay for 10l.; of which 2l. is intended by the kind donor for my own temporal necessities, and 8l. for the Orphans, so that we have more than enough for this day. —There came in still further this evening, in five small donations, 6s. 10d., by needlework 6s., and by sale of articles 1l. 6s. 6d.

Dec. 11. Anonymously put into the box at Bethesda, 2s. 6d., and from
C. M. W. 1l.

Dec. 14. There was now again only ONE PENNY in my hands this morning. About eleven oclock I received a note, enclosing 2s. and 10s. The brother who kindly brought the note which contained the money, gave at the same time 2s. 6d. for the Orphans. As only 16s. was needed to purchase the necessary provisions for this day, and one of the labourers was able to add 1s. 5d. of his own, we were supplied.

Dec. 15. Only 2s. 3d., the contents of an Orphan-box, 1l. by sale of stockings, and 2s. 1 1/2d. from the boxes in the Orphan-Houses, have come in. This, with 5s. which one of the labourers was able to give, supplied the need of today.

Dec. 16. Nothing has come in. 3s. 5d., which one of the labourers was able to give, was all we had. At six oclock this evening, our need being now very great, not only with reference to the Orphan-Houses, but also the Day Schools, &c., I gave myself with two of the labourers to prayer. There needed some money to come in before eight oclock tomorrow morning, as there was none to take in milk for breakfast (the children have oatmeal porridge with milk for breakfast), to say nothing about the many other demands of tomorrow, being Saturday. Our hearts were at peace, while asking the Lord, and assured that our Father would supply our need. WE HAD SCARCELY RISEN FROM OUR KNEES, when I received a letter containing a sovereign for the Orphans, half of which was from a young East India officer, and the other half the produce of the sale of a piece of work, which the sister, who sent the money, had made for the benefit of the Orphans. She wrote: "I love to send these little gifts. They so often come in season." Truly, thus it was at this time.—About five minutes later I received from a brother the promise of 50l. for the Orphans, to be given during the next week; and a quarter of an hour after that, about seven oclock, a brother gave me a sovereign, which an Irish sister in the Lord had left this day, on her departure for Dublin, for the benefit of the Orphans. How sweet and precious to see thus so manifestly the willingness of the Lord to answer the prayers of His needy children!

Dec. 17. This morning we three again waited unitedly upon the Lord, as there was not enough for the necessities of the Orphan-Houses for this day. Moreover, the teachers in the Day Schools need supplies. Between ten and eleven oclock I received by the first delivery a letter, containing half a sovereign with these words: "The young lions do lack and suffer hunger; but they that seek the Lord shall not want any good thing. Dec. 16, 1842." It was not stated whether this money was for my own personal need, or for the Orphans, or any other object. I took it for the Orphans.— Thus we had enough, except about 2s. 6d., to provide all that was needed for today and tomorrow. Between seven and eight oclock this evening, a brother sent half a crown to the Boys-Orphan-House, stating that he had been thinking much about the Orphans in the course of this day, but that he had not had time to send this money sooner. Thus, by the kindness of the Lord, we have the exact sum which is required, and are again brought to the close of another week.—Between nine and ten oclock this evening came in still further, by the sale of articles, 2l. 7s. Thus the Lord has not only helped us to the close of the week, but given us also a little with which to begin another week.

Dec. 19. Yesterday came in by the profit of the sale of ladies bags 1l., and in two donations 2l. By this 5l. 7s. which came in since Saturday evening, we should have had enough for the ordinary household expenses of today; but as our stores of oatmeal, rice, peas, and Scotch barley, are either entirely or nearly exhausted, and as some calico for shirts and lining, besides many other little articles are needed, and as especially the teachers in the Day Schools are greatly in need of pecuniary supplies, I had been especially entreating the Lord, that He would be pleased to send us larger supplies. I rose from my knees about half-past ten this morning, and about a quarter to eleven I received a let letter from A. B. with an order for 100l., to be used as most needed in the work. Of this sum I took for the Orphans only 25l., and for the other funds 75l. (in consideration of 50l. having been promised to be paid this week for the Orphans); and thus we are in every way again most seasonably helped. "Bless the Lord, O my soul, and forget not all His benefits!"—There came in still further by three donations 3l. 10s.

On Dec. 20 and 21 there came in 2l. 15s. 3d. for the Orphans.

Dec. 22. Though there had come in above 36l. for the Orphans, during the last four days, yet as our stores needed to be replenished, and there had been several other expenses to be met, we were again today in need of farther supplies, when I received the 50l. for the Orphans, which had been promised during the last week. Thus I was able also to supply the labourers in the Orphan-Houses with some money for their own personal need.

REVIEW OF THE YEAR 1842.

I. As to the church.

68 brethren and sisters brother Craik and I found in communion, when we came to Bristol.

848 have been admitted into communion since we came to Bristol.

916 would be, therefore, the total number of those in fellowship with us, had there been no changes. But

131 have left Bristol.

59 have left us, but are still in Bristol.

51 are under church discipline.

74 have fallen asleep.

315 are therefore to be deducted from 916, so that there are only 601 at present in communion.

73 have been added during the past year, of whom 27 have been brought to the knowledge of the Lord among us.

II. As to the supply of my temporal necessities:

1. The Lord has been pleased to send me from the saints among whom I labour in Bristol, in provisions, clothes, etc. worth to us at least £10 0s. 0d.

2. In anonymous offerings in money, put up in paper, and directed to me, and put into the boxes for the poor saints or the rent, at the meeting places £113 1s. 8d.

3. In presents in money, from saints in Bristol, not given anonymously £47 8s. 1s.

4. In provisions and clothes, from saints not residing in Bristol, worth to us at least £10 0s. 0d.

5. In money from saints not residing in Bristol £149 6s. 3d.

Altogether £329 16s. 0d.

Jan. 21, 1843. From Dec. 22 up to this day the Lord was pleased to send in the donations for the Orphans so, that there was always some money received, before all was expended. — The 50l. which was given to me on Dec. 22, and between 50l. and 60l. which had come in since, was now today, Jan. 21, 1843, all spent, after the expenses of today, Saturday, had been met, when there was given to me this evening a silver cup, a gold seal, a broken gold seal, a gold buckle, a watch hook, and a brooch. There came in also by sale of articles 2s. 6d., and by a donation 10s.

Jan. 23. Yesterday came in. 9s. and today 2l. 13s.

Jan. 24. Today came in 5l. 7s. 7d.

Jan. 25. This day I received 3l. 3s. 2 1/2d.

Jan. 28. The last money had been again paid out yesterday morning, when I received 5l. last evening with Eccles. ix. 10. This morning was sent to me from Clapham, 2l. 8s. Thus we were able to meet the expenses of today, which were 4l. 5s.

Feb. 3. Since Jan. 28 there had come in 13l. 5s. 1d., which had fully supplied all our need; but now all was again spent, after this days expenses had been met, on account of which I gave myself to prayer with my wife this morning. This evening I received in answer to it 7s. by sale of articles.

Feb. 4. This morning a brother gave to me 1l. Thus we have 1l. 7s.; but as this is not nearly enough for today, we have given ourselves still further to prayer, and are now looking for supplies. While I am writing this, the Orphan has brought the letter bag to fetch 2l. 15s., which is the need of today; I am therefore looking out for help to make up this sum. —I opened the boxes in my house, in which I found 3s. 6d. With this 1l. 10s. 6d. I had to send off the boy, waiting for further supplies. —This afternoon, about five, came in by sale of articles 1l. 4s. 7d. Thus we had enough, and one penny more than was needed, and we are brought to the close of another week. O Lord, how can Thy servant sufficiently praise Thee for condescending so to listen to his requests! His soul is amazed at Thy condescension, and yet, not amazed when he considers that Thou doest it for the sake of Thy dear Son, in whom Thou dost continually look upon Thy servant! —There came in still further this evening 2s. 6d.

Feb. 6. Yesterday was intrusted to me altogether for the Orphans 2l. 17s. 6d., in eight different donations. Thus I was able to send the supplies which were needed this day in the Orphan-Houses, which required all that had come in yesterday. When now there was again nothing at all in hand, I received, about one oclock 10l., with the following lines: "From the widow to the Orphans, a thank-offering to Him who careth for them both." Through the same donor I received at the same time from a lady and gentleman 2l. In the evening came in further 10s., by the profit of the sale of ladies bags, and 2s. 6d. as a donation.

Feb. 10. As during the last three days only 1l. 6s. had come in., all our money was now again expended, and nothing in hand towards the supplies of tomorrow, Saturday, when I received this afternoon 10s., being the profit of the sale of ladies bags. This evening came in still further with Eccles. ix. 10, 1l., by sale of articles 2s., and from a brother 2s.

Feb. 11. By what came in yesterday afternoon and evening, we had 1l. 14s. towards the expenses of this day. But, as this was not enough, I asked the Lord still further for help, and, behold, this mornings post brought me a post-office-order for 2l. from Stafford, of which 1l. 7s. 6d. is for the Orphans. Thus we have 3l. 1s. 6d., which is quite enough for this day.

Admire with me, my dear Reader, if you know the Lord, His seasonable help. Why does this post-office-order not come a few days sooner or later? Because the Lord would help us by means of it, and therefore influences the donor just then, and not sooner nor later, to send it. Surely, all who know the Lord, and who have no interest in disowning it, cannot but see His hand in a remarkable manner in this work.— Nor will the godly and simple minded reader say:—"There is no difference between this way of proceeding, on the one hand, and going from individual to individual, asking them for means, on the other hand; for the writing of the Reports is just the same thing." My dear Reader, there is a great difference. Suppose, that we are in need. Suppose, that our poverty lasts for some weeks or even some months together. Is there not, in that case, a difference between asking the Lord only from day to day, without speaking to any human being not connected directly with the work about our poverty, on the one hand: and writing letters or making personal application to benevolent individuals for assistance, on the other hand? Truly, there is a great difference between these two modes. I do not mean to say that it would be acting against the precepts of the Lord to seek for help in His work by personal and individual application to believers, (though it would be in direct opposition to His will to apply to unbelievers, 2 Cor. vi. 14-18); but I act in the way in which I do for the benefit of the Church at large, cheerfully bearing the trials, and sometimes the deep trials connected with this life of faith (which however brings along with it also its precious joys), if by any means a part at least of my fellow believers might be led to see the reality of dealing with God only, and that there is such a thing as the child of God having power with God by prayer and faith. That the Lord should use for so glorious a service one so vile, so unfaithful, so altogether unworthy of the least notice as I am, I can only ascribe to the riches of His condescending grace, in which He takes up the most unlikely instruments, that the honour maybe manifestly His. I add only one word more: Should Satan seek to whisper into your ears: Perhaps the matter is made known after all, when there is need (as it has been once said about me at a public meeting in a large town, that when we were in want I prayed publicly that the Lord would send help for the Orphans, which is entirely false); I say, should it be said, that I took care that our wants were made known, I reply: Whom did I ask for any thing these many years since the work has been going on? To whom did I make known our wants, except to those who are closely connected with the work?—Nay, so far from wishing to make known our need, for the purpose of influencing benevolent persons to contribute to the necessities of the Institution under my care, I have even refused to let our circumstances be known, after having been asked about them, when on simply saying that we were in need, I might have had considerable sums. Some instances of this have been given in the former part of this Narrative. In such cases I refused, in order that the hand of God only might be manifest; for that, and not the money, nor even the ability of continuing to carry on the work, is my especial aim. And such self-possession has the Lord given me, that at the times of the deepest poverty, (whilst there was nothing at all in hand, and whilst we had even from meal to meal to wait upon the Lord for the necessities of more than 100 persons), when a donation of 5l. or 10l. or more has been given to me, the donors could not have read in my countenance whether we had much or nothing at all in hand. But enough of this. I have made these few remarks, beloved Reader, lest by any means you should lose the blessing which might come to your soul through reading the account of the Lords faithfulness and readiness to hear the prayers of His children.

Feb. 13. Monday. After having paid out on Saturday all there was in hand, though having quite enough for that day, we had now again to look to the Lord for means, as we generally need several pounds on Mondays. At this time also our faithful Lord did not disappoint us. For there came in late on Saturday, by the sale of articles given for sale, 1l. 8s. 11d., and by sale of stockings, knitted by the boys, 5s. I received also since then by the profit of the sale of ladies bags 10s., by the boxes in my house 1s. 9d., and by two donations 6s. There was also yesterday put into the chapel boxes, half-a-crown with these words: "Trust in the Lord, and wait patiently for Him." Thus we had 2l. 14s. 2d., which was enough for the need of this day.

Feb. 14. I have received nothing since yesterday morning. Nothing therefore was in hand when money was sent for, except 1s. 6d., which was sent up from the Orphan-Houses, by the messenger who came for this days supplies, and which had been received yesterday at the Infant-Orphan-House. I opened the boxes at my house, in which I found 1s. WHILE THE BOY WAS WAITING FOR THE MONEY, the sister who sells the articles which are given to be sold for the benefit of the Orphans, and who knows nothing about our present need, came and brought 12s. for some things which she had sold. With this 14s. 6d. we are able to supply the need of today, as nothing but some bread and milk require to be purchased.

Feb. 15. 2l. 14s. came in from the neighbourhood of Rotherham, besides 1s. 9d. Thus we had enough for this day.

Feb. 16. Yesterday afternoon I received 9s. from two poor sisters at Portsmouth. This, with 9d., which was left of the money which I received yesterday, after the days need had been met, was all I had at the commencement of this day. In the course of the morning was sent by a lady of Ashton, 10s. more. Thus we had 19s. 9d., which sufficed for this day.

Feb. 17. Only 2s. 6d. had come in as a donation, and 2s. 4d. by knitting. This 4s. 10d. was all I could send, hoping in the Lord for more. The information I had from the Boys-Orphan-House was, that the 4s. 10d. supplied the matrons with all that was absolutely needful for today. This evening at nine oclock I received from sister E. Ch. 8s. 9d. for Reports. This is a most precious help, as without it there would be no means to take in the milk tomorrow morning.

Feb. 18. This morning between seven and eight oclock I took the money which came in last night, to the Orphan-Houses, so that we were supplied for the breakfast. We had now to look to the Lord for several pounds, to meet the demands of this day, being Saturday. Between 10 and 11 oclock I again with my wife besought the Lord, entreating Him, that He would be pleased to help us, when a FEW MINUTES AFTER, in this our great need, I received by the first delivery a letter from Barnstaple, containing 5l. for the Orphans. How truly precious, to see thus so manifestly the hand of God day by day stretched out on our behalf!

Feb. 20. Monday. Most seasonable as the help had been, which the Lord so kindly had sent on Saturday morning, and fully as it had supplied our need for that day; yet there was nothing left, after all the expenses had been met, so that we had even on Saturday still further to wait upon the Lord for fresh supplies for this day. Now at this time likewise the Lord has appeared on our behalf. About nine oclock on Saturday evening arrived by post a small parcel from Yorkshire, which contained 6 pitcher purses, 2 night caps, a watchguard, and 6l. 1s. 4d. Of this money 5l. is to be applied for Missionary purposes, 1s. 4d. for the Orphans, and 1l. as it may be needed. This 1l. I took therefore for the Orphans.

—Yesterday morning I received as a widows mite 1l. for the Orphans; and into the chapel boxes was put 10s. with Eccles. ix. 10, and also half-a-crown anonymously. Thus the Lord has been pleased to send us altogether 2l. 13s., whereby we are able to meet this days expenses.

Feb. 21. We were comfortably helped through yesterday, but having provided for all the demands, there was again nothing left in my hands for today. How kind therefore of the Lord to incline the heart of the same brother, who had given me 50l. a few weeks since, to intrust me with 1l. 2s. 6d. more last night, about nine oclock! By this donation our need for today is supplied.

Feb. 22. Only 3s. 9d. came in yesterday by sale of Reports.

When this morning the letter bag was sent from the Orphan-Houses for supplies, I found a note in it, containing this: "For today there is no need of mentioning any sum, as we can make that do, which the Lord may please to send." The 3s. 9d. was all I had to send, waiting upon the Lord for more—There came in further in the course of the morning by sale of stockings 3s., and by sale of other articles, given for that purpose, 2s. 6d. Our need also led us to open the boxes in the Orphan-Houses, in which we found 11s. 6d. Thus we had a altogether, 1l. 0s. 9d., whereby we were helped through this day.

Feb. 23. Last evening I received from Bath a small parcel, containing a small telescope, a set of mother-o-pearl counters, 7 silver buckles, and a broken silver brooch. This morning the bag was brought for money, but I had nothing in hand. WHILST THE BOY WHO BROUGHT THE LETTER BAG WAS WAITING, to receive the answer, the sister who disposes of the articles which are given for sale, (and who was no more acquainted with the state of our funds than any other person), brought 11s. 4d. With this we began the day, again trusting in the Lord for further help.

Feb. 24. Nothing more came in, in the course of yesterday morning; but a little after four oclock I received a letter from Jersey, containing a post-office-order for 1l. for the Orphans. The donor writes thus: "Herewith you will find a post-office-order for 1l., being this years subscription. I had a desire to defer it to the 1st of June; but owing to my mind having been deeply worked on the present day, that this was the acceptable time, I make no scruple of availing myself of this evenings post, which I hope will be acceptable." Jersey, 20 Feb. 1843—How manifest is the hand of the Lord in this matter! He stirs up this donor, who lives at such a distance, to remember our need, whose money indeed came in a most acceptable time. — Thus we were again helped for yesterday. A few minutes after having received the 1l. from Jersey, a brother near Bruton sent me 15s. The money, given by this donor, being always left entirely to my disposal, I took this 15s. towards the need of the Orphans for today. This mornings post brought me half-a-sovereign from London. The letter contained only these words: "London, Feb. 22, 1843. Psalm xxvii. 14." I put this half-sovereign to the Orphan-Fund. There came in also by knitting 1s. 4d., and through the boxes in my house 6 1/2d. Thus we had for the need of this day again, by the good hand of our Lord upon us, 1l. 6s. 10 1/2d.

Feb. 25. Saturday. Yesterday afternoon and evening 12s. 8d. came in by knitting, and 1s. 9d. besides. This was all we had wherewith to begin the day. There came in still further in the course of today: by the boxes in the Orphan-Houses 5d., by knitting 7s. 8d., by a donation 1s., by sale of Reports 4s., by sale of an article, given for that purpose, 10s., and one of the labourers gave 6s. Thus the Lord gave us again 2l. 5s. 6d. for todays need, and we are helped to the close of another week. — As a fresh proof, that our loving Father is still mindful of us, we received this evening a parcel and a box from Plymouth: the former contained a musical box and a piece of worsted work, the latter 10 china ornaments: all to be sold for the benefit of the Orphans.

Feb. 27. Monday. Nothing at all has come in since Saturday. When therefore this day began, we had no means to provide what was needed. My comfort, however, was, that our Father knew that we were needy, and that kept me at this time also in peace. Between 10 and 11 oclock this morning I received 1l. 10s. from Guernsey. The brother, who sent the money, writes, that he had delayed in sending it, and hoped

136

that "this was the Lords time," which indeed it is, for we are thus supplied for this day.

Feb. 28. Yesterday afternoon. 3s. were put into the box in my room, which our need brought out, as again this day began without our having anything in hand. I received still further to day from a brother at Crediton. 2l., being the produce of an Orphan-box in his house. —This evening I was at a Scripture-Reading-Meeting, at a brothers house. On leaving I found half-a-crown in one of my gloves, evidently put there on purpose, which I put to the Orphan-Fund, and it was immediately taken to the Orphan-Houses. Thus we were helped through this day also, but have nothing in hand towards tomorrow. There came in also for knitting 2s. 11d. Thus we had 2l. 8s. 5d. for this day.

March 1. There came in this morning by sale of some articles 1l. 5s. About dinner time a clergyman, who had had one of my Narratives lent to him by one of the labourers in the Orphan-Houses, returned it with 1l. 10s. for the Orphans, from himself and his two sisters. Thus we were again provided with all we needed for today. —This evening the Lord helped still further. I received with Eccles. ix. 10, 3l. From sister M. B. came in 1l., by knitting of the Infant-Orphans 3s. 6d., and by two donations 6s.

March 2. This day the Lord has again looked upon us in His faithful love, and sent us help, whereby I am enabled to replenish our stores with rice, peas, and Scotch barley, and am also able to put by the rent. There was found in the boxes in the Orphan-Houses 2l. 3s. 7d., which had been put in by some visitors, who saw the Orphan-Houses yesterday afternoon. There were also given to me 63 old silver coins, the greater part of them old English coins, the others old Spanish and French coins, also one crown piece current. There came in also by sale of articles and donations, besides the money for the silver coins, 16s. 10d. Thus the Lord has dealt bountifully with us these two days, after many days of poverty.

March 6. Monday. The last money had been given out last Saturday, and only 6d. had come in yesterday, whilst our need for today, I knew, would be about 2l. About a quarter of am hour before I was called on for money, I received from a brother at Plymouth a post-office-order for 2l. 11s. 6d., and by the same post, anonymously, a French cambric handkerchief and half-a-crown. Thus our present need was again more than met.

March 7. There came in today 2l. 13s. 10d.

March 8. Today we required 3l. 10s. to supply comfortably all that was needed in the Orphan-Houses, but only 2l. 1s. 10d. was in hand. How kind therefore of the Lord to send me a large donation, whereby we were richly supplied! The particulars of it are these: —On Oct. 25, 1842, I had a long conversation with a sister in the Lord, who opened her heart to me. On leaving me I told her, (because I thought it might prove a comfort to her at some future time,) that my house and my purse were hers, and that I should be glad if she would have one purse with me. This I said, I repeat, because I judged that at some future time it might prove a comfort to her in an hour of trial, having at the same time, (to judge from a circumstance which had occurred two days before,) every reason to believe, that she had not 5l. of her own. This sister, after I had said so, readily took me at my word, and said, I shall be glad of it, adding presently that she had 500l. The moment I heard that, I drew back, and said, that had I known that she had any money, I should not have made her this offer, and then gave her my reason why I had supposed she had no property at all. She then assured me that she possessed 500l., and that she had never seen it right, to give up this money, else she would have done so; but that as God had put this sum into her hands, without her seeking, she thought that it was a provision which the Lord had made for her. I replied scarcely any thing to this; but she asked me to pray for her with reference to this matter. This whole conversation about the money occupied but very few minutes, and it all took place after the sister had risen and was on the point of leaving me. —After she was gone, I asked the Lord, that He would be pleased to make this dear sister so happy in Himself and enable her so to realize her true riches and inheritance in the Lord Jesus, and the reality of her heavenly calling, that she might be constrained by the love of Christ, cheerfully to lay down this 500l. at His feet. From that time I repeated this my request before the Lord daily, and often two, three, or four times a day; but not a single word or line passed between me and this sister on the subject, nor did I even see her; for I judged that it would be far better that she retained this money, than that by persuasion she should give it up, and afterwards perhaps regret the step she had taken, and thereby more dishonour than honour be brought on the name of the Lord. After I had thus for 24 days daily besought the Lord on behalf of this sister, I found her one day, on returning home, at my house, when she told me, that she wished to see me alone. She then said to me, that from the time she had last conversed with me, she had sought to ascertain the Lords will with reference to the 500l., and had examined the Scriptures, and prayed about it, and that she was now assured that it was the will of the Lord, she should give up this money. After she had told me this, I exhorted her, well to count the cost, and to do nothing rashly, lest she should regret the step she had taken, and to wait at least a fortnight longer before she carried out her intention. Thus we separated. On the 18th day after this conversation. I received the following letter.

"Dear Brother,

"I believe the Lord has not permitted you to grow weary of remembering me, but that He has still enabled you to bear me upon your heart in His presence. All is well with me, dear brother. Your petitions have been heard and answered; I am happy and at peace. The Lord has indeed manifested His tender care of and His great love towards me in Jesus, in inclining my heart cheerfully to lay all I have hitherto called my own, at His feet. It is a high privilege.

I write in haste to ask you (as we have now one purse) to receive the money at a bank in Bristol; I will direct it to be sent in my name, to be delivered into your hands. Etc."

As this whole circumstance is related only for the profit of the reader, and as I knew that the sister still had my letters on the subject in her possession, I wrote to her, requesting her to send them to me, at the time when I published the last account about the Orphan-House, etc. and extracts of them were given in the last Report, in so far as they might refer to the subject or tend to edification. These extracts are here reprinted. My reply to the above was this:

21, Paul Street, Kingsdown, Bristol,

Dec. 6, 1842.

"My dear Sister,

"Your letter found me in peace, and did not in the least surprise me. Dealing with God is a reality. Saints have power with Him through Jesus. It is now forty-two days since you first mentioned this matter to me. I cannot but

admire the wisdom of God and His love to you in allowing
me to speak to you as I did [i.e. offering her to have one
purse with me; when I thought she had no earthly
possessions at all], that thus this great privilege might be
bestowed upon you, to give up this little sum for Him. Since
that hour I have daily prayed for you, and often thrice or
more in the course of the day, that the Lord would make
you so happy in Himself, and help you with such faith to
lay hold on all which He has given you in Jesus, that you
might be constrained by love cheerfully to lay down this
little sum at his feet. Thus I prayed again at six oclock this
morning for you. Nor have I had the least doubt from the
commencement, that the Lord did hear my prayer; yea, so
fully have I been assured that I had the petition, that again
and again I have thanked Him that He had answered my
prayer, before I saw you eighteen days since, and before
your letter came this morning. Moreover, I have been fully
assured since you were last here, that He was carrying on
His work in your soul with reference to this matter, and
that no subtle suggestions of Satan, nor educational
prejudices, nor misinterpretations of the Scriptures were
able to prevail; for I had asked the Lord, by His Spirit to
overcome them in you, and that, if a brothers word should
be needed, He would be pleased to incline your heart to
write to me: and, as no letter came, I felt fully confident, you
were going forward in this matter in peace. When I had seen
you this day six weeks, and learned about this little sum, I
determined, never to say or write to you another word on
the subject, but to leave you in the hands of the Lord. Thus
I purposed again during the last eighteen days; for it was
not the money given up, that I cared for in you, but the
money given up unto the Lord, and from right motives. On
this very account I advised you to wait one fortnight longer,
though you had come to the conclusion; but now, having
done so, and seeing that you are fully purposed in the Lord

to be poor in this world indeed, that the more abundantly you may enjoy His riches, His inexhaustible riches, I change my advice. My word now, beloved sister, is this: "Whatsoever thy hand findeth to do, do it with thy might," and "If ye know these things, happy are ye if ye do them."

Delay then no longer, even as also you have no desire to delay: and the Lord will bless you abundantly in doing so, inasmuch as you do it unto Him. As you desire to intrust me with this money, I do not refuse it, knowing many ways to lay it out for Him. Etc." Then only follows the direction how the money is to be paid into my bankers hands.

On Dec. 18, 1842, I received a reply to my letter, which answer was begun to be written on Dec. 8th, but finished on the 16th. I give a few extracts of the letter: "Since I last saw you, dear brother, I have not had the slightest doubt as to what I ought to do: the word of God has been so clear to me on this head, that I have been kept resting on it; and, in answer to your prayers, no temptation has been allowed to prevail, indeed, I think I may add to arise. But I feel that temptations may come, and that I may in seasons of trial not always have faith to be able to rejoice in this privilege. My heart is so deceitful and my faith so weak, that I shall greatly need your prayers still. Will you then, if the Lord enables you, pray that I may never offend my Father by regretting in the least measure this act of obedience, which He has by His grace inclined me to carry out. I shall pray the Lord still to lay me on your heart. I felt so sure, that you were helped to pray for me, that I had thanked the Lord for His grace. I am glad you did not write, although I much value your advice; but I wished to be led by the Lord alone, after He had used you as the instrument in the first instance, and in such a way too, that I am quite sure He intended to bless you to my soul in this matter. I have asked my heart whether I am really doing this to Him. My heart assures me that I am, and not from any other motive than obedience to the written word. Before I ever saw you I had asked the Lord to make me willing to give this little sum into your hands, if it were His will I should; but His time to make me willing had not then come; even then I had, in a measure given it to you, having written a paper, desiring in case I should fall asleep in Jesus, that you might get possession of it; I had it signed by two witnesses, and I always carried it about with me when I travelled, sealed and directed to you. When I wrote this, I little thought what grace the Lord had in store for me. You will forgive my being thus tedious, but I am sure you will praise the Lord with me for His gracious dealings with me. Etc."—At the end of this letter, which was finished on Dec. 16, the sister tells me, that unexpectedly a hindrance had arisen to her having possession of the money, so that it was not likely it could be paid over to me till about the end of January, 1843.

When this letter came, it would have been naturally a great disappointment to me, as the sister had told me in a previous letter that the money should be paid into my hands, and as just at that time in a variety of ways it was desirable that I should have considerable sums. The Lord, however, enabled me immediately to lay hold on that word, "We know that all things work together for good to them that love God," Rom. viii. 28, and my soul was in peace, though we had only enough money in hand to provide for one or at the most for two days the necessary provisions in the Orphan-Houses. It was but the next day, Dec. 19, 1842, when I received 100l. from A. B., and on Dec. 22, I received 50l. from a brother in Bristol, besides other donations: so that within one week, after I had had grace to delight myself in the will of God, He gave me about 200l., whereby I was able to meet all the heavy expenses of replenishing the stores, &c., on account of which I should naturally have been tried in the payment of the money being delayed.

In reply to the letter, which I received from this sister on Dec. 18, I wrote another on. December 31, 1842, of which I give an extract on this subject. "The hand of the Lord is indeed most manifestly to be seen in this matter, concerning the money: the way in which your own mind was led; my speaking under the circumstances under which I did, when you were already risen to leave the room; the reason why I did so, i.e., mere sympathy with your circumstances, and thinking that some day or other my brotherly offer might be a comfort to you, though you should never need it, and all this when I believed that at that time you did not possess 5l.—I have continued to pray for you, or rather the Lord has enabled me every day once, twice, thrice, or even more, to remember you. The burden of my prayer still has been, that He would be pleased to make you very happy in Himself and enable you to enter into the inheritance which awaits you; further, that you may not be permitted in the least to regret the step which you have taken, but rather consider it a privilege to be permitted to give this little sum back to Him who gave it to you, and who gave Himself for you.—With reference to the delay, I cannot but rejoice. This gives you abundant opportunity to ponder the matter, and afterwards to state to any (who, judging as those who know not how rich the saints are, might blame you,) that you did not do the thing in haste. I consider this delay to be for the furtherance of the honour of the Lord. You know my advice to you, to wait at least a fortnight. That you have seen much of your unfaithfulness, &c., I consider to be an especial blessing which the Lord has bestowed upon you, lest this step you have taken should become a snare to you. Humblings last our whole life. Jesus came not to save painted but real sinners; but He has saved us, and will surely make it manifest. I have a passage laid on my heart for you, read the whole of it carefully: 2 Corinth. viii. 1-9, especially verse 9. Etc."

Day after day now passed away and the money did not come. The month of January was come to an end, and February also, and the money had not come. Thus more than one hundred and twenty days were gone by, whilst day by day I brought my petition before the Lord, that He would bless this sister, keep her steadfast in her purpose and intrust me with this money for His work in my hands. Amidst it all my heart was assured (judging from the earnestness which He had given me in prayer, and that I had only desired this matter to the praise of His name), that in His own time He would bring it about. But I never wrote one single line to the sister on the subject all this time. At last, on the one hundred and thirty-fourth day after I had daily besought the Lord about this matter, on March 8th, 1843,1 received a letter from the sister, informing me that the 500l. had been paid into the hands of my bankers.

I now wrote to the sister to inquire, whether she wished the money to be expended upon any particular objects, or whether she would leave me altogether free to expend it, as I might be led.

In reply to this she wrote me: "Dear Brother, I would still leave this little sum in the hands of Him to whom it has been given. May He alone be your guide in disposing of it. If I did express one wish, it would be, that you would make use of a part for your own or your familys present necessity." This latter point I declined entirely, thinking it not wise to take a part of this money for myself, to avoid even the appearance as if in any measure I had sought my own things in this matter, instead of the things of Jesus

145

Christ.

The 500l. were thus portioned out: 100l. for the School-Bible-Tract and Missionary Fund. 50l. for the Employment Fund.8 50l. was taken at once for the Orphan-Fund, and afterwards also the remaining 300l. when, as I shall presently relate, the Lord pointed out to me to go forward in the Orphan work, and to establish a fourth Orphan-house.

I have related the particulars connected with this donation so minutely, in order to show, that though we may have long to wait upon the Lord, yea, though for one hundred and thirty-four days we may have daily the same petition to bring before Him, yet at last He will give us the desire of our hearts, if our petitions are according to His mind. And now I only give a few lines of a letter which I received on. July 3, 1844, from the sister who gave this donation, together with my letters for which I had asked her, in order that I may show her state of mind on the subject, after she had had it more than twenty months before her, and after she had for sixteen months actually given up the money. She writes thus: "I am thankful to say that I have never for one moment had the slightest feeling of regret; but it is wholly of the Lords abounding grace. I speak it to His praise."

On March 31, 1843, I called at the Orphan-Houses, to make certain arrangements, and one of the sisters told me by the way, that she had been asked by Miss G, who with her father occupied the house, No. 4, Wilson Street, to let me know that they wished to give up their house, if I would like to take it; but she had replied that it was of no use to tell me about it, for she was sure that I had no thought of opening another Orphan-House. When I came home, this matter greatly occupied my mind. I could not but ask the Lord again and again whether He would have me to open another Orphan-House, and whether the time was now come that I should serve Him still more extensively in this way. The more I pondered the matter, the more it appeared to me that this was the hand of God moving me onwards in this service. The following remarkable combination of circumstances struck me in particular. 1, There are more applications made for the admission of Orphans, especially of late, than we are at all able to meet, though we fill the houses as much as the health of the children and of the labourers will possibly admit. 2, If I did take another house for Orphans, it would be most desirable it should be in the same street where the other three are, as thus the labour is less, and in times of great need we are near together for prayer, the distribution of the money, &c. But since the third Orphan-House was opened in Nov. 1837, there never has been one of the larger houses in the street to be let. 3, There are about fifteen children in the Infant-Orphan-House, whom it would have been well some time ago to have removed to the house for the older girls, had there been room; but when a vacancy happened to occur in that house, there were generally several waiting to fill it up, so that unintentionally the female children in the Infant-Orphan-House remained where they were; but this is not well, nor is it according to my original intention for the Infants were intended only to be left till they are seven years old, and then to be removed to the houses for older boys and girls. This my original plan could be executed better for the future, and at once for the present, were I to open another Orphan-House. 4, I know two sisters who seem suitable labourers for this fourth Orphan-House, and who have a desire thus to be engaged. 5, There are 300l. remaining of the 500l. which I so lately received. This money may be used for the furnishing and fitting up of a new Orphan-House. So much money I have never had in hand at one time during the last five years. This seemed to me a remarkable thing, in connexion with the four other reasons. 6, The establishing

147

of a fourth Orphan-House, which would increase our expenses several hundred pounds a year, would be, after we have gone for five years almost uninterruptedly through trials of faith, a plain proof that I have not regretted this service, and that I am not tired of this precious way of depending upon the Lord from day to day; and thus the faith of other children of God might be strengthened. —But most important, yea decidedly conclusive, as these points were; yet they did not convince me that I ought to go forward in this service, if the Spirits leading were not in connexion with them. I therefore gave myself to prayer. I prayed day after day, without saying anything to any human being. I prayed two and twenty days, without even mentioning it to my dear wife. On that very day, when I did mention it to her, and on which I had come to the conclusion, after three weeks prayer and consideration in the fear of God, to establish another Orphan-House, I received from A. B. 50l. and 1l. through him from a sister. What a striking confirmation that the Lord will help, though the necessities should increase more and more. At last, on the 24th day, having been now for several days fully assured, that God would have me go forward in this service, I went to inquire whether Mr. and Miss G. still wished to give up the house. But here I found an apparent hinderance. Having heard no wish expressed on my part to take the house, and the sister in the Orphan-Houses, with whom Miss G. had communicated, not having given her the least reason to think that I should do so, Mr. and Miss G. their altered their plans, and now purposed to remain in the house. However, I was to call again in a week, when I should receive an answer. I was not in the least discomforted by this obstacle. "Lord, if Thou hast no need of another Orphan-House, I have none," was the burden of my prayer. I was willing to do Gods will, yea to delight myself in His will. And just on this very ground, because I knew I sought

148

not my own honour but the Lords; because I knew I was not serving myself, but the Lord in this thing; and because I knew that with so much calm, quiet, prayerful, self-questioning consideration I had gone about this business, and had only after many days, during which I had been thus waiting upon the Lord, come to the conclusion that it was the will of God I should go forward in this service: for, these reasons I felt sure (notwithstanding what Mr. and Miss G. had told me), that I should have the house. I also especially judged, that thus it would be, because I was quite in peace, when I heard of the obstacle: a plain proof that I was not in self-will going on in this matter, but according to the leading of the Holy Ghost; for if according to my natural mind I had sought to enlarge the work, I should have been excited and uncomfortable when I met with this obstacle. After a week I called again on Mr. G. And now see how God had wrought! On the same day on which I had seen Mr. G., he went out and met with a suitable house, so that when I came the second time, he was willing to let me have the one which he then occupied in Wilson Street, and as the owner accepted me as a tenant, all the difficulties were removed, so that after the first of June we began fitting up the house, and in July the first Orphans were received.

Of the donations which came in from March 8 to the end of May, 1843, and which were many, I only notice:

on April 10 a brother gave 5l., which had been saved out of house furnishing, by doing it in a plainer way.

At the end of May, 1843, I entered upon a remarkable part of my life, upon which I must dwell somewhat at length, especially as it will, by Gods blessing, still further show the Reader the preciousness of depending upon God for every thing.

149

It was in September or October 1841, that one day a German lady, a native of Wirtemberg, called on me. She said that she had come to England to perfect herself in English, and purposed afterwards to return to Germany to establish a boarding school for young ladies, and especially for English young ladies. Having heard that I was a German, she came to obtain my advice, and to request me to interest myself for her in getting her pupils to instruct in German, in order thus to support herself while in England. After having conversed with her for some time about these things, and given her the information which she desired, I then spoke to her about the things of God, in which conversation I soon found, that though she might have had some religious feelings from time to time, yet that she did not know the Lord. On leaving me I gave her the first and second part of my Narrative, which I thought she would read because it contained the experience of a German, and thus she would also have exercise in English. I then followed with my prayers the reading of the book, that God would be pleased to bless it to the conversion of her soul. After some time she called on me again, telling me that she had been deeply interested in reading my Narrative, and asked me whether I had any objection to her translating the book into German, with the view of getting it published on her return to Germany. My reply was that I had no right to object to it; for, in so far as translation into another language was concerned, the book was everyones property. I might have mentioned that I did not think her yet sufficiently acquainted either with the English language or the state of things in England, especially religiously, and that, as she was not converted herself, she could not give the exact translation of the book, though she were qualified with reference to the two former points; but, as I had the spiritual benefit of the individual in view, I thought thus with myself; this person has no employment at present, and by

150

translating this book she will be kept from the many snares connected with idleness; she will by this means also make progress in English, which she is desirous of doing; but, most of all, the fact of translating a book for the press will oblige her more accurately and attentively to consider what is contained in it, than she would be obliged to do, were she simply to read it through several times, and therefore this work may, with Gods blessing, be instrumental in doing good to her soul. The last point weighed particularly with me; I therefore did not discourage her, though at the same time I did not encourage her, but left the matter to herself. As, however, she left me with the impression that she was going to translate the book, I asked the Lord to convert her soul in doing so. After a time Mrs. G. called on me again, and brought me a part of the manuscript, that I might read it over. I took it, but could not promise her to read it; for I had little prospect of doing so, for want of time. Nevertheless I read a few pages, which I found rather better translated than I had expected. After this she brought me at two or three other times considerable parts of the translation, which, however, I had never time to read. By this time the winter had passed away, and it was come to March, 1842, when all of a sudden, one Wednesday afternoon, I was seized with sharp pains, something like spasms, which were so acute that, though they passed off after about an hour, they left me so weak, that I was not able to go out to our usual meeting on that evening. About seven oclock, just when I should have been at the meeting but for this illness, Mrs. G., who for several weeks had been at Trowbridge, to finish the translation, and to instruct a young lady in German, came to take leave of me. She said she now purposed to return to Wirtemberg. Though I was very weak, yet, under these circumstances, I could not decline seeing her, as it would be in all human probability the last time that I should do so. I therefore besought the

Lord to strengthen me for this service (which I soon perceived He had done), and, after a short conversation with her about her circumstances, I began to speak to her about her soul, and soon found she was heavy laden, burdened under her sins, and broken in heart. With many tears, she told me that she was a great sinner, an exceedingly great sinner. Every word she spoke gave me the impression, that all she now needed was to have the work of Christ pointed out to her, i.e. the power of His blood in cleansing from all sin, by faith in His name. I spent about two hours with her, and she left me with many tears. —I also had said to her at the beginning of the conversation with reference to the translation of my Narrative, that if she still desired to publish it, she should seek to get the assistance of a pious clergyman in Germany, who understood English well—On the next morning about nine Mrs. G. called again upon me, telling me that she could not leave Bristol without seeing me once more. She now spent about three hours more with me, in which she told me that, during the night, which she had chiefly spent in prayer and reading the word of God, she had found peace in the Lord Jesus, and that she was now happy in Him. She further told me, that, after she had translated a part of my Narrative, the Spirit of God began to work upon her heart, by convincing her that she was a great sinner. The further she went on, the more she felt what a sinner she was, till at last, when she was come towards the end of the book, she came to the conclusion to return to Germany. I now gave her some advice in reference to her return, and also what she should do with reference to her spiritual welfare, after her return to Wirtemberg. After this she left me. About two or three weeks after (in April, 1842) I received a long letter from her, written on her way homeward, by which I was still further confirmed that, although Mrs. G. was only a mere babe in Christ, yet that she was a babe, and that a real work of grace had been

152

begun in her heart. I then wrote to her, but from that time till towards the end of May, 1843, I heard no more of her. Towards the end of May, 1843, however, I received a long letter from her, dated Stuttgart (capital of the kingdom of Wirtemberg). In this letter Mrs. G. gave me an outline of her history during the year after she had returned to her country. Suffice it here to say, that she had sought in vain to find Christians with whom she could be united in fellowship according to the truths she thought she saw in my Narrative, and according to what she had seen and heard at our meetings in. Bristol. At last, about New-year, 1843, she became acquainted with a little baptist church, which was separated from the State church, and she was after a time baptized and received into fellowship among them, which took place in Feb. 1843. Soon, however, she found things different, as to church order, etc., from what she had seen amongst us in Bristol, or from what she had learnt from my Narrative, especially with reference to close baptist principles, which in the highest and strongest degree were practised among the brethren at Stuttgart: and she wrote to me, to ask my view about that point, as she felt pained at separating from true believers, because they might not be instructed about believers baptism. Her letter was accompanied by another letter from one of the brethren of the baptist church, Dr. R—, a solicitor or barrister to the upper tribunal of the kingdom of Wirtemberg. The letter of the latter testified of the gracious spirit of the writer, but also that he likewise held the separating views of close communion, and that he, having read the translation of my Narrative in manuscript, seemed to be drawn and knit to me affectionately, but wished to have, upon Scriptural ground, my views about open communion.

Before I received these letters, I had been repeatedly asked, during my fourteen years residence in England, why I did

153

not labour in my native country. The importance also of doing so had been pointed out to me; nor was I myself insensible to this; but my answer had always been: "I must labour where the Lord will have me to be, and as I have never seen it to be the Lords will, that I should labour in Germany, I ought not to do so." About fourteen months before I received these letters, it had been also more than ever laid on my heart by brother R. C. He had seen something of the religious state of the Continent, and he had heard still more about it, and he had found, almost every where, that when he set truth before brethren, they said, It is Scriptural, you are right; but if we were to practice this, what would be the consequences? what would become of us and our wives and children? or something of that kind. Brother C. therefore came on purpose to see me, on his return from Denmark, to lay it on my heart to visit Germany, on account of my being a native and having been led by the Lord as I had. He told me especially that he considered it of importance that I should publish my Narrative in German, in order that thus the faith of the brethren., with the Lords blessing, might be strengthened, and that they might be led to act according to the light which they had. All this seemed to me very important: but my answer was as before; I cannot go till the Lord calls me. Scarcely had I read the letters from Mrs. G. and Dr. R—, but I felt: now is the time come when I am to go to Germany; and from that time I gave myself to prayer about it. When I afterwards communicated my feeling on the subject to brother R. C. he said; I am not surprised about it, for from the time that I spoke to you on the subject, I have been constantly asking the Lord to bring it about.

—The reasons that pointed it out to me as the Lords will, that I ought to go to Germany to labour there for a season, were these. 1, I knew not of one single body of believers, who were gathered on scriptural principles. In all the States of Germany, with scarcely any exception, believers are connected with the State Churches, and the very few believers of whom I had heard that they were separated, I knew to be close Baptists, who, generally, by their most exclusive separate views, only confirmed believers in remaining in the Establishment. Especially of the Baptist Church at Stuttgart I had much reason to believe this. It seemed to me therefore important to go to Germany, and labour there for a season., if it might please the Lord to condescend to use me to put a light on a candlestick, howsoever dimly it might be burning at the first, so that by means thereof the light might be spread in other parts of Germany. 2, As I am a German, and therefore familiar with the language, there seemed to me an especial call that I should take on myself this service, particularly as my experience in connexion with several bodies of believers, during the 13 1/2 years previous to this time, would be of great help in this service. 3, It seemed further to me to be the Lords will that I should go to Germany, in order that I might publish my Narrative of the Lords dealings with me (which Mrs. G. had not been able to accomplish), and that not simply in the form of a translation, but so that it should be prepared for the press just as the necessities of the believers in Germany (who, with scarcely any exceptions, are not only connected with the Establishment, but have no idea that there is any where else any thing besides Establishment) might require it. Thus, I judged, something would be given to Germany of the practical working of labouring out of the Establishment; of meeting only as believers in the name of the Lord Jesus, irrespective of any particular religious party or sect, and that in dependence upon the power and presence of the Holy Ghost in the Church of Christ; of dependence upon the Lord alone for every thing; of recognising no other book but the Holy

Scriptures for our rule concerning every thing, &c.; and thus my Narrative, if the Lord allowed me to publish it, might be working still, after I had left Germany. 4, Up to that time I had never known an open door for me to labour on the Continent, at least not in Germany; for in the Establishment I neither could labour with a good conscience, according to the light which the Lord had been pleased to give me, nor should I have been permitted to have done so; and I was not acquainted with believers on the Continent out of the Establishment; and as to preaching in the open air, or going somewhere and taking a place for preaching, any thing of this sort was out of the question; for I was too well acquainted with the police of Germany, not to know that that would not be permitted. But now I heard of an open door. At Stuttgart, I judged, I might labour in expounding the truth in this close Baptist Church, and seek to bring these dear brethren out of their sectarian views. 5, But that which in connexion with these four reasons had likewise much influence upon me, was this: During the fourteen years that I had been in England, I had never had my mind drawn to labour on the Continent, and now the very opposite was the case. It was but two or three days before I received those letters from Stuttgart, that I had again expressed my mind as to labouring in Germany, i.e. that I felt no call from the Lord to do it, and had no drawing towards it. Now the case was altogether otherwise. I could not but pray about it; I could not but feel drawn to go to Germany in love to the Lord and in pity towards the poor Church of Christ in that country. Naturally there was nothing inviting; for I saw a hard struggle before me with reference to the brethren who were to be won for the truth, and to be brought out of their errors; in the Continental manners and the long and beautiful journey on the Rhine I saw, through grace, no charm, and certainly I saw nothing in them which would

156

induce me to leave home, but the reverse; the fourth
Orphan-House was on the point of being opened, and I,
naturally, was very reluctant to be absent from it just then;
the labour would be great in Germany, and work would
heap up greatly for me in Bristol, during my absence. But
with all this:—the leading of my mind to Germany still
remained.

The more I prayed about these points, the more I judged it
to be from the Lord, that I should go for a season to
Germany. It was but a few days, before I had the fullest
assurance in my soul, (after much prayer, much self-
examination in the fear of God, and after much looking at
these five points), that it was the will of God I should go;
yet even then I did not speak publicly about it.

After having come to the conclusion, that, as far as I could
see, it was the will of God that I should go, I began
prayerfully to look at the difficulties there were in the way,
which were principally these. 1. the New Orphan-House
needed to be opened, and all the work in connexion with it
was to be done before I could leave; because I could not
judge it to be of God, that this work, which was begun,
should remain unfinished, except absolute necessity pointed
it out, as otherwise it would be a waste of money, a breach
of promise to the relatives whose children were to be
received, &c. I therefore asked the Lord to help me through
all this work, which was not a little, before I could leave. 2. I
judged it for various reasons important, not to leave the
work of the Orphan-Houses, Day-Schools, &c., without
leaving such a sum of money behind, as would, at least for
about two months, defray the probable current expenses for
the work, therefore a few hundred pounds I thought it
desirable to leave behind, in order that the burden of the
work might not be left upon the shoulders of my dear

fellow-labourers. I had therefore by prayer to get this sum
from the Lord, for the obtaining of which I had no natural
prospects whatever. 3. Another obstacle in the way was,
want of money for traveling expenses to and from Stuttgart,
and means for staying there at least for a time, and that not
only for myself, but for my dear wife; for I judged, for
various reasons, that it was the will of God she should
accompany me in this service, but principally because her
health was not equal to being left in Bristol, with the
responsibility of the work resting upon her in my absence.
This again would require a considerable sum, I mean
considerable for me, a poor man. The means I then had of
my own as far as I now remember, were not enough, if they
had been multiplied by fifty. This obstacle was to be removed
by prayer. 4. One of the especial reasons for which I saw it
to be the Lords will that I should go to Germany was, the
publishing of my Narrative, at a cheap price (2s. for both
parts), or to be given away gratuitously, so that the poor
might have it. But this could not be obtained, except I
published it on my own account, to avoid the publishers
putting a higher price upon it. Then again, as so much
expense of time was connected with printing it, I intended, if
once I went to Germany, to print not less than 4000 copies;
and what is even that number among the many millions
whose language is German. But whence was the money to
come for all this; an expense which, though printing and
paper are very much cheaper in Germany than in England,
yet I knew would cost between one and two hundred
pounds. For this, then, also, I, a poor man, betook myself to
the living God, being fully assured, that, as He had pointed
out to me His will with reference to my going, He would
also most assuredly provide the means. Nay, I had a secret
satisfaction in the greatness of the difficulties which were in
the way. So far from being cast down on account of them,
they delighted my soul; for I only desired to do the will of

158

the Lord in this matter. In honesty of heart, I had examined the matter, as standing before God. I wished only to know His will, that I might do it. I judged, it was His will that I should go to Germany, and therefore determined in His fear that I would go. When I therefore saw the difficulties, they cast me not down, but cheered me; for as it was the will of God, according to my judgment, that I should go, I was sure He would remove the obstacles out of the way; and therefore the greater the obstacles, the more abundantly plain the proof, that I had come to a right judgment, if they were removed by prayer; but if after all I had been mistaken, which I could not think I had been, then, the sooner I was undeceived the better. How different such a state of heart, from what it would have been, if somehow or other the love for a Continental tour, or the desire to go up the beautiful Rhine, had beguiled me: then I should not have liked to look at the difficulties, or at least I should have sought to have them removed by my own efforts. But as it was, I did nothing but pray. Prayer and faith, the universal remedies against every want and every difficulty; and the nourishment of prayer and faith, Gods holy word, helped me over all the difficulties. —I never remember, in all my Christian course, a period now (in October 1881) of fifty-five years and eleven months, that I ever SINCERELY and PATIENTLY sought to know the will of God by the teaching of the Holy Ghost, through the instrumentality of the word of God, but I have been ALWAYS directed rightly. But if honesty of heart and uprightness before God were lacking, or if I did not patiently wait upon God for instruction, or if I preferred the counsel of my fellow men to the declarations of the word of the living God, I made great mistakes. —5. A fifth difficulty in the way was, to find a sister, as matron, for the new Orphan-House, who, as far as I could see, would be suitable; for there were reasons why the sister, of whom I had first thought, could not be engaged for this work. This was no small difficulty in the way, not only as a point important in itself, but also because I could not proceed with the fitting up of the house, &c., till such a sister had been found.

In the beginning of June, I began therefore to give myself to prayer, along with my wife and her sister who lived with us, making it a point, every morning after family prayer, to retire together for the express purpose of asking the Lord to remove these five difficulties, if it were indeed, as I judged, His holy will, that I should labour for a season on the Continent. In addition to this we day by day asked His blessing upon the brethren at Stuttgart among whom I was looking forward to labour, and upon unconverted persons with whom I might come in contact on the Continent in the ministry of the Gospel publicly or privately. We asked Him also especially to prepare the hearts of the brethren in Germany for my service, to help me in writing the book, to bless it, &c. We asked Him further, to be with the Church in Bristol, during my absence, to use my absence as a means of making the gifts, which He had bestowed among us, more abundantly manifest, to help the labourers in the Orphan-Houses and Day-Schools during my absence, &c. Thus we were, morning by morning, waiting upon the Lord, and enlarging our petitions as the Holy Spirit might lead me in prayer. But whilst we were thus day by day waiting upon the Lord, the difficulties, instead of being removed, appeared to increase. For instance: instead of money coming in for the Orphans, the Day-Schools, and the other objects of the Scriptural Knowledge Institution, there was considerably more expended than came in, so that we were getting almost poor. Instead of finding a sister, who seemed suitable as matron for the new Orphan-House, I had the prospect of losing another sister out of the work, who considered it her place to leave Bristol. But notwithstanding all this, my soul was at peace, being fully assured, that I could not be mistaken, as I had come through sincere, patient, and prayerful consideration of the whole matter at last to the conclusion, it was the will of the Lord that I should go to Germany, to labour there in the Word, and publish my Narrative in the German language. Faith therefore saw all the difficulties already removed. Faith could give thanks, while the difficulties yet remained. Faith could triumph, though there seemed the death blow coming, since there not only was no money coming in, but the considerable sums, lately in hand, were rapidly diminishing; and, instead of finding a sister for the new Orphan-House, another sister seemed on the point of leaving. Thus forty days had been passing away, whilst day after day we had been waiting unitedly upon the Lord; but the obstacles were greater than ever, yet my confidence in the Lord, that He would remove the difficulties in His own time, was greater than ever also. It was on July 12 that I said to a sister, being led to it by the certain prospect of one of the dear labourers in the Orphan-Houses going to leave; "Well, my soul is at peace. The Lords time is not yet come, but, when it is come, He will blow away all these obstacles, as chaff is blown away before the wind." It was only ONE QUARTER OF AN HOUR after, when the following paper was put into my hands, whereby I obtained power over 702l. 3s. 7d.

"1st, The poor brethren and sisters of our dear Lord and Saviour. In connexion with the Employment-Fund or otherwise [i.e. might be given away in connexion with the Employment-Fund or otherwise.]

2nd, Sending help in the Gospel of Christ to the dear brethren in Germany, or publishing the Narrative.

3rd, The dear Orphan-Children.

4th, To complete the payment of the expenses incurred by building a chapel for the meeting of the saints at Barnstaple.

I leave the sums, to be used in these several objects, under the Lord, to the judgment of the Lords servant, brother Müller, knowing assuredly that He whose steward he is will direct and guide him in this and every other matter.—His holy name be praised for the REAL JOY I feel today in doing a thing, which a few weeks since was a trying act of obedience. Surely, the statutes of the Lord are right, rejoicing the heart. In keeping of them there is great reward. —July 10, 1843."

Thus three of the hinderances were at once removed; for I was by this sum furnished with travelling expenses, and with what might be required for my stay in Germany, had means to publish 4000 copies of my Narrative, and was able to leave means behind for the work in Bristol, sufficient for at least two months. When I received this note, I was not in the least excited, but took the circumstance as quietly as if it were a matter which could not be otherwise. I had been sure, that, when the Lords time was come, He would send the means, and according to my faith it was now granted to me; and a proof, that up to the last I did believe, was, that when the money came, it did not surprise me. The 702l. 3s. 7d. was not portioned out (except what was sent to Barnstaple), till my return, as I could not know how much each object might require. It was thus spent. 1, For the chapel at Barnstaple, 80l. 7s. 1d. 2, For poor saints, 112l. 2s., spent in a great measure in providing them or their children with linen and clothes, and for the Employment-Fund, 50l. 3, For publishing 4000 copies of the two parts of my Narrative in German, our travelling expenses to and from Stuttgart, our stay for nearly seven months in Germany, and other expenses connected with my service in Wirtemberg, 267l. 4s. 11d. 4, The remainder of the 702l. 3s. 7d., being 192l. 9s. 7d., I put to the Orphan-Fund, not that so much was in hand on my return from Germany; for I had drawn on the strength of what was in the hands of my bankers.

Shortly after I had received the 702l. 3s. 7d. on July 12, the Lord was pleased to remove the other difficulties also; for a sister was found for the matrons place in the new Orphan-House, and after this the Lord helped me through the work connected with fitting up the house for the reception of the children. The Lord likewise made it plain to the sister who had purposed to leave her situation, that she should remain in Bristol. Thus all the difficulties were by prayer and faith removed, after we had been, day by day, more than fifty days waiting upon the Lord.

On Aug. 3rd, I received a valuable donation of plate, jewellery, china, linen., books, etc., which was a still further proof of the Lords readiness to supply all that might be needed during my absence in Germany, and also of His having heard our requests that He would be pleased to send in means before my departure. Most of these articles were readily disposed of, so that, even before I had set out, about 60l. had come in for them.

On Aug. 9, 1843, my dear wife and I left Bristol in company of a German sister, Miss W. The latter, together with a Swiss brother, had been led to see the truth of believers baptism, and had much wished to be baptized; but as the baptist church at Stuttgart had refused them baptism, except they would promise never to take the Lords supper any more with unbaptized believers, or with those who belonged to any State Church, to which they could not conscientiously submit, they had undertaken the journey of nearly 800 miles

163

to come to Bristol, to be baptized by me, as they both had read the translation of my Narrative in manuscript, and thus knew that we receive all who believe in the Lord Jesus, though they should not agree with us in all parts of truth. They had arrived in Bristol about a fortnight before my departure for Germany, and were baptized at Bethesda a week after their arrival, when I gave an address in German, and used the words of the German translation of the Holy Scriptures which contain the institution of baptism, as neither the brother nor sister understood English. The brother, who had been a teacher and cashier in a considerable establishment in Wirtemberg for educating young gentlemen, and who had lost his situation when his views with reference to baptism became known, remained in England as teacher of the French and German languages, and the sister travelled back with us to Germany.

During the time of my absence from Bristol, I kept no journal, and therefore I cannot give a minute account of all that transpired, and that might be interesting to the believing reader; but as some letters which I wrote to one of my sisters-in-law are preserved, and also all the letters which I wrote to the brethren in Bristol, among whom I labour, I shall be able by giving these letters, to furnish a pretty full account of my service in Germany up to my return.

The following Letter to my sister-in-law gives some account of a great part of our journey.

Weinheim, Aug. 19, 1843.

My dear L.,

Thus far we have now been brought through the goodness

of the Lord. If you look at the map where Mannheim is, you will, I think, find a small town, called Weinheim, the place where we are now at Mrs. Ms. Weinheim forms with Heidelberg and Mannheim a triangle, about 10 miles from Mannheim, and the same from Heidelberg. On the Lords day evening last I wrote to you from Rotterdam, which letter, I hope, you safely received. On Monday morning at seven, Aug. 14, we left Rotterdam, with sister W. in one of the Rhine steamers, in which we sailed till about half-past eight in the evening, when we arrived at Emmerich, the first Prussian town, where we stopped for the night. The weather was beautiful, as indeed it has been every day of this week. There was nothing remarkable as to natural things, except a large noble river, and on the banks of the river clean pretty cottages of the Dutch people. The Lord enabled me to do a little for Him. I distributed German tracts among those who could read German; but many of them were Dutch persons, who could understand me in speaking to them, but could not read German. I had a long but affecting conversation with four Jews, who, though disagreeing among themselves as to their religious views, were all agreed in their complete rejection of Jesus of Nazareth, as the Messiah, and, as usual, blasphemed. I conversed with many persons, but found only one aged person, who, I think, as far as I could learn, was a christian. After having given him a tract, having heard my testimony for Christ, he came with tears and asked me to sell him another tract. After having told him that I gladly gave him the tract, he then asked me to give him a third and a fourth for the old clergyman and the schoolmaster of his place, and said, Oh! if you could but stop, how glad the old clergyman, a pious man, would be to see you. —There were two other interesting things that day. Very soon after we had started, perhaps two hours after, a gentleman left, to whom I gave a tract in German and English, as he could also read English.

He then told me he had seen me reading the Bible, but did not like to interrupt me. I told him my errand to Germany. His reply was: "Brother, the Lord bless thee." On asking him who he was, he told me he was a Baptist minister at Amsterdam, and on his way to the brethren at Utrecht, in Holland. He now much regretted not to have had conversation with me. In the afternoon, a gentleman, an officer on pension, who, with his lady, had heard my confession for Christ, while I was conversing with a person sitting close by, asked me very politely, on his leaving, for a tract. — There were two little cabins in the steamer, each with two berths, one of which I engaged for Mary and myself it being much cheaper than to go on shore, though we should not do so again, as our sleep was greatly interrupted, there being much noise till twelve oclock, and commencing again soon after three in the mornings, so that for three nights our sleep was greatly interrupted. Yet I do not mention this in the way of complaint, for we have only to sing of mercy. However, as in spiritual things, so in natural things, we learn daily. The noise only arose from the needful occupations, but it could scarcely have been greater than it was, if persons had purposely tried to disturb us. — At half-past five on Tuesday morning the steamer began again to ply. While I was sitting on deck, between five and six, reading the Bible, a Dutchman came to me to speak about the things of God. He understood me pretty well, but I understood him only imperfectly. He questioned me about the connexion between faith and works, and how man can believe, being a fallen being in Adam. I fear it was more intellectual than heart-work with him, but I made use of the opportunity, to preach Jesus before all, who through this conversation had been drawn round us. This day also I had opportunities of giving away tracts, and of speaking to several, particularly to a young Prussian soldier, and other young men. But all were dead. Most listened and received the tracts, but there were some who boldly rejected. On the second day we sailed from half-past five in the morning till about half-past ten in the evening, when we arrived at Cologne, where we stopped. Our German sister went on shore, and took leave of us, to go on by another companys vessel, for which she had previously paid; dear Mary and I remained alone on board. The third day we had very few passengers on board. Two Irish gentlemen and an English gentleman came on board, to whom I gave English tracts. One of them soon left, and the other two declared themselves on the Lords side. Two other Jews, who had come on board, likewise rejected the truth, yet I conversed with them till they blasphemed. This third day we sailed from ten in the morning till about half-past seven in the evening, when we arrived at the Prussian fortress Coblentz. Mary and I now took a little walk. In the town I gave some tracts to a Prussian soldier, for himself and some of his comrades, for having given us some information; and in going back to the steamer we heard an English lady before us speaking English to a little boy who was with her. We joined her, and offered her some English tracts, which she accepted, also some German tracts for the Roman Catholic servant. Today we have seen beautiful scenery. Fourth day, Aug. 17, One of the Irish gentlemen asked me to read to him and his friend a chapter in the Bible. This day also we glided along through most beautiful scenery. Travelling is a very dangerous thing. I would exhort every one, especially to be aware what he is about, before he sets out on a journey. Much as I had prayed about this journey, and sure as I have been and still am, that the Lord sent me on this errand, I was yet made to feel how difficult it is to keep the heart in the right frame whilst looking at such beautiful scenery. It surpassed all I have before seen of the kind. I suppose we have not had less than forty instances of ruined castles, fortresses, &c., brought before us this day; the ancient

Roman glory—the glory of the German knights, and of the German emperors, whose works, castles and fortresses we saw in ruins, how loudly does it speak of the changeableness of all earthly things, and yet how pernicious often the effect upon the new nature, while looking at these things. The Rhine is wide, the castles often quite close to the river, and hundreds of millions of vines, you might say, without exaggeration, and tens of thousands of vineyards all along the river for perhaps a hundred miles or more. It is beautiful; but how poor, how very poor this beauty in comparison with Jesus! Through grace I would not pay one shilling to see it again, nor go one mile to see it again, for the sake of seeing it.—On the fourth evening, after having sailed that day from seven in the morning, we arrived about five or six oclock at Mayence, sister W. having joined us again. We found it very refreshing to have a few hours quiet in an hotel, and then all three together took a walk. In this town, where printing was invented, Gods precious word is not valued. Almost all are Romanists. It is a large, magnificent, and busy town, and a strong fortress. The railroad also was just in sight on the opposite side of the river. There was scarcely a trace to be seen of that poverty which you see so often in large towns in England, but all bespoke abundance, though I know there is not the abundance of the English gold. Yesterday morning, Aug. 18, we ought to have left at eight oclock by the steamer, in which we had taken our places from Rotterdam to Mannheim, but the steamer, by which we ought to have gone, did not arrive. We waited hour after hour, till at last, near four oclock in the afternoon, we left Mayence for Mannheim by a steamer of another company, having thus to lose the money we had previously paid. We were on board of this steamer about seven hours, till near eleven in the evening, when we arrived at Mannheim. There were at least 14 English passengers on board, besides many

168

Germans and French. I distributed English and German tracts, and had conversation with several. There was a dear young sister, a French lady, with whom I had much conversation. She had been with her little brother to a bathing place near the Rhine. I saw her reading the Epistle to the Romans, and thus took the opportunity to converse with her. She had been at school in Paris till within a few months, and is now, as she has no parents, living with her aunt, a pious woman near Strasbourg. It was very refreshing to be able to help this solitary one, who knew no one on board, and who was very glad to have a little counsel. In parting I gave her a copy of my Narrative, some English tracts, a German tract, and an Orphan Report, as she has begun to learn English, and has a friend, a believer, who understands English well. I had also a pretty long conversation with a German young gentleman, a Roman Catholic, about the way to heaven. This morning, Aug. 19, we called on our sister N. at Mannheim, if it might please the Lord to use us to benefit and restore her soul. We found out her residence after some inquiry, and she seemed very glad to see us. After having our passports signed, and taken up some money from the banker, we left Mannheim at two oclock in the afternoon, and arrived here at four, where we were very affectionately received by brother T. H. and dear Mrs. M. We are now staying in an old building, formerly a Roman Catholic cloister, where I this evening expounded the Scriptures.

Aug. 20, 1843. This morning I expounded the Scriptures at
family prayer in English, then at eleven oclock we broke
bread in the cloister, being five in number, and this
afternoon, at four oclock, I expounded again, when
altogether 10 English gentlemen and ladies, who are staying
here, were present. Tomorrow morning I purpose to see the
pious Lutheran clergyman resident here, and about one
oclock, the Lord willing, we shall leave by the mail and
arrive at Stuttgart on Tuesday evening, Aug. 22. The heat
has been exceedingly great all the last week, so that we have
constantly been obliged to sleep with the window wide
open. Farewell, dear helper. Our love to dear sister E. from
whom we shall be very glad to hear, and to whom you will
please to communicate all in our letters that may be
interesting to her. Our tender love also to our own dear
child. How gladly should we see and kiss her, but though
we cannot do that, yet we pray for her. Love also to S. My
especial love to all my dear fellow-labourers in the church.
My love to all the dear brethren and sisters in the Orphan-
Houses and Day-Schools. Our love to all the saints.

Your affectionate brother,

GEORGE MÜLLER.

We are now just 600 miles from Bristol.

I make a few remarks in connexion with this letter.

I found it injurious to my inner man that for three nights I
had had very little sleep. My own experience has been
almost invariably, that if I have not the needful sleep, my
spiritual enjoyment and strength is greatly affected by it. I
judge it of great moment that the believer, in travelling,

should seek as much as possible to refrain from travelling by night, or from travelling in such a way as that he is deprived of the needful nights rest; for if he does not, he will be unable with renewed bodily and mental strength to give himself to prayer and meditation, and the reading of the Holy Scriptures, and he will surely feel the pernicious effects of this all the day long. There may occur cases when travelling by night cannot be avoided; but, if it can, though we should seem to lose time by it, and though it should cost more money, I would most affectionately and solemnly recommend the refraining from night travelling; for, in addition to our drawing beyond measure upon our bodily strength, we must be losers spiritually. The next thing I would advise with reference to travelling is, with all ones might to seek morning by morning, before setting out, to take time for meditation and prayer, and reading the word of God; for although we are always exposed to temptation, yet we are so especially in travelling. Travelling is one of the devils especial opportunities for tempting us. Think of that, dear fellow believers. Seek always to ascertain carefully the mind of God, before you begin any thing; but do so in particular before you go a journey, so that you may be quite sure that it is the will of God that you should undertake that journey, lest you should needlessly expose yourself to one of the special opportunities of the devil to ensnare you. So far from envying those who have a carriage and horses at their command, or an abundance of means, so that they are not hindered from travelling for want of means, let us, who are not thus situated, rather thank God that in this particular we are not exposed to the temptation of needing to be less careful in ascertaining the will of God, before we set out on a journey.

Stuttgart, Aug. 30, 1843.

171

My dear L —,

My last letter I finished on the 20th, and posted it on the
21st at Weinheim. On. Monday morning, Aug. 21, I saw a
pious clergyman at Weinheim, a true brother, and a nice
man. But we came, without my seeking it, upon the subject
of separation from the state church, for which I could not be
sorry, as I had an opportunity of stating truth to him which
it may please the Lord to use hereafter. Mrs. — — gave us a
rich silk dress, quite new, and a few silver articles for the
Orphans. So even here the Lord makes it manifest that He is
mindful of this work. About one oclock in the afternoon we
left Weinheim. At Heidelberg, about ten miles from there, a
person came into the mail in which Mary and I were, whom
I found out in a few moments to be a brother; and a few
minutes afterwards the widow of a much tried pious
clergyman, who herself also loves the Lord Jesus, seated
herself likewise. We had now, from three oclock till about
half-past nine in the evening, when we arrived at
Heilbronn, a most pleasant and profitable time, being all
four believers. I told this brother much about England, and
also about the Orphans, and on separating from him he
gave me a gold coin, about seventeen shillings in value, for
the Orphans. It was indeed a most precious gift to me, and a
fresh proof in what a variety of ways the Lord is able to
send help. We remained the night at Heilbronn, that we
might not have to travel the night, left the next morning at
eleven oclock, and reached the apartments of our sister G.
about eight in the evening on Aug. 22. We were received in
the most affectionate way, and she has done every thing to
make us comfortable; but the very great heat and the change
of living have hitherto drawn upon both of us. I think,
that, with the Lords blessing, we shall be better after a few
days. Indeed I have been rather better yesterday and today.
On the same evening of our arrival here I went to the post-

office and found your first letter, and last Monday morning I received your second also. The next afternoon, Wednesday, Aug. 23, I went to Brother Dr. B., with whom I spent about two hours; and in the evening from half-past eight till ten oclock I met the four elders of the Baptist Church at his house. The next evening from half-past eight to ten was a meeting of the little church, which consists of about 50 brethren and sisters, of whom almost all were present. I stated the object of my coming to Germany, in so far as it was wise to do so, and also a little about the church in Bristol. The next evening, Aug. 25th, I expounded the scriptures from half-past eight to ten oclock. All the meetings are in the evenings from half-past eight to ten, so that we generally come home at half-past ten, and go to bed about half-past eleven. Persons have their supper before they go to the meetings. On Saturday evening we had again a meeting, at which I began to give an account of the Lords dealings with me, from the beginning, as being the best means of leading me to speak about many important truths. It was desired that I should expound the scriptures at all their usual meetings, i.e. twice on the Lords days, and twice in the week; and, on all the other evenings, there should be extra meetings, at which I should give an account of the Lords dealings with me. On the Lords day therefore I expounded twice with much help, feeling scarcely any difficulty with reference to the German language, though I have not before preached in it for fourteen years and a half. On Monday, Aug. 28th, I went on again with my Narrative, and last night I expounded again with much help. But now, as the truth is beginning to be spoken, the devil will also begin to seek to work. But the Lord Jesus will triumph. There is a great crisis before us. Several have been already attracted by the preciousness of the truth, and others already wish I had never come to Stuttgart. They are not asleep over what I say, and that gives me pleasure. I fear it will come in a very few days to a storm, except the Lord prevent. Nor am I quite sure whether the police will allow me quietly to work here, when it gets known what I am doing, as the liberty is not so great as I had thought. But it would have been worth while to have come here, only to have spoken these few times. There is now here on a visit to us an English sister, Mrs. F.

Your affectionate brother,

GEORGE MÜLLER.

Immediately on my arrival at Stuttgart, yea, the very first hour that I was there, so heavy a trial of faith came upon me, that it was one of the sharpest trials which I ever have had. The cause of it I am not at liberty to mention. But so much as this, it was in connexion with my going to Stuttgart, and, humanly speaking, the thing would not have occurred, had I not gone thither. The trial was of a double character; for it was not only the thing itself, great as the trial of my faith was on that account; but it was as though the question were put to me in the strongest way: — Are you willing to make sacrifices in connexion with your service here? And do you really lean upon me, the living God, in your service here? But thanks to the Lord, Satan did not prevail. My heart was enabled to say almost immediately: — "All things work together for good to them that love God." I know this also does work together for my good. I know it is the very best thing for me. — Thus peace was almost immediately restored to me, and I was enabled to leave the matter quietly in the hands of the Lord. Nor was it many days before I could say from my inmost soul, if even then I could have had it in my power to alter the thing, which occasioned the great trial, and the consequences of which were then still remaining, and were remaining all the time while I was in Germany, yet I would not have wished it to be altered. And since my return to England I have again and again had reason to admire the goodness of the Lord in having allowed this thing to be as it was, for it proved in the end in every way good to me. May the believing reader leave himself more and more unreservedly in the hands of the Lord, and he will find it to be just as the writer has found it, i. e. that our greatest trials often turn out to be our greatest blessings.—Had I gone, however, in my own strength to Stuttgart, and had I not been led to treasure up so many petitions in heaven before I went, I should, in all human probability, have been quite overcome by this very first trial.

This was not the only trial which befel me there, but they were so many, so great, and so long continued, that I required every particle of experience, wisdom, and grace, humanly speaking, which the Lord had been pleased to intrust me with. I could not but again and again admire the wisdom of the Lord in having sent me only in the year 1843 to Germany, and not several years before, as I often had been advised to go long before I did. For had I gone without having the experience which I had gathered in my service among the saints during the 13 1/2 years previously, and without having had my soul exercised before God in trials of patience, and hope, and faith, as it has been since November 1830, humanly speaking, I should have been overwhelmed. But, as it was, my soul, through grace, having learned to deal with God about every thing, I was sustained by casting all my care upon Him, and looking to Him for help, and expecting help from Him, though every thing looked dark in every way. And thus it came, that all the difficulties were overcome one after another. But more about this when I come to relate some of the peculiar difficulties in connexion with my service at Stuttgart.

I also mention here, that during the eight years previous to my going to Germany to labour there, it had been laid on my heart, and on the hearts of some other brethren among us, to ask the Lord that He would be pleased to honour us, as a body of believers, by calling forth from our midst brethren, for carrying the truth into foreign lands. But this prayer seemed to remain unanswered. Now, however, the time was come when the Lord was about to answer it, and I, on whose heart particularly this matter had been laid, was to be the first to carry forth the truth from among us. About that very time the Lord called our dear brother and sister Barrington from among us, to go to Demerara, to labour there in connexion with our esteemed brother Strong, and our dear brother and sister Espenett, to go to Switzerland. Both these dear brethren and sisters left very shortly after I had gone to Germany. But this was not all Our much valued brother Mordal, who had commended himself to the saints by his unwearied faithful service among us for twelve years, had from Aug. 31, 1843, (the day on which brothers Strong and Barrington sailed from Bristol for Demerara), his mind likewise exercised about service there, and went out from among us eleven months after. He, together with myself, had had it particularly laid upon his heart, during the eight years previously, to ask the Lord again and again to call labourers from among us for foreign service. Of all persons he, the father of a large family, and about 50 years of age, seemed the least likely to be called to that work; but God did call him. He went, laboured a little while in Demerara, and then, on January 9, 1845, the Lord took him to his rest. —When we ask God for a thing, such as that He would be pleased to raise up labourers for His harvest, or send means for the carrying on of His work, the honest question to be put to our hearts should be this:

Am I willing to go, if He should call me I Am I willing to give according to my ability? For we may be the very persons whom the Lord will call for the work, or whose means He may wish to employ.

The Reader will notice, in the preceding letter, that all the meetings in the evening were very late. The time of the meetings was one of the many difficulties with which I had to contend; for if the times had been on purpose ill chosen, they could scarcely have been worse. On the Lords day mornings the meetings were at nine; thus the mothers of families either could not come at all, or had to hurry through their work, and come without having had any time to themselves. On the Lords day afternoons they were at two, when the heat of the sun in the summer, which is most oppressive, and the effect of the dinner, both combined together to make the persons sleepy, so that individuals not more than half a yard from me, though interested about what was going on, were sometimes fast asleep. In the evenings the meetings commenced at half-past eight, when persons were not only worn out from working nearly up to that time, but also, in general, had just had a heavy supper, which was sure to make them sleepy, thought they might be never so desirous to listen. But, by the grace of God, none of these things moved me. I knew the Lord had sent me to these dear saints, and that, therefore, by His help, I could overcome all these difficulties. And these difficulties were overcome; for after a little while I was able to show to the dear brethren and sisters that the Lords day morning meeting was too early, and we had it half an hour later. The Lords day afternoon meeting at two oclock was entirely given up, on account of its being an unseasonable time, and it being better to have only two meetings instead of three, as almost every one could attend two meetings, which was quite enough for one day, and gave some time for parents to

177

be with their children, or gave some more time than usual for reading the Scriptures, a point at which I aimed from the beginning. For when I came to Stuttgart, I found it just as I have found it in some places in England on my first beginning to labour there, even that the dear brethren and sisters had little relish for the word of God, and as a proof of this never referred to it at the meetings; but, before I left Stuttgart, I had the joy of seeing either all, or almost all, having the word of God open before them whilst I was expounding it. —Instead of the afternoon meeting at two, we met at four oclock, when the oppression of the heat in the summer is not so great as at two, whereby also the lateness of the evening meeting was avoided on the Lords days. Also on the week evenings we had the meetings half an hour sooner, that is at 8 oclock instead of half-past 8, and I affectionately advised the dear saints to take a very light supper on those evenings when we met, that blessing might not be hindered. Earlier than eight on the week evenings, and later than half-past nine on the Lords day mornings, we could not have the meetings, on account of the habits of the country. It can scarcely be perceived by brethren in England how great the difficulties are, with which brethren have to contend in many foreign countries in seeking to spread the truth, not only on account of the climate, or the police, etc., but also on account of the habits of the people; so that I would affectionately beseech all, who take a hearty interest in the spread of the truth, to help by their prayers all who labour in the word and doctrine in foreign lands, so that through the power of the Holy Ghost they may be enabled to overcome all those hinderances.

I now insert my first letter to the brethren in Bristol, written by me from Stuttgart, soon after my arrival, which will show to the reader my position there more clearly. The letter is, with the exception of a very slight verbal alteration,

178

which I made in revising it for the press, just as it was written.

Stuttgart, Sept. 7, 1843.

To the Brethren meeting at Bethesda and Salem Chapels, Bristol.

My dear Brethren,

It was yesterday four weeks since I left Bristol, and I now write these few lines that you may know how I am situated in the service, on account of which I left England, in order that thus you may the better be able to remember me in your prayers, according to my need. My journey to this place was full of mercies and blessings in a variety of ways, but I must delay giving you the particulars, till it may please the Lord to allow me again the privilege of labouring among you. I arrived at Stuttgart on Tuesday evening, Aug. 22. On the next evening I met the five brethren who labour here in the little church. On Thursday, Friday, and Saturday also I had meetings with the little church, at which I either expounded the Holy Scriptures or communicated to the brethren things about Bristol, which might be profitable to them. The following Lords day I spoke twice at their meetings, and in the evening I broke bread in my room with a few saints, as the Baptist church break bread only once a month. On Monday and Tuesday evenings I continued to meet the whole little church. Up to that time all went on quietly; but I knew well that it was only the quietness before a storm, and that shortly a hot battle would commence. And thus it was. On Wednesday last week, i.e. Aug. 30, I was requested to meet the elders of the church.

When we came together, the brother who appears to take the lead among them, and who is the only one who speaks at their meetings, told me that the time was drawing nigh when the church would take the Lords supper, and that they had a rule which they considered to be Scriptural, which was, neither to take the Lords supper with any one who was not himself baptized by immersion after he had believed, nor with any one who, (though thus baptized himself) would take the Lords supper with any who had not thus been baptized. Nor did they take the Lords supper with any brother who would take it with any yet belonging to the state church. After this brother had stated to me his views, I stated my own convictions from the Holy Scriptures on these points, and I was quietly heard for about an hour and a half whilst I was speaking without interruption. The Lord was so with me, that when I came home I did not remember any one thing that I could have wished to have stated which had not been stated. The whole having taken up more than two hours, and it being now past ten oclock in the evening, we proposed to meet again on the next day, Thursday afternoon, at five oclock. We did so, and several other brethren besides the elders were present. The subjects were now discussed from the Scriptures. Brother—maintained that no one was born again except he was baptized, no one had a right to say his sins were forgiven, except he were baptized, and also that the apostles were not born again until the day of Pentecost. Whilst seeking to defend these unscriptural statements, he also affirmed that our Lord Himself had been born again at His baptism, and that the last three years of His life He had not been under the law, but had ceased to be under the law when He was baptized. I had been accustomed during the eight days that I had been going in and out among the brethren to hear all sorts of unscriptural statements, into which they had fallen through laying an undue stress upon

180

baptism, and especially through considering baptism as a
covenant into which God enters with the believer; but
when now the foundation truths of the Gospel were also
attacked, when of our Holy Lord it was said that he was
born again at his baptism, (which made Him out to be like
one of us), and when it was said that He had not been
under the law during the last three years of His life;—I saw
it needful first of all to see whether we were agreed about
the foundation truths of the Gospel. But as we had now
been together from five to half-past seven in the evening,
and as at half-past eight the public meeting began at which I
had to speak, I proposed to separate and to meet again on
Friday afternoon from five to seven. This was done, I now
first of all pressed the first points. Brother—stated in the
presence of the elders and six or seven other brethren, that
he had made an unscriptural statement, and that our Lord
needed not to be born again. I then went to the other point,
whether the Lord was under the law up to the time when
He died on the cross, or only up to the time when He was
baptized. Many passages were brought forward to show
that our Lord was under the law up to the last moments of
His earthly life, which is clear from Gal. iii. 13, Phil. ii. 8,
Heb. x. 1-13, and many other passages. At last he was
convinced about this also and acknowledged his error. But
many other points, equally unscriptural, he was unwilling
to renounce, such as, that baptism is a covenant with God,
and that there cannot be forgiveness of sins except
individuals have been baptized after believing. He also
maintained that I was sinning in breaking bread with
unbaptized believers, and with those who belong to the
state church, and that if the church here allowed me to
break bread with them, they would be defiled, as I made
myself a partaker of the sins of others, which sins I brought
with me; and other such unscriptural statements were made
by this brother. Thus we spent again about two hours and

a half in intercourse, whilst this teaching elder and one of the other elders considered me unfit to take the Lords supper with them on the coming Lords day, but the two other elders and several other brethren who were present were quite ready to break bread with me, and with any who love our Lord Jesus. Brother—now said, there must be a separation. I then entreated the brethren not to think of a separation. I represented to them what a scandal it would be to the ungodly, and what a stumbling block also to the believers who are yet in the state church. I further told them that I had not come to Stuttgart to make a separation between the brethren, but only to lend them a helping hand according to the ability which the Lord might give me. I lastly said: As we have now spent more than six hours together in intercourse, let us meet together tomorrow evening some hours for prayer. To this the brethren agreed, and we accordingly met on Saturday evening at eight oclock for prayer. The subject of our prayer was, that the Lord would be pleased to unite us together in the truth, and make it manifest on which side the truth was. After we had thus prayed for about two hours, brother—prayed at the end, and related (in what he called prayer) his experience before his conversion, his conversion, his being convinced about baptism, my coming to Stuttgart, his readiness to receive the unbaptized in consequence of my intercourse with him, and how then a great horror had befallen him, and that now he had come back to his former view, only to receive the baptized, and how now his peace had been restored to him, and that he purposed to live and die in this belief. When we arose I told him that the Lord Himself had decided the matter, and had shown on whose side the truth was; for that he, if in peace, as he had said, could not thus have related his experience, and called it prayer. This prayer tended greatly to show the other brethren that he has not the truth. —I should have stated that I said to the brethren

182

at the commencement of this meeting, that, as I and my wife were the only persons on whose account they could not break bread on the coming day, and as nothing ought to be done in a hurry, to whatever conclusion they might come, we would gladly withdraw ourselves, and break bread in our room. This was not accepted, as there was much disunion among the brethren, as they told me, and had been before I came, and that my coming had now only brought matters to a point. I stated once more, at the end of the meeting on Saturday evening, Sept. 2, that we ought to dread a separation, and that we ought to pray that we might be of one mind, and that I was ready to meet them by day or by night for prayer or searching the Word on the subject. Thus we separated. The next morning, Sept. 3, I spoke again at the meeting, having been by all the elders requested at my arrival here to expound the Scriptures at all their meetings, or to communicate to them any thing that might be profitable. On this morning I spoke principally on the Lords supper, and on what fits for it; on what is meant by feeding upon Jesus, and what fits for it; on the point that it is not a part of truth, but Jesus round whom believers should unite together; and on the truth, that, if any one is a believer, he is entitled to all the privileges of the saints. These points I had not chosen on purpose for that morning, but they came in course in speaking on Exodus xii., on which chapter I had spoken four times before. After I had finished, I was going to pray at the close, when I was interrupted by brother—, the principal and teaching elder (as to outward authority). He stated that he must contradict me, for I had said: 1, The bread and wine in the Lords supper meant the body and blood of our Lord, whilst, as he believed, and as the word said, it was the real body and blood of our Lord. 2, He believed that as circumcision made a man an Israelite, and fitted him thus for the partaking of the Paschal Lamb, so without baptism no one is fitted to partake of the Lords

183

supper, which is set forth by the Paschal Lamb; whilst I had said that every one who believes in Jesus was by this his faith made a spiritual Israelite, and had a right to the Lords supper and to all the privileges of the children of God. He stated further, that this was against the rules of their church, and that, as I took the Lords supper with unbaptized believers, and with those who had not quite left the state church, I made myself partaker of their sins, and that therefore, as being defiled with these sins, I could not be admitted to the Lords supper. From the commencement of his speaking he was very irritated, but now continued in a passionate way: I am ruler in this church, and you (addressing himself to me) are no longer permitted to speak at our meetings. Moreover he said, "Whosoever takes the Lords supper with Müller will no longer be considered as a member of the church;" and then in anger he left the meeting. During all this time, the Lord, in the riches of His grace, kept me in perfect peace and calmness. I answered brother—not a single word. When he was gone I fell upon my knees, asked the Lords blessing upon the word which I had spoken, asked the Lord to forgive brother—, and to teach me what I should do now. After this I dismissed the meeting. When all was over, one of the elders, brother R., one who seeks after truth, and rejoices in the true liberty which the Lord enables me to preach, and one who had been sighing under the iron hand of brother—for a long time; this brother, I say, requested me before all, according to the first arrangement, to continue the meetings and to tell them all that might be profitable to them. He was, however, immediately interrupted by another elder, who sees with brother—, and told that he had no right to do so. I then stated again that I had only come from England in love, and that I would not force myself upon them. I then left.—By the time of the afternoon meeting I had received light from the Lord that I should not go to the meeting. I saw that as I had been cast out, together with all the other brethren who owned me as a brother, and as all my tenderness in seeking to avoid a separation had been useless, I had now on the other hand to go steadfastly forward, leaving it with the Lord to decide on which side the truth was. I therefore remained at home. The two elders who were won for the truth, went to the meeting in the afternoon, at which brother—sought to disprove what I had said, and after the meeting they stated that they were purposed to own me and all who believe in the Lord Jesus as brethren in the breaking of bread.—On the same evening seventeen of us met in my room for the breaking of bread, as we were in peace; of these seventeen twelve were belonging to this little Baptist church, two Swiss brethren, one English sister, my wife and I. We had a peaceful meeting. Thus the Lord so soon, so unexpectedly, has brought the matter to a point, though in a painful way. The matter would be, however, more painful, did I not see it of great importance that the disciples who hold the truth should be separate from those who hold such fearful errors as: The forgiveness of sins received through baptism; baptism a covenant between us and God; regeneration through baptism and no regeneration without it; the actual death of the old man through baptism, it being drowned, so that only the body and the new nature are alive; and many other fearful errors, to which these poor deluded brethren have been led by laying such undue stress upon baptism. As to poor brother — —, he had denied some months since the inspiration of Luke, the Acts, and the Epistle of James, which point he only gave up when several brethren stated that they must leave on that account, and he has fallen into many other grievous errors; but there has been no one who has had sufficient spiritual courage steadfastly to resist him. Now there is joy with many that the Lord has set them free.—On Monday last, Sept. 4th, I had again a meeting with the brethren and sisters whose

eyes the Lord has opened, and others also came, not
belonging to this Baptist church. On. Wednesday I had
again a meeting, and today, Sept. 8, and tomorrow evening I
purpose to meet the brethren again.—All is only a
beginning. But there is a beginning. That which I longed
for, the chief object of my journey to the Continent, that
there might be also in Germany a little living church, but
based on Scriptural principles, which might be a light to
other places; the beginning of that has now been made, but
it is a small beginning. The minds of the dear brethren have
been so darkened through this mixture of error and truth,
that about every thing they need instruction. However, the
Lord will help further. I am of good cheer, because I know
that the Lord is on my side, and that He has sent me here,
and that He keeps me here. How gladly would I leave this
very day, were it His will; but I know that at present I
ought to labour here.—I have so circumstantially and
minutely related all to you, that you may the better know
how to help me with your prayers. The errors and sins of
our brother —— I have only related, that you the more
clearly may see how my coming here is of God, in order that
these dear children of God, who have suffered so much for
the Lords sake, and who are sincere, though in much error,
might be led on and delivered out of these snares of the
devil. But many, unaccustomed to examine Scripture, hold
fast the former ways; yet those, who are sincere, the Lord
will deliver after awhile. How long I may continue here, I
know not; but the moment I see the Lords leading to
England, I shall be delighted to go back. At present my
temptation is not to stay longer than I ought to stay; but
rather to leave sooner than I ought to leave. Help me,
therefore, dear brethren, that I maybe willing to do and
suffer all the will of God here. As to further particulars, the
Lord willing, you shall have them either verbally or by
writing. Should any of you like to write to me, or my dear

wife, we shall be glad to hear from you; and if the letters be written on thin paper and left at my house, they will be forwarded to me. We remember you daily in our prayers, as you also, no doubt, remember us. May the Lord bring us in His own time again together in peace. Pray earnestly for all the brethren who labour among you. My dear wife salutes you. The saints here salute you.

I am, dear brethren.,

Affectionately your brother and servant,

GEORGE MÜLLER.

I make the following remarks in connexion with this letter.

I. In the beginning it is mentioned, that on the evening of the day after my arrival I met with the five brethren who laboured in the Baptist church at Stuttgart, that is with the teaching elder or president, the three other elders, and the brother who acted as deacon. At this very meeting, nay at the very commencement even of this meeting, I saw what a difficult position mine would be, and what abundant help I should need from God. That which led me to think so was this. During the day that I had been at Stuttgart, I had perceived, that all the brethren and sisters called one another "Thou," which is in Germany the sign of great familiarity, and which is used between very intimate friends or between parents and children, or husband and wife, or brothers and sisters of the same family, &c. Here now I found that males and females of all ages and different stations in life called one another "Thou." When I therefore met with those five brethren I stated the substance of the following objections, against this practice, not however in the form of objections, but either in the way of affectionate inquiries or brotherly suggestions. My objections against it were these: 1, I did not think it would have, in general, a desirable effect upon believers of different sexes to speak to one another thus in the way of so great familiarity. 2, I did not think it would work well for brethren and sisters in service to speak thus to their master and mistress, especially if it should happen that the mistress was an unbeliever, and therefore not in fellowship with them, and a sister were as a servant to say to her master "Thou." 3, I thought it would not work happily and healthfully for a very young brother and sister to be expected to call aged brethren and sisters "Thou," as if on terms of great familiarity, from the moment they were baptized and thus received among them into fellowship. 4, But that which far more strongly operated upon my mind than any of the previous reasons was this, It seemed to me to substitute an outward form for the inward power and reality. I stated to them, That if the calling one another "Thou" were the result of realizing that all the children of God have one and the self-same Father in heaven, that they are really, and not nominally only, brothers and sisters of the same heavenly family, and heirs of the same precious inheritance, and bought by the same precious blood of the Lord Jesus; if it were the result of these truths being enjoyed and realized within, I should see not the least reason against it, in general; but I feared that it was merely an outward thing, judging from the fact, that however it might have been with a brother and sister previously, the moment they were baptized they were called "Thou" by every one of their number, and they were expected to call every one "Thou" in return. And I judged it to be a pernicious thing, if thus the "Thou" was forced upon persons; for on the part of those who were comparatively high in life it would be considered sooner or later an unpleasant burden, and on the part of the poorer classes it would lead to carnal gratification in being able to treat those in the way of great familiarity who were considerably above them with reference to this life. The thing itself, then, if done from right motives, from the entering into our position as saints with reference to God and to each other, would be most precious; but the thing done, merely because it was customary among them, and observed in order to keep up uniformity, would work most perniciously.—In reply to my remarks of this kind, it was stated, that the use of the word "Thou" was scriptural, that in the Holy Scriptures we never read, when one single person is spoken to, "You," but always "Thou." To this I answered that it was so, but that we must remember that in the Holy Scriptures we find governors and kings addressed by poor men in the term "Thou;" for this was the only form of speech in use, whilst in Germany, where the "Thou" is not used except to denote near natural relationship or familiarity, it ought not to be used, except there be that inwardly corresponding to what we outwardly seek to convey by the term; else it will lead to formality, if not to hypocrisy, and sooner or later the pernicious tendency of this outward thing, to which there is nothing inwardly corresponding, will most surely be felt. It appeared to me far better not to make any profession of familiarity and intimacy by the use of the "Thou," when the heart does not go along with it, and rather to continue to say to one another "You" till there be the drawing of heart to heart by the love of Jesus, than to force the "Thou" upon the brethren and sisters. I felt the more strongly about this, as I had witnessed more than once among believers in England the injurious effects of doing things because others did them, or because it was the custom, or because they were persuaded into acts of outward self-denial, or giving up things whilst the heart did not go along with it, and whilst the outward act WAS NOT the result of the inward powerful working of the Holy Ghost, and the happy entering into our fellowship with the Father and with the

Son. I had seen, when these things had been done from wrong motives, that there had been regret afterwards, and the returning back as much as possible to what had been given up or forsaken. Moreover, though I had been only one day in Stuttgart when we had this meeting, yet I had heard enough of the state of things, to make me think the calling one another "Thou" was in many instances a mere outward form.—My brotherly suggestions were not received, but strongly opposed by two or three out of the five brethren, and it was pretty plainly hinted, that, perhaps, I was too proud to be called "Thou;" and the moment I perceived that, I said that I wished every brother, the very poorest of them, to call me "Thou" (and I encouraged them in doing so, by calling every one "Thou"), but that I could not, with my light, call any of the sisters "Thou," nor did I do so up to the day of my departure.

There was another thing of the same character, that is the kiss. In Germany, as on the Continent generally, the kiss is the sign of affection and familiarity among men as well as among females, and the brethren and sisters at Stuttgart always had been in the habit of kissing one another after having partaken of the Lords supper, that is all the brethren had kissed each other, and all the sisters had kissed each other. Now this again, if the result of real inward affection, and springing from the entering into our heavenly relationship and oneness in Christ Jesus, would be most beautiful, and would be the "holy kiss" of which the Apostle Paul speaks; but I had no reason to believe that this was generally the case among the brethren and sisters at Stuttgart, but rather that it was merely the result of custom and form, and that it was done because it was expected to be done, for it was the churchs order, after the Lords supper to kiss one another. It was on this ground that it seemed to me to be most pernicious; and I could have known how it would work, even though I had not been actually told, that sometimes sisters had stayed away from the Lords supper, because they did not feel comfortable in kissing all the female members of the church. When therefore I began to break bread with the brethren, after we had been separated by the close baptists, I did not kiss one brother after the breaking of bread; but I made a point of it to kiss every one of them on that very day at a later meeting, when I left them to go to my lodgings, in order that no one might be able to say it was pride or want of love in me that I had not kissed them. Thus I did on the second Lords day, and on the third. On the fourth Lords day a brother said, after the breaking of bread, Brethren shall we give one another the brotherly kiss, and I was then ready at once, like the rest, to kiss all the brethren; but the next time there was no kissing, and thus the mere cold form was banished, and every brother felt free to kiss another brother when his heart bade him to do so, without being bound to it by custom or form.

I have so circumstantially dwelt on these apparently little things, because I think them, in principle, matters of the deepest importance. Every thing that is a mere form, a mere habit and custom in divine things, is to be dreaded exceedingly: life, power, reality, this is what we have to aim after. Things should not result from without, but from within. The sort of clothes I wear, the kind of house I live in, the quality of the furniture I use, all such like things should not result from other persons doing so and so, or because it is customary among those brethren with whom I associate to live in such and such a simple, inexpensive, self-denying way; but whatever be done in these things, in the way of giving up, or self-denial, or deadness to the world, should result from the joy we have in God, from the knowledge of our being the children of God, from the entering into the preciousness of our future inheritance, etc.

191

Far better that for the time being we stand still, and do not take the steps which we see others take, than that it is merely the force of example that leads us to do a thing, and afterwards it be regretted. Not that I mean in the least by this to imply we should continue to live in luxury, self-indulgence, and the like, whilst others are in great need; but we should begin the thing in a right way, i.e. aim after the right state of heart; begin inwardly instead of outwardly. If otherwise, it will not last. We shall look back, or even get into a worse state than we were before. But oh! how different if joy in God leads us to any little act of self denial. How gladly do we do it then! How great an honour then do we esteem it to be! How much does the heart then long to be able to do more for Him who has done so much for us! We are far then from looking down in proud self-complacency upon those who do not go as far as we do, but rather pray to the Lord, that He would be pleased to help our dear brethren and sisters forward, who may seem to us weak in any particular point; and we also are conscious to ourselves, that if we have a little more light or strength with reference to one point, other brethren may have more light or grace in other respects.

II. It may be asked, whether I consider brother — —, with all his errors, his fearful errors, to be a brother. My reply is, that so far as my own personal acquaintance is concerned, I am not able to form a judgment about it; but from all I have heard about his godly life formerly for many years, I think there is very much reason to believe that he is a child of God. I have related all this and made it public (which I naturally greatly dislike, on account of brother — — being my brother, and therefore his sin is my own shame), in order that other children of God may be profited by it. There are two most instructive points connected with the history of the Baptist Church at Stuttgart and of our brother — —

in particular.

1, These children of God had been right in considering believers baptism to be Scriptural, and in separating from the state church of Wirtemberg. But upon these two points they had laid undue stress. Though believers baptism is the truth of God; though separation from state churches on the part of children of God who know that a church is "a congregation of believers" is right, because they see in state churches nothing but the world mixed up with some true believers; yet, if these points are made too much of if they are put out of their proper place, as if they were every thing, then there must be spiritual loss suffered by those who do so. Nay, whatever parts of truth are made too much of, though they were even the most precious truths connected with our being risen in Christ, or our heavenly calling, or prophecy, sooner or later those, who lay an undue stress upon these parts of truth, and thus make them too prominent, will be losers in their own souls, and, if they be teachers, they will injure those whom they teach. That was the case at Stuttgart. Baptism and separation from the state church had at last become almost every thing to these dear brethren. "We are the church. Truth is only to be found among us. All others are in error, and in Babylon." These were the phrases used again and again by our brother — —. But God never allows this state of things without chastisement. This spiritual pride had led from one error to another. Oh may it be a warning to me and to all believers who may read this, and may God in mercy give and preserve to them and to me a lowly heart!

2, Another thing, on account of which the church at Stuttgart is a warning, is this: When these dear brethren left the state church of the Kingdom of Wirtemberg, on account of which they had many trials, they did not meet together in dependence upon the Holy Spirit, but they took some Baptist church, whether in H— or E— I know not, for a model, and there was to be a teaching elder among them. Instead of being content to own their weakness, and give themselves to prayer that the Lord would be pleased to give them a teacher, brother — — becomes their teaching elder, and this having been done, he alone speaks at all the meetings (with few exceptions). Now, as his own mind laid such an undue stress upon baptism, and as there was no free working of the Holy Spirit, so that any other brother might have brought out at their meetings what the Lord might have laid upon his heart, what could there have been expected otherwise than that after a time the whole noble little band of disciples, who had taken so trying a stand as to be separated from the state church, should become unsound in the faith. May God grant unto us to be profited by it, dear believing reader, so that in our own church position we do our utmost to give to the Holy Spirit free and unhindered opportunity to work by whom He will!

I have related all these things, painful as they were to me when I was in them, and painful as they are now to me in the remembrance, if it may please God to make them a warning to other dear children of God.

Stuttgart, Oct. 14, 1843.

To the Saints, meeting in the name of Jesus, at Bethesda and Salem
Chapels, Bristol.

My dear Brethren,

I have judged that your love to the Lord and to me will make you desirous of knowing further particulars about the work here, and I write therefore a little concerning the state of things here. — Since the date of my last letter I have sought to instruct the dear brethren, who had been led by the Lord to own me as a brother with whom they could and ought to have fellowship, and who, therefore, had been disowned by those with whom they had formerly been associated. The state of things concerning the others, who think they do God service in the way in which they treat us, is very affecting. They not only keep entirely aloof from our meetings, but with those of our number, whom they consider seducers and perverters of the truth, they will not speak, nor greet us again when they are greeted. In this state of things nothing remained for us but to speak to the Lord about them, and I, therefore, proposed last week, that we should have especial prayer meetings for these dear, but awfully deluded, brethren. This was heartily responded to, and we now meet from time to time for especial prayer on their behalf. I mention this that you may help us with your prayers in this particular also. The iron rule, and the want of being able to exercise spiritual judgment is so felt, that only one of the brethren and sisters in the neighbouring little towns and villages, who belonged to the Baptist Church, has ventured to meet with us; but amidst it all I am in peace, knowing that the Lord Himself sent me here, and that the truth at last will assuredly triumph. Indeed I know that except these brethren own the sin of which they have been guilty against me, the Holy Spirit, who has been grieved, will not work among them, and the spiritual death among them will open the eyes of the upright ones. Such an instance came before me last week, when a sister of the Baptist Church came to our meetings, and said that she could not remain any longer where she was, as it was as if God had departed from them. We now meet every Lords day morning from nine to eleven, for the exposition of the word, and from four to six in the afternoon for the breaking of

195

bread. On Tuesday and Thursday evenings, from eight till
nearly ten, I expound the scriptures, and on Wednesday and
Friday evenings, from eight to ten, I meet with the brethren
to read the scriptures. There is the greatest teachableness
among the dear saints with whom I meet; but just because
they have been so long fed with error instead of truth, they
need to be taught almost every thing. But hitherto the Lord
has so helped me, and so made the dear brethren willing to
bow before the word of God, that we have gone on most
happily, and without any disagreement. The last five
meetings of this kind we have spent in considering the
truths contained in Romans xii., Ephes. iv., 1 Cor. xii. and
xiv., &c. They are now gaining light in apprehending the
presence and power of the Holy Spirit in the church, and
His indwelling in every individual believer, together with
the practical application of these truths; and I cannot but
hope, that if the Lord, even now at once, were to remove me
from them, they would be able to witness in some measure
for God, with regard to their church position. But even
these truths will take up several such evenings yet, in order
that the dear brethren not only may be grounded in them,
but also be profited by my experience in these particulars
during the last thirteen years, that they may not fall into
the same errors, or be exposed to the same difficulties. When
that subject is done with, I have to undertake another
work, perhaps as difficult as any I have had since I have
been here, and I mention it to you, that you may help me
with your prayers, that the Lord would be pleased to give
me His especial help in that matter also. I understand that
all the dear precious saints with whom I meet, have fallen
into the awful error, spread almost universally among even
true believers in this country, that at last all men will be
saved, and even the devils themselves. This awful error I
must attack as soon as the subject which we now consider
is finished; but pray earnestly that the Lord would give me

such spiritual power, as that these dear brethren may be brought, through Gods truth, out of this delusion also. I hope in God concerning this matter. He will help me. He has in so many ways made it so abundantly plain that He Himself sent me here, that He will help me in this matter also. —Last Lords day we were twenty in number at the breaking of bread, including my dear wife and myself; among them was the first fruit of my labours here, in the way of conversion. She is a young lady of nineteen years, the daughter of the procurator of the upper tribunal, Dr. R, one of the former elders of the Baptist Church, who for my sake was cast out. This young sister was baptized about four miles from here, in a river, about eight oclock in the evening, by moonlight, as the dear brethren feared the tumult and concourse of the opposers in the day time. I advised her father to baptize her, in order that at once, even in this respect, there might be nothing in the judgment of the dear saints, as if a ministerial person, according to the use of the word in the world, were needed, and also that thus the attention of the police might not needlessly be directed towards me, as they are so particularly opposed to baptism. Hitherto I have been left unmolested and unhindered, although I have been nearly eight weeks here, and although it is becoming known throughout the city, and beginning also to spread throughout the country that I am here. —The work still remains small as to outward appearance, as generally, besides the believers in fellowship, there are not more than about ten or twelve persons present; but I dare not take a large place to meet in, humanly speaking, and judging from what hitherto has been always done, but I must go on quietly instructing the saints, or preaching to the few sinners who come, in the hope that God, through my instructing the brethren, will open the eyes and hearts of others, after I have left. There is one brother among us, who learned the way of God more

197

perfectly in Switzerland, and who often had spoken about it, before I came, but who was neither much listened to, nor received into fellowship, because he was not baptized. —In the mean time I also go on with preparing my Narrative in the German language for the press, having found out that there is sufficient freedom of the press here to allow of my getting it printed; but I make but little progress, as my time is, in a variety of ways, here also taken up, and as I have too little mental strength to continue very long at a time working with my pen. Nevertheless, I have about the fifth part ready for the press. I am more and more assured that Germany needs my service in this respect, and that the Lord has called me for this work. About the time of my return to you I can say nothing, as the Lord has not given me any light concerning it; but this I must say, that my wife and myself shall consider it a happy day indeed, when the Lord allows us to see you again. But, His servants we are, and we desire grace to tarry as cheerfully here, as we shall be glad to go back to Bristol, when the Lord sends us back. Only help us in the mean time with your prayers, (as we also pray for you), that the Lord would enable us in this dark land to glorify His holy name. Farewell, greatly beloved brethren. My heart longs after you to behold you again; yet I am happy here, and will cheerfully wait the Lords own time here. I repeat, that if any of you have it in your heart to write to us, and will leave the letters at my house, they will be forwarded to me. My dear wife sends her love in Christ to all the dear brethren and sisters.

Your affectionate brother and servant in the Lord,

GEORGE MÜLLER.

I make again a few remarks in connexion with this letter.

198

I. One of my especial aims in my service among the dear brethren at Stuttgart was, to seek to ground them in the truth. To this end we had, from the beginning of our being separated from the Baptist Church, two meetings in the week, from eight to ten oclock in the evening, when we considered together, upon the ground of the word of God, those points of truth on which these dear brethren appeared to me most to need instruction. I judged it not enough to expound the Scriptures at their public meetings, but to give an opportunity to any brother or sister, at these private meetings, to state any difficulties that they might have on their minds. At first we considered particularly the great truths of the gospel, so that any remaining errors, connected with fundamental points, might be corrected. After that we began the consideration of Romans xii. 3-8, Ephes. iv. 7-16, 1 Cor. xii. and xiv., and the other passages which stand in connexion with the truths taught in these portions. The brethren had seen almost immediately that, according to the example of the first disciples (Acts xx. 7), it would become us to meet every first day of the week for the breaking of bread. Thus far they had light, and that light, I judged, ought to be carried out at once. We therefore from the beginning met every Lords day for the breaking of bread, with the exception of two or three who had for a few weeks some little doubt remaining on their mind, whether, on account of the frequency of the observance, this ordinance might not lose its beneficial effects; but as we left them free, to act according to the light they had, they soon saw the greatness of the privilege of being allowed so often to show forth the Lords death, and they therefore met regularly with us.—As, however, on my arrival at Stuttgart, the dear brethren had been entirely uninstructed about the truths relating to the power and presence of the Holy Ghost in the church of Christ, and to our ministering one to another as fellow members in the body of Christ; and as I had known enough of painful consequences when brethren began to meet professedly in dependence upon the Holy Spirit without knowing what was meant by it, and thus meetings had become opportunities for unprofitable talking rather than for godly edifying; and as I felt myself bound to communicate to these dear brethren the experience I had gathered with reference to these very truths since June 1830: for these reasons, I say, I thought it well to spend evening after evening with them over the passages above mentioned. Thus week after week passed away. We broke bread, but it was understood, and I wished it to be understood, that I was the only speaker. This I did that in every possible way I might have opportunity of instructing the brethren, and because they knew not yet what was meant by meeting in dependence upon the Holy Spirit. But, at length, after we had for about eight weeks or more spent two evenings a week together over those passages, and others setting forth the same truths, and full opportunity had been given, carefully to look at all the points connected with them, and when now there seemed a measure of apprehension of the mind of God in those passages, then we met for the purpose of carrying out what the brethren had learned, and therefore, at the next time when we met for the breaking of bread, I took my place among them simply as a brother; yet as a brother who had received a measure of gift for the benefit of his fellow members, and upon whom therefore responsibility was laid to use that measure of gift, and who, by the grace of God, felt this responsibility laid upon him, and who was willing to act accordingly. I do not mean at all to say that even then this matter was perfectly understood, for a few times still things like these would occur: — A brother read a portion of the Word, and then would say, "Perhaps our brother Müller will expound to us this portion." Or, a brother might speak a little on a subject, and then would say, "Perhaps our brother Müller will enter somewhat more fully into this subject." At such times, which occurred twice or thrice, I said nothing, but acted according to the desire of those brethren, and spoke; but afterwards, when we met privately, at our scripture reading meetings, I pointed out to the dear brethren their mistake, and reminded them that all these matters ought to be left to the ordering of the Holy Ghost, and that if it had been truly good for them, the Lord would have not only led me to speak at that time, but also on the very subject on which they desired that I should speak to them.

II. At these scripture reading meetings, of which I had about forty with them, we went on very peacefully and happily, though I had many things to bring before the brethren which were quite new to them, and some points also to which they had been exceedingly opposed. The Lord enabled me to seek His help for this service, and He granted it to me.

III. I never had a moments hesitation in owning these brethren, and meeting with them at the breaking of bread; for I could not say of any of them that they wilfully held those errors, but that it rather arose from the truth never having been brought before them. I therefore judged, that it was my duty to seek to instruct them in the truth, and then they would be led to renounce their errors.

IV. I had from the beginning great hope that the dear brethren would be brought out of their fearful errors. I never was overwhelmed by the prospect of the difficulties before me, but had confidence in God, that through Him I should conquer. My assurance was built on the following grounds: 1, I considered the remarkable way in which so unexpectedly, and after the overcoming of so many difficulties which had been in the way, I was sent to them. I therefore judged that the Lord had sent me to them for blessing. 2, He had given me grace to pray much for the saints at Stuttgart before I had ever seen them, and He helped me to continue in prayer for them whilst with them. This I judged was, in order that He might answer my request on their behalf. 3, They were not like persons who had had the truth set before them, and wilfully rejected it, but they had never had it set before them. 4, The Lord, in His grace, enabled me to deal patiently with them. They were deeply entangled in error, very deeply. Pressing things hastily upon them, I knew, would only make matters worse; but patiently hearing all their objections; meeting time after time over the Word, and seeking the Lords blessing in prayer on those meetings both before and after, being willing not to press a point too much at once, but giving time to the Holy Ghost to work upon their hearts; dealing thus with them, even as the Lord had inclined my heart, I judged that He would give me the desire of my heart, and deliver them out of their fearful errors.

V. I cannot help noticing here the strange mistake under which the religious public was with reference to my being at Stuttgart. It was this: Some weeks after my arrival the report was spread, and widely too, (for it was printed in one of the religious periodicals), that I was a Missionary sent by the Baptists in England, to bring back the Baptists in Wirtemberg to the State Church, as it was the view of the Baptists in England that it was not wrong to be united with the State Church. This having been stated in print, (though I knew not of it till I was on the point of returning to England), my stay at Stuttgart, I suppose, was rather liked by religious persons in connexion with the State Church, and it is not at all unlikely that that may have contributed to my being permitted to work quietly week after week, and month after month, without the police in the least interfering with me, though it not only was well known, that I was there, but well known too what I was doing in the way of holding meetings, etc. I recognise the hand of the Lord in allowing this mistake to be made.

VI. For many weeks the number of those who frequented the meetings was very small. Very few, besides those who were in communion with us, attended them. The highly sectarian and exclusive spirit which had been manifested by those brethren, who belonged to the Baptist Church, was a great hindrance in the way; for it was naturally supposed that we were of the same mind with them. But after nearly five months had passed away, there began to be a different effect produced. The number of those who attended increased, and increased to more than twice or thrice as many as used to come at first, and, humanly speaking, had I seen it to be the Lords will to remain one month longer, the result might have been still greater. But as I saw as clearly the time of my departure from Stuttgart as that of my going thither, I was not influenced by any outward appearance; for I felt certain that, for various reasons, I ought to return to my service in Bristol.—In this circumstance also I cannot but see the hand of God. Had the meetings all at once been much attended in the beginning, it might have attracted the attention of the police, and possibly a ticket of permission to reside any longer at Stuttgart might not have been granted to me; but, as it was, there was nothing whatever outwardly to attract the notice of the world, for we were few in number, met in a very poor neighbourhood, and in a poor meeting place, and I had thus opportunity to instruct the saints.

Stuttgart, Nov. 11, 1843.

To the Brethren meeting in the name of Jesus, at Salem and Bethesda

Chapels, Bristol

Dear Brethren,

I have judged that it might be profitable to you, with the
Lords blessing, to hear again a few particulars of His work
here, and I have also thought that the love you bear me will
make you desirous to know how I am, and what the Lord is
doing with me, and therefore I again write you a little,
which is no burden to me, but a sweet pleasure. Yet I assure
you, dear brethren, I need not write to you, in order that I
may be reminded of you; for I think of you daily, and pray
daily for you, as I am sure you do for us: and it will, indeed,
be a sweet pleasure to us and joy in the Lord, to behold
your faces again; but, in the meantime, we desire grace, not
to feel ourselves as in banishment, but so to realize, that this
is our present place of service, and so to walk with Jesus,
that we maybe very happy, even now, though so far, and for
so long a time absent from you. It is now thirteen weeks
and three days since I left Bristol, but I have not, during all
this time, even for one single minute, been permitted to
question whether the conclusion, that I should serve the
Lord for a season in this country, was of Him or not; but
during all this time, as also many weeks before I left Bristol,
my heart has had the fullest assurance concerning this
matter. It has been also very kind of the Lord, that He has
not even suffered me to be tempted, through a great variety
of trying events, which might have occurred either here or
in Bristol, to question my call for this service; but, on the
contrary, every days experience almost, here, confirms my
mind, and every letter from Bristol also shows, how that
Gods finger is in this matter. And thus, my dear brethren, it
must be always, when we are taking any step according to
the will of the Lord: the result must be peace and blessing. I
desire therefore quietly to, tarry here, till the same Lord,

who put me at this post, shall call me away from it.

—I now enter upon the narrative of a few facts which I wish to communicate to you, that you may be led yet more highly to prize the spiritual privileges, and especially the religious liberty, which you enjoy in England.—About nineteen months since a brother and sister here, who were connected with the little Baptist Church, (the only body of believers in this country who are separated from the State Church) desired to be united by marriage. As they had conscientious objections to be married according to the usage of the State Church, a statement was sent to the director of this city, the first magistrate, in which this brother and sister expressed their desire and declared that they would submit themselves to everything to which they could with a good conscience, such as having their names three times publicly called at the church, paying the clergymans fees, &c.; but that they could not conform to the marriage ceremony at the church, and they therefore begged to be exempted from this; and they finally claimed for this the rights of the subjects of the kingdom of Wirtemberg, to whom full liberty of conscience is granted by the constitution of the Government. After a time they received a complete denial to this request from the Ecclesiastical court, called the Consistory. They now gave in a full statement of their views, why they left the State Church, why they could not conform to the marriage ceremony in the State Church, &c., and sent this statement, if I remember right, to the highest court, the ministry of the kingdom. It was again refused. And so also by the king himself. Many months had in the meantime elapsed, and the patience of the brother and sister at last began to fail, and as the sister (at that time) saw scarcely any objection to be married at the church, the brother was at last overcome, and he went and gave in the banns at the church. This was in the middle of June last

205

summer. The nearer, however, the marriage day came, the more tried the brother felt, and all peace left him. At last he came to the conclusion to leave himself quite in the hands of the Lord while in the church, and to do no more than he could do with a good conscience; yet he did not know anything definite, nor did he tell his intended wife anything. He asked the brethren, with whom he was in fellowship, to pray for him, who accordingly met at the time when he was to be married. It was on a Lords day afternoon after the public service, and several hundreds of people had remained. The clergyman, a believer, who, no doubt, knew of the former expressed conscientious objection of this brother and sister, did not at all use the printed liturgy, but only gave, as I hear, a scriptural address as the occasion called for, which our brother found profitable. After this the brother and sister made the usual solemn declaration that they would take each other as husband and wife, &c. This, our brother considered all that could be required of him as a subject. But now remained the clergymans blessing and confirmation of the matrimony, which in the literal English translation is as follows: "As you then have solemnly promised to each other conjugal love and fidelity, I therefore confirm in the name of the Father, the Son, and the Holy Ghost, as an appointed minister of the Christian church, this your conjugal union as a union, which according to Gods order, is indissoluble. What God has joined together, let no man put asunder." Now, while the clergyman was pronouncing the first of these words, the brother walked a step or two back from the altar, with his wife, and interrupted the clergyman in words to this effect: "I do not belong to the State Church, and I therefore cannot accept the blessing of the State Church, or the confirmation of the State Church, with reference to our marriage. Our Union was made in heaven, and therefore needs no earthly confirmation. I have gone as far as I could with a good

206

conscience, but further I can do nothing."—The clergyman
now stated "I pronounce your marriage as void, and I shall
give notice of your behaviour to the magistrates."—The
whole matter made a great stir, the people rushed out of the
church, and our brother, with his wife, having gone orderly
back into their pews, fell on their knees and prayed, and
then walked home.—The first thing that now followed was,
that the relations on the part of the wife sought to separate
the brother and sister by all possible means, removing the
furniture out of their intended rooms, sending policemen,
and not suffering the brother to live where he had purposed
to live after marriage, so that the newly married couple had
to take up their abode in the house of a brother in the Lord
now in fellowship with us, who is the brother of the young
wife. On the next day the newly married brother went to
the clergyman, and humbly stated to him, that that, which
had occurred on the previous day, was not in the least
intended as an insult to him, but that he had been forced to
act thus to maintain a good conscience. But he again
declared the marriage as void, and said that he should
legally proceed against him. Either on the same day, or the
day after, our brother and sister had to appear before the
director of the city, and after having been for hours
examined, the marriage was declared as void, and they were
ordered to separate from each other, otherwise the laws
against concubinage would be put in force against them.
Our brother and sister meekly declared, that they would
gladly submit to the Government in every thing, in which
they could submit with a good conscience, but that they
should not separate from each other, as they considered that
they, according to divine and human laws, were married.
After some time they had to appear a second time, and, if I
remember right, a third, if not a fourth time; but they
always gave the same declaration before the city director,
and added that they claimed the rights of the subjects of

Wirtemberg, according to which there was secured to them perfect liberty of conscience. So the matter remained. Nothing more occurred till Monday, Oct. 23rd, when the said brother was ordered to appear before a court called the "Criminal Court" at half-past two, his wife at three, and the brother who had taken them in and lodged them, at half-past three in the afternoon. I ought to have said before, that all three belong to those saints who for my sake were separated from the Baptist Church here. Brother R. and I therefore met for prayer while they were before the judge, and continued in prayer from half-past two till half-past five. All three experienced the fulfilment of that word: "Take no thought how or what ye shall speak: for it shall be given you in that same hour what ye shall speak." Matt. x. 19. The Lord was very nigh to them. They were able firmly, but meekly, to bear testimony for the truth. Even the sister, though alone before the judge, was greatly helped. She has been, ever since the event at the church, quite of one mind with her husband. The crime alleged against the other brother at this court was, that, after he knew that the magistrates had declared the marriage illegal, he still lodged them in his house; to which he declared that he considered the marriage legal. This led to the reasons, and a long and blessed testimony for the Lord was borne before the judge. The crime alleged against the husband before this court was, that he had intended this as an insult against the church, which he denied, but stated that he had gone as far as he could, and that he would rather suffer any thing than act against his conscience. On Thursday, Oct. 26th, these three dear saints had to stand before the same judge, each again alone, from half-past two till half-past five, whilst brother R. and I were again in prayer for them. The Lord again abundantly helped them. Even the judge, though a Roman Catholic, sought both times to favour them as much as possible, and the investigations of the whole affair were as

208

favourably taken down for them on paper by him, as if a brother in the Lord had written them down. We know how that came. The Lord heard the prayers of His children, and also acted according to the just mentioned promise. To both brethren was permitted to hand in on the next day a written statement, on what scriptural grounds the husbands conscience led him to act as he did; and the other brother, on what scriptural grounds he could not obey the magistrate, in refusing to lodge his sister and brother-in-law, when their marriage had been declared illegal. Brother R. and I now wrote two long statements about the affair with scriptural proofs, which, on the next day, were delivered to the Court. On Friday, Oct. 27, the brother, the husband, had to stand the third time that week before the judge, who, among other things, told him, that until the matter by the proper court was decided, the police would separate him and his wife. Thus the matter stands. Our brother and sister may any day be separated; if so, they will be only separated as long as they are in prison; when they come out, they feel themselves before God bound to come again together; and should the matter be forced, they must leave the country. Moreover, if the matter is pressed, the husband may be from six months to two years imprisoned for the act at the church. But the Lord reigneth, and men can go no further than the Lord gives them permission. Our brother who lodged them is liable to six months imprisonment; but the Lord reigneth. Nothing is to be done here, except to pray and to be ready to suffer for the Lords sake, in order that real liberty of conscience may be obtained. Such a case never occured here before. The courts know not themselves what to do. The judge who investigated the case, in order to lay the written investigation before the proper court, said publicly: "I wonder how they will manage this affair." With reference to my own judgment about the matter, it is this: If any brother and sister were now to be married to whom the Lord has given the same light, they should not go at all to the church, but simply give information to the magistrates, have their names called at church, declare themselves ready to pay the fees, and state before the brethren that they mean to consider themselves as united by marriage; and if the government after this oppresses them, to leave the country. I cannot regret that matters have been as they have. The government itself forced our brother, so to say, to do what he did: and good will come out of it for the church. —We are now waiting for what the Lord will do in this matter, and to see whether these dear saints will have to bear imprisonment or not.

Another event has occurred: On Oct. 24th, the elders of the Baptist Church, and therefore two of the brethren with whom I now meet for the breaking of bread, were ordered to appear before the director of the city to hear a communication from the ministers of state with reference to their request about being permitted to marry, without going to church. As this order now came to them as being of the Baptist Church, whilst our brethren no longer belong to the Baptist Church, but consider themselves united with all who love our Lord Jesus, they sent a written statement to the director of the city, stating that they had ceased to belong to the Baptist Church. Thus, without our seeking it, the position which we hold, even if it had not been so before, is now made known. Still, hitherto nothing has been done to us, nor any hinderance laid in our way. Indeed a few days since, through a particular circumstance, the city director had my passport put into his hands, with the inquiry whether a ticket of permission to remain in Stuttgart should be granted to me, or not, and there were no objections made. So I still teach and preach Christ freely,

210

and all that the Lord has taught me, although to a very small number; for the people are afraid of us. In the mean time I speak to souls as I may meet them in the fields, or when persons ask for an alms without the city, for in the whole of Stuttgart I never saw one beggar. I also make considerable progress with my Narrative, much more than at the first, and have nearly one-half ready for the press.

When we took our position here of receiving all who love our Lord Jesus, irrespective of their agreeing with us in all points, one brother came among us, who had been always refused by the Baptist Church here, because he was not baptized. After this brother had been about six weeks among us, he himself desired baptism. He was baptized on the evening of Oct. 28. Thus we have been able to give a practical proof of the truth which we hold.

Our number has only been increased by the arrival of our brother T. H., the son of our brother H., whom you know. He resides in the same house with us. — I repeat that it will give us joy to hear from any of you. We remember before the Lord those of you by name, of whom it has been written to us that they are in trial. My dear wife sends her love to all the dear brethren and sisters.

I remain, my dear brethren,

Your brother and servant in the Lord,

GEORGE MÜLLER

P.S. — I only add that the two brothers and the sister, by their meekness and godly walk, much commend the truth, and are precious instruments chosen of the Lord, to carry the truth before the rulers of the land.

Dec. 31, 1843. During this year 75 have been received into communion among us in Bristol, and 13 saints have fallen asleep. Being absent from Bristol, I am not able to give the present exact state of the church there as to numbers. — The Lord has been pleased to give me during this year for my temporal necessities.

1, Through the saints among whom I labour in Bristol, in provisions, clothes, etc. worth to us, at least £10 0s. 0d.

2, Through anonymous offerings in money, put up in paper, and directed to me, and put into the boxes for the poor saints, or the rent, at the meeting places £130 8s. 4 3/4d.

3, Through presents in money, from saints in Bristol, not given anonymously £106 12s. 0d.

4, Through presents in money from saints not residing in Bristol £79 1s. 6d.

Altogether £326 1s. 10 3/4d.

To this is to be added that the expenses connected with our journey to Germany, and with our temporal necessities, and all the various expenses coming on us in connexion with our stay in a foreign land, from Aug. 9, to Dec. 31, were met out of the 702l. 3s. 7d., which had been given to me, as has been stated, for several purposes, but especially also for the expenses connected with my service in Germany.

Is it not again most manifest from this statement, that during the year 1843 also I served a most kind Master even with reference to temporal supplies? And this I delight to show. If I had been striving with all my might to obtain a good income during the year 1843, I could not have had more; for in one way or another the Lord gave me about 400l. without asking any one for any thing, and therefore I had far more than I needed either for myself and family, or for giving me ability to use hospitality. I find it more and

213

more pleasant, even with reference to this life, to walk in the ways of the Lord, and to rely upon Him for all I need; and often, when I recount on my walks for meditation the mercies of the Lord towards me, I am constrained to say to the praise of the Lord, that if I had remained in my unconverted state, and therefore continued a servant of Satan, I could not have been nearly as well off, even with reference to this life, as I am now in the service of the Lord Jesus. I find, that the more the Lord enables me, not to seek my own things, but the things of Jesus Christ, the more He takes care that my temporal necessities shall be richly supplied.

Jan. 1, 1844.—Last evening I met with the whole little church at Stuttgart to tea, and the last hours of the year, till about 12 oclock at night, we spent together in prayer.

On Jan. 15th, I wrote another letter to the brethren in Bristol, which is here subjoined.

Stuttgart, Jan. 15, 1844,

To the Saints meeting in the name of Jesus, at Bethesda and Salem
Chapels, Bristol.

Beloved Brethren.,

I have it in my heart once more to write to you a little about the work of the Lord here, before my return to you, and I do it the more readily, because I have confidence in your love, being assured that you are as glad to hear from me, as I am to write to you. With reference to all the time since I left you, and in particular with reference to the time since I

214

last wrote to you, I have abundant reason to say, that goodness and mercy have followed us. Never, since I first saw it to be the will of God, that I should labour here for a season, which is now more than seven months, have I been permitted to question, that this conclusion was formed under the guidance of the Holy Ghost; and ever since I left you, which is now five months and six days, every thing has proved, that I left you according to the will of God. It is precious, beloved brethren, to go on an errand when the Lord Himself sends us, and to be at a post where the Lord Himself has placed us for then all goes on well. Far better to wait months, or even years, than to take a step in uncertainty, or being but half assured that it is the will of God, that we should take that step. —But as fully as I was assured that I should leave you for a season, so, as far as I can see at present the mind of the Lord, does it appear to me now, that the time is fast approaching, when our Lord will give us again the great joy and precious privilege of seeing you face to face. Truly, we may say, through grace, and without hypocrisy, "We, brethren, being taken from you for a short time in presence, not in heart;" indeed nothing but grace has kept us here so long. And now the time seems to be fast approaching when we shall leave this, and I am by prayer and labour endeavouring, to see your face soon. If the Lord will, my Narrative, (which, with a particular reference to the spiritual necessities of the Church in Germany, I have been preparing for the press, and is nearly finished), will be printed within five weeks from this day, so that I hope we shall be able to leave this towards the end of February. Yet, in the mean time, there remains much work for me still to do, both with reference to writing and labouring among the brethren here; therefore continue, dear brethren, even as you have done hitherto, to help me with your prayers; and we also, by the help of God, will continue to intercede for you, as we do with joy.

As there have occurred a number of important events among us, since I wrote to you last, I proceed now to give you some account of them. —In the early part of November last year, brother R., the Doctor of Law, asked me to unite with him and a sister in prayer, as that sister (not one in fellowship with us, but belonging to the State Church) was going to be divorced from her husband, and she had desired that we should spend the time with her in prayer for her husband, while this act would be settled in the judicial court. This sister had had to suffer exceedingly during the space of many years from her husband, who hated her greatly for the Lords sake. Three times she had been obliged to leave him, because of his awful treatment; but three times, especially through the peace-making efforts of brother R., who was her legal counsellor, she returned to her husband, and lived for a season with him, till at last each time her health sank under the sufferings she had endured from him. At length, about two years since, she left him again, with the intention not to return to him any more. This led to a divorce by law, a thing not uncommon on the Continent; and in that hour in which we met for prayer, the matter was settled. In consequence of this, as she had three children, and brought a comparatively considerable property to her husband, the law proceeded to secure this money for the benefit of herself and children, as the husband had wasted all his own property. This act was settled on December 9th, on which occasion she had to meet her husband at his house with the appointed government officers; and she requested our brother Dr. R., as a friend to accompany her. Brother R. (who had been for fifteen years the peace-maker between this husband and wife, and who had three times succeeded in favour of the husband, though the legal adviser of the wife) was nevertheless greatly hated by the husband, who repeatedly spoke to him in public courts of law thus: "You shall never baptize me." Or, "Now my wife

216

will soon be free to marry her priest," (meaning brother R.,) &c. All this brother R. had been able to bear with the greatest meekness, though thus publicly insulted, when acting as solicitor or barrister at the judicial courts. Now on the 9th of December, brother R., as I said, went with this divorced sister to her husbands house. When all the business was done, the husband came close to brother R., in the presence of several magistrates, put a pistol to his side and fired it at him, then took another pistol, put it to his own breast, fired and sank down dead immediately. But while he himself died immediately, brother R. has been wonderfully preserved. He wore a thick wadded coat, and had four papers in his side pocket, through all of which the ball passed. Then, to show the hand of God, the ball met in the other clothes such obstacles (all being double in that spot,) that it only entered a very little way into the body and lodged upon one of the ribs. After the fire was extinguished, (for our brothers clothes were set on fire, so near had the poor sinner put the pistol to him,) our brother walked home, and shortly after a surgeon extracted the ball, and on the seventh day our brother was so far restored, that the whole little church here could be gathered around his bed, together with his relations, and we united together in praising the Lord for His wonderful help; and on the fifteenth day our brother was already so far restored, that he was able to assemble himself again with us for the breaking of bread. Half an inch higher or lower might have taken his life; but the balls (for the pistol was loaded with two, one of which fell out of his clothes,) though most maliciously so prepared that they might do much mischief on entering the body, found so much resistance that the power, through the soft clothing being every part double in that spot, was spent before touching the body. Surely, the Lord is round about us Even the ungodly in this city have been forced to marvel; but now the devil spreads the report that that wicked person shot our brother, because he purposed to marry his wife.

At last also the sentence has come from the judicial court appointed for that business, with reference to the married brother and sister about whom I wrote to you. Both of them are sentenced to fourteen days imprisonment, and their marriage is declared to be illegal and only concubinage, so that when the imprisonment is over, they will be separated by the police, and sent back to prison, should they still seek to live together as they must do, being married in the sight of God. Further, the brother who lodged them after their marriage, is sentenced to four days imprisonment, because he helped on, as it is said, concubinage. Finally, the husband is sentenced to pay 4/6 of the legal expenses, his wife 1/6 and the other brother 1/6. If here were only the question about money, or suffering imprisonment, we must bear it, and account it an honour, to suffer for Christs sake; but as the sentence is, that this marriage is concubinage, which according to God and to man it is not, and as the liberty of the Wirtemberg subjects allows them to appeal to a higher court, and as brother R. can do all this business, I have with brother R. and some other brethren judged, that in this case, like Paul, we ought to appeal to a higher court, if by any means we may keep the government from committing this grievous sin of unjustly punishing those godly persons. Should this, however, be in vain, we must yield to the power, the brethren must bear the imprisonment, and this dear couple must leave the country.

Our position here as saints was unquestionably known from the beginning by the police, who watch us closely; but nothing was officially done in the matter till very recently, which was occasioned in the following way. The Baptist church here have two or three times a year, or as often as the city director (the head of the police) requires it, to give in the list of names of those who belong to the church, who have been added, and who have been separating themselves or have been excluded. At the close of the year that was now done again, when the considerable number who had left it on my account, were noticed by the city director, who then sent for the teaching elder or president of the Baptist church, who told him all about me, and that I had occasioned this business. This now drew forth an order from the city director to brother R., in which he was requested to state—1. Who had separated themselves with him, (names, station in life, and place of abode)?—2. Whether we meant to form a separate church?—3. Who were the elders?—4. And who at present belonged to our number? This was very briefly replied to by giving the names of those who separated themselves, the additional two names of those who have been added since, that we meant to be in communion with all who love our Lord Jesus, and that this was the reason, why we had separated ourselves from the Baptist church. To this no reply has been sent; nor has any one as yet put the least hinderance to my freely teaching and preaching Jesus Christ, though it is now five months and six days since I have been labouring here.

The Lord is also now beginning to work among the brethren belonging to the Baptist church here, in answer to our and your prayers, and those of many other dear saints in England, Switzerland, &c. Several are beginning to feel that their position is not a right one, but none have yet fully and publicly renounced their errors, which, I trust, will soon be the case. May we continue to pray concerning this matter. Moreover, the prejudices against us are wearing off on the part of some other persons, so that the number who attend our meetings is rather increasing. There seem also several who are somewhat concerned about their souls, and a few children of God belonging to the state church come. Another brother was also added to our number about a fortnight ago, so that we are now two-and-twenty altogether, who break bread. This is a small company certainly, but though it be only like a taper on a candlestick, yet there is some light, however little, and I trust that, with Gods blessing, this light will be more and more bright in Germany, where it is so much needed. The Lord is also blessing my labours among the dear brethren here, so that they grow in knowledge, and, I trust, in grace also; likewise those errors, of which I wrote to you, are giving way, but they are not overcome fully yet, and I shall have a conflict still about them, before I leave: still the Lord has kept us in peace, by giving me wisdom to deal gently with the brethren, remembering the years in which they were built up in error. Help me also with your prayers, that I may find a bookseller to take my book on commission for sale; for I have offered it to three, and they have refused it. One glimpse was enough for one, in seeing that I did not belong to a State Church. Surely I have conflict here step by step; but God helps, and through Him I shall do valiantly in this thing also; nevertheless I beg your prayers. — And now, finally, I entreat you, beloved pilgrims, help me with your prayers, that I may do and suffer all the will of God here gladly, that I may live to His honour while remaining here, that I may be helped in the remainder of my work, that I may not leave a day before, nor stay a day beyond the Lords time, and that the Lord would give us a prosperous journey and voyage in His own time. My dear wife unites with me in love to all the dear brethren and sisters. We often pray for you, and remember by name those who are in particular trial through bereavement, or from other causes. Farewell.

Your affectionate brother and servant in the Lord,

I add a few remarks in connexion with this letter: —

I. The wisdom of our brother R., in being present at the judicial settlement of the money affairs of the sister, who was legally divorced from her husband, may be questioned, on account of the expressions used by the husband. As to myself, knowing the particulars more fully than the reader can, I do not for a moment think that the man thought our brother had any intention of marrying his divorced wife, for all these expressions were evidently only used to insult Dr. R.; but my objection would rather spring from this, that I question whether a christian has any business at all with such concerns. The Lord in a most remarkable way protected Dr. R.; but this by no means proves that he was in his proper place.

II. I also say a few words more about the brother and sister whose marriage was considered illegal. The appeal to the highest court was of no avail, also the final appeal to the King was useless, and about July, 1844, the brother and sister were imprisoned for fourteen days, and the brother, who had taken them in, four days. The Lord was with them, and blessed them much in the prison, as they wrote me. The brethren had free access to them, and once even the greater part of them met in the prison and broke bread together. This exceeding great leniency was granted to them, I think, through the judge who had to investigate their affairs. When their imprisonment was expired, they were ordered to separate, which however they did not do, considering themselves married in the sight of God. For a long time the government only threatened, without separating them by force; at last, however, in March, 1845, after having taken from him his right of citizenship at Stuttgart, and having thus deprived him of the privilege of carrying on his business as a master cabinet-maker, the husband was taken by force from his wife, and escorted by a policeman to his parish, which is about nine miles distant. This was done after the government had suffered them to live together as husband and wife above twenty months, and after they had had a child more than ten months old, which however the Lord took to Himself about a week before the parents were thus separated. This affair has occasioned the loss of the business of this brother; and if an alteration be not shortly made in the laws of the country, with reference to liberty of conscience concerning marriage, (which they hope for, as they mean to appeal to the representatives of the people,) they purpose to emigrate to England.

Though our brother and sister might have acted more wisely, and not have brought the matter to this public act at the church; yet we must keep in mind that their position had been trying, as for more than a twelve-month they had delayed being married, in hope of obtaining permission from the government not to have to go to the State Church; and as no one of the brethren had ever been thus situated; and as they themselves had not much light, yet wished to maintain a good conscience: on these accounts, I say, we cannot but feel for our brother and sister in their trial, and remember them in love.

Were it again to occur, that a brother and sister of the little church at Stuttgart should desire to be united in marriage, and have conscientious objection to be married in the State Church, I gave it as my judgment to the brethren, that they should humbly and meekly make known their intentions to the city director, have their banns called in the Church, pay the fees of the clergyman, etc., and afterwards make known to the whole little Church that they took each other in marriage, signify the same to the city director, and not go to the State Church. If after this they should not be suffered to live together, then to emigrate.

III. After I had been between two and three months at Stuttgart, and the brethren had been instructed in some measure, both at the public meetings and at the Scripture Reading Meetings, about many important truths, I at last began decidedly to go forward at our private meetings, after much prayer, to the exposing of the fearful errors, which they almost all held, in thinking that at last all men would be saved, and even the devils themselves. We had not, however, had more than two or three meetings on this subject, when Dr. R. was shot; and as this occasioned his absence for some time, I thought it better not to go on with the subject; and when he was sufficiently restored, it was wished that we should consider all the passages connected with the Lords supper. As on this point also the brethren needed instruction, I readily yielded the point, judging that I had to show them, by being willing to wait, that I sought not my own gratification, in considering their views about universal salvation. Thus five or six meetings were spent in considering all the portions of the Holy Scriptures which speak about the Lords Supper. But now, this having been finished, I proposed that we should resume considering the Scriptures, with reference to universal salvation, and I found that they had been led into this error, because 1, They did not see the difference between the earthly calling of the Jews, and the heavenly calling of the believers in the Lord Jesus in the present dispensation, and therefore they said, that, because the words "everlasting," etc., are applied to "the possession of the land of Canaan," and the "priesthood of Aaron," that therefore the punishment of the wicked cannot be without end, seeing that the possession of Canaan and the priesthood of Aaron are not without end. My endeavour, therefore, was, to show the brethren the difference between the earthly calling of Israel and our heavenly one, and to prove from Scripture, that whenever, the word "everlasting" is used with reference to things purely not of the earth, but beyond time, it denotes a period without end. 2, They had laid exceeding great stress upon a few passages where, in Luthers translation of the German Bible, the word hell occurs, and where it ought to have been translated either "hades" in some passages, or "grave" in others, and where they saw a deliverance out of hell, and a being brought up out of hell, instead of "out of the grave." 3, They had taken passages out of their connexion.—The mode which I now pursued was, to refer to all the very many passages which they had written down, and to expound them according to the connexion in which they stood, seeking to show the brethren this connexion. In addition to this, I requested them to allow me to speak on those passages without being interrupted, in order that, being able pretty fully to enter upon this subject, there might be free opportunity given to the Holy Ghost to work conviction in their hearts; and, as they were greatly in favour of universal salvation, they might thus be kept from controversy, to which they would have been inclined, without having heard what I had to say from the Word of God against universal salvation; for I had previously given them full opportunity to bring out their own views. After having thus proceeded for several evenings in our private meetings, I saw that the greater part were fully convinced about the errors they had held, and the others had no desire to contradict, though they had perhaps not grace enough to say plainly that they had been in error. Nor did I in the least enforce that any acknowledgment should be made to me. These meetings took place during the last three weeks of my stay at Stuttgart. Thus, by having received grace from the Lord to deal patiently with the brethren, and to wait upon God even for the right time to attack these errors, I was helped to conquer in this thing also.

IV. I add also a few words more with reference to my Narrative, which I published at Stuttgart. When I had proceeded a considerable way in preparing it for the press, I found especial help from God, in being directed through a kind brother, whom I had known eight years before at Stuttgart, to a paper manufacturer, from whom I could buy the paper for 4,000 copies on advantageous terms, and also to a very honourable and promise-keeping printer. The printer engaged to print two sheets a week and kept his word to the end, so that as long as six weeks before my departure, I was able to say that, if the Lord would, I should depart on the 26th of February, and on that very day I was able to depart. Important as it was, for many reasons, that I should return to my service in Bristol when I did, I cannot but see the hand of God in directing me to so honourable a person as the printer was, in whom also, I trust, is somewhat of the fear of God. — It has been often mentioned to me in various places, that brethren in business do not sufficiently attend to the keeping of promises, and I cannot therefore but entreat all who love our Lord Jesus, and who are engaged in a trade or business, to seek for His sake not to make any promises, except they have every reason to believe they shall be able to fulfil them, and therefore carefully to weigh all the circumstances, before making any engagement, lest they should fail in its accomplishment. It is even in these little ordinary affairs of life that we may either bring much honour or dishonour to the Lord; and these are the things which every unbeliever can take notice of. Why should it be so often said, and sometimes with a measure of ground, or even much ground: "Believers are bad servants, bad tradesmen, bad masters?" Surely it ought not to be true that we, who have power with God to obtain by prayer and faith all needful grace, wisdom and shill, should be bad servants, bad tradesmen, bad masters.

When now the Narrative was nearly printed, I had to look out for a bookseller who would undertake the sale of the book on commission. My reason for this was, not the money which might thus be obtained, for truly glad should I have been to have given away all the 4,000 copies at once, had I known of suitable opportunities; but in order that by means of the book-trade the Narrative might be circulated even a thousand miles off or more, where I had no opportunity of reaching. Here now it was again that I met with difficulty, as I had done step by step in the other parts of my service in Germany. Three booksellers refused to undertake the sale of the book. The objection evidently was, that I did not belong to the State Church, and one of them plainly told me so. But by the help of God I was not discouraged. I knew the Lord had sent me to Germany: I knew also that it was His will that I should publish an account of His dealings with me in the German language; for He had so unexpectedly laid this matter upon my heart; He had so remarkably provided the means for it, without my asking any one but Himself for them; He had given me such especial help in preparing the book for the press; He had given me such an abundance of prayer about this part of my service, both many weeks before I left England, and day by day all the months that I had been in Germany. For these reasons it was that I had the fullest assurance that this difficulty also would be overcome. I therefore now began to give myself to prayer with my dear wife concerning this very matter. Day by day we waited upon the Lord for about four weeks, and then I applied to another bookseller, who without any hesitation undertook the sale of the book on commission, so that I retained 2,000 copies for gratuitous distribution, and 2,000 he was to have.

Dear reader, there is no difficulty which may not be overcome. Let us but use the power which we have with God as his children by prayer and faith, and abundant blessings may be drawn down from Him.

V. On my departure from Stuttgart, the number of the brethren who met for the breaking of bread was twenty-five. On the very last Lords day I had the joy of seeing the third elder of the Baptist Church, who had at first thought me so much in error, come among us, and unite with us in the breaking of bread, having for some time had his mind more and more opened to the truth. The day before I departed, not only the brethren and sisters among whom I had laboured took leave of me with many tears, but also nineteen brethren and sisters of the close Baptist Church came to my lodgings, and affectionately bade me farewell, and many with tears. The Lord indeed, in His rich mercy, had so far answered my prayer concerning this my service, that I left a testimony behind in their consciences.

On Feb. 26, 1844, my dear wife and I departed from Stuttgart, and on March 6th, we reached Bristol. Exceedingly as we had longed to return to Bristol, as soon as we could see it to be the Lords will; yet so greatly had our hearts been knit to the dear saints whom we left behind, that it was a sad pleasure to depart, and our only comfort was, that we left them in the hands of the good Shepherd.

I resume now the account about the Orphan-Houses, and other objects of the Scriptural Knowledge Institution.

During all the time of my absence from Bristol, the Lord

227

bountifully supplied our need. For though the money, which I was able to leave behind on my departure, would not have supplied the Orphan-Houses with more than about one-half of what was needed, yet the Lord helped so seasonably, and sent in so many donations, that there was not once, during all this time, the least difficulty with reference to means. There came in for the Orphans, between Aug. 9, 1843, and Mach 6, 1844, about 450l., besides very many articles of clothing, pro visions, books, trinkets, old silver, etc.

On Aug. 11th, 1843, A. B. sent 50l., which, being left to my disposal, was put to the School-Bible-Missionary and Tract Fund. I received information about this donation on the evening of Aug. 22nd, during the first hour after my arrival at Stuttgart. It was a precious earnest, that the Lord would also be mindful of the need of the Institution during my absence from England. Indeed, it cannot be described, how sweet to me just then, under the circumstances in which I found myself, in an especial trial of faith to which the Lord called me in that very hour, as before stated, was this fresh proof of the Lords watchful care over His work in my hands.

Nov. 21, 1843. At a time when all means were exhausted, and when for many reasons large supplies were needed for the School-Bible-Missionary and Tract Fund, whilst I was daily waiting upon the Lord with my dear wife in Germany, bringing the work in Bristol before Him, and beseeching Him also to give us pecuniary means for it, that His enemies might have no cause for triumphing, was sent to me a letter from Bristol, containing another from the East Indies, in which the writer gave me an order for 100l. for the work of the Lord in my hands, giving me at the same time full liberty to use the money as most needed.

228

A few days after A. B. sent another 50l. for the work of the Lord in my hands. By these two donations, both of which I put entirely to the funds for these objects, we were not only helped to meet all present demands, but were richly supplied.—Thus, at so great a distance from the work, we were yet able by our prayers effectually to serve the Institution!—Truly, it is precious in this way to hang upon God! It brings its abundant reward with it! Every donation, thus received, so manifestly comes out of the hands of the Lord Himself.

Dear Reader, just look once more upon this circumstance! Hundreds of miles we were from Bristol, and by our bowing our knees before our Heavenly Father at Stuttgart, we not only could bring down spiritual blessings upon the work in Bristol, but also temporal means. Thus, simply by prayer, we obtained whilst in Germany, for the work of God in Bristol, within about one week, nearly 200l.; for there came in some other donations for the Orphans also.

On Jan. 6, 1844, there came in 50l. from one who is VERY FAR PROM BEING RICH, of which 10l. was given for the School Fund, and 40l. for the Orphans. The donor is satisfied with food and raiment, labouring cheerfully, and wishing rather to spend than to keep, or lay up treasure on earth.

March 25, 1844. After a comparatively great abundance with regard to the Orphans, for a whole year and seventeen days, during which time we were not once in difficulty as to means, which had not been the case for nearly five years previous to the commencement of this period, we are now again quite poor, there being NOTHING AT ALL left in my hands, after I have paid out this day more than 50l. for rent and salaries. But through the grace of God I am able to trust as heretofore in the Lord, and therefore my heart is in peace.

229

—Evening. I received this afternoon 11s. 2 1/2d., 2s. 7d., by sale of articles came in 1l.19s. 9d., by sale of Reports 3s., and by a donation 2s. 2d.

March 26. This morning my wife and I besought the Lord unitedly for means, and received almost immediately afterwards 5l. from Birmingham, in answer to our prayer.

March 27. I received 8s., and there was anonymously put into the box at Bethesda 2s. 6d. This morning at half-past nine a sister came to me, and brought me a sovereign for the Orphans, saying: "Whilst I was lying this morning at six oclock on my bed, I thought, here I am so comfortable, and perhaps the Orphans may be in need, and I resolved to bring you this." The donation came most seasonably and as the fruit of our prayer.—I received also 1l., the profit of the sale of ladies bags.

March 30. Saturday. There is 6l. 19s. 9d. in hands This will be at least enough till Monday morning.—There came in this morning 1l. 1s. by a donation, before the money was sent off to the Orphan-Houses, so that I had 8l. 0s. 9d. to send, which will be enough, I suppose, till Tuesday morning.

April 1. There came in since the day before yesterday 1l., which was anonymously put into the box at Salem Chapel, 15s. was given by a young sister as the produce of some work which she had done for the benefit of the Orphans, and I 6s. came in by sale of articles. Having had this 2l. 11s. coming in I was able to meet extraordinary expenses which came upon me today, not having expected that anything beyond the ordinary housekeeping money would have been needed.

April 2. The need of today was 3l. 0s. 6d. Yesterday I had

paid away all the money in hand, but in the afternoon came in by sale of articles 2l. 17s. 5d., by the boxes in the Orphan-Houses 5s. 6d., and by needle-work of the Orphans 4s. 3 1/2d.: so that we were able to meet the demands of today.

April 3. Today 1l. 14s. was required. I opened the boxes in my house, in which I found 3s. 1 1/2d. Thus I had 8s. 10d. with what was left yesterday, and the remainder, being 1l. 5s. 2d., one of the labourers was able to give of his own.

April 4. Last evening was given to me 11s, and 10s.; and this morning 5s. came in. Thus we have 1l. 6s., and the need of today is 1l. 7s. One of the labourers was able to add the 1s.

April 5. Yesterday came in by sale of articles 3l., and this morning I received from Clapham 1l. 10s., and through a believer in Bristol 2l. 6s. This afternoon came in still further from a brother in Bath 5l. We have therefore received altogether this day 11l. 14s. from the bountiful hand of our Heavenly Father.

April 6. One of the labourers in the Orphan-Houses gave me still further today 5l., and from Kensington I received 1l. 6s. We are thus again provided for the probable expenses of two or three days.

April 7. Today a sister gave me 2l. for the express purpose of providing a little treat for the dear Orphans, and 15s. 6d. came in besides.

April 8. It has often occurred in our experience, that after we have had to pass for some time through a season of comparative poverty, in which day by day we have had to wait upon the Lord, our Father alters His way of dealing with us, and opens His bountiful hand, by supplying us for several or many days at once. Thus it is now. During the last three days we received more than was required for each of those days, and it was still more abundantly so today; for this afternoon a person, residing at Keynsham, gave me 1l., and this evening a brother gave me 50l. When I received this 50l., we were not in absolute need, but had enough for two or three days; yet I see the kindness of the Lord in sending this donation, as I had been repeatedly of late praying for means, and as we are thus enabled to do things which are not absolutely needful just now, though desirable, and as we have thus the continued proof of his willingness to send means.

April 14. From the end of Nov. 1843, till about the middle of March, 1844, there was always as much in hand as was needed for the School-Bible-and Tract Fund; for besides the help, which we received through the two donations of 50l. and 100l., a number of smaller donations came in after. But now for some weeks past all means were again gone, and on the last three Saturdays all the usual remuneration could not be given to all the teachers in the Day-Schools. In addition to this, the greater part of the common sort of Bibles and Testaments, for circulation among the poor and for Schools was gone. I had also often prayed for means to assist Missionary brethren. Under these circumstances I received this morning from A. B., who has been already repeatedly referred to, as having been used by the Lord to help us in our need, the sum of 50l.

May 4. Besides the 50l. which was given on April 8th, for the Orphans, and the money we had in hand before the 50l. was given, there has come in since then 36l. 2s. 8d.; but today, Saturday, we have again only 5l. 6s. 6 1/2d. left, which, however, is enough for today, and a few shillings will be left for the beginning of next week.

May 6. On Saturday came in by sale of articles 1l. 11s., and by a donation 10s., and yesterday was put anonymously into the Chapel boxes 2s. 6d. So we have more than enough for the expenses of today.

May 8. By the produce of some little boxes, made by a sister, there came in 5s. 6d., by a donation. 2s. 6d., by the contents of an Orphan-box from Crediton. 6s. 10d., and by sale of articles 10s. By these small donations all that is needed for today is met. The brother, who sent me the 6s. 10d, from Crediton, wrote, that he did not like to wait till this little sum had increased, before he sent it, as it might be just now needed; and thus it was.

May 9. The Lord has again helped for today and tomorrow. Last evening
I received through a brother 5s., and this morning the boxes in the
Orphan-Houses were opened, in which 5l. 3s. 1 1/2d. was found; some
one also bought a Report and gave 1s. for it.

May 13. On the 10th there came in 2l. 1s. 9d., on the 11th 10l. 10s. 4d., on the 12th 5l. was sent from Barnstaple by three sisters, and 3l. 6s. came in besides. By I the income of these three days I was not only able to meet their own demands, but I had enough for today, though I required no less than 13l. 15s.

May 15. Yesterday there was only 1l. 5s. left, not nearly enough for what was required today. When I came home last evening, having spent a part of the afternoon at the Infant-Orphan-House, where I found that several articles were needed, I heard that a gentleman had called and wished to be shown into my room, where he had written a paper, which he had put with some money into the Orphan-box. On opening it I found the paper to contain four sovereigns. Thus we are helped for the present.

May 16. Only 5s. came in, through the boxes at my house.

May 17. Yesterday I paid out all TO THE LAST PENNY I had in hand. When now there was nothing left, 2l. came in by the sale of some books, and 1l. 0s. 6d. by two donations, whereby I was able to meet this days need.

May 18. This morning 1l. 17s. 10d. came in. We have thus, with the little which was left yesterday, 2l. 15s. 11d. for this day, Saturday but I know not whether that will be enough. —Evening. This evening at six oclock one of my sisters-in-law returned from Plymouth, where she had been staying for a little while, and brought from a sister in the Lord 2l., from another sister 1l. 15s., and also a parcel from some sisters in the Lord in the neighbourhood of Kingsbridge, containing 14s., and the following articles: a pair of shoes, 3 pairs of socks, 3 pairs of cuffs, a pair of mittens, 3 little mats, a pincushion cover, a comb, 3 books, 4 clasps, 2 brooches, a gold pin, a chain, a vinaigrette, a Turks head cushion, and 10 yards of calico. Also a parcel from Plymouth, containing 2 veils and a scarf. Also from another sister, 2 netted handkerchiefs.

—The money I took at once to the Orphan Houses, where I found, that, to meet the present expenses, 3l. 10s. more was required than what I had been able to send in the morning, as altogether about 6l. 5s. was needed for this day. How kind, therefore, of the Lord, to send this money so opportunely, though only towards the evening of the day! Thus we had enough, and a little left towards the need of Monday.

May 20. Monday. Yesterday came in 4s. 3d., and today 8s. 5d. As this, together with what had been left in hand, was not quite enough, one of the labourers added 6s. 6d. of his own. Thus we had 1l. 18s. 2d. for the need of today.

May 23. We are still supplied by the day. We had received from the Lord during the last days also what we required, but we were poor, having nothing at all in hand. Under these circumstances with reference to means for the Orphans, and in as great need for the other objects of the Institution, two persons, professed believers, called on me today, who were going from house to house in the street where I live, to ask money for a chapel debt. I remonstrated with them, and sought to show them how the name of the Lord was dishonoured by them, in calling upon the enemies of the Lord for pecuniary assistance towards, what they considered, the work of the Lord. I sought to show them, that if their work were of God, He would, in answer to their prayers, send them help: and if not, ought they not to give up, what was not His work, and not force the matter by calling promiscuously from house to house upon believers and unbelievers. Their reply was: "The gold and silver are the Lords, and therefore we call upon the unconverted for help for His work." My reply was: "Because the gold and silver are the Lords, therefore we, His children, need not go to His enemies for the support of His work." Now, at that very moment, while I was thus speaking for the Lord, having then nothing at all in hand for the Orphans or the other objects, the postman brought a small brown paper parcel and a letter. My conversation seemed, for the time at least, fruitless; for those two individuals, having left, went as before from house to house; but when I came back to my room, I found the blessedness of the scriptural way; for that parcel, which the postman had brought, while I was conversing, came from Ireland, and contained two post-office orders for 5l. each, and a worked stool cover; the letter which had been brought, and which was from Seaton,

235

contained 1l. for the Orphans; and 1l. 1s. 5d. had been sent, having been taken out of the boxes in the Orphan Houses: so that altogether, whilst those two persons were with me, 12l. 1s. 5d. had come in. Half of the 10l. I put to the Orphan-Fund, and half to the other funds, there being nothing in hand to supply the teachers in the Day-Schools during this week.

May 24. Today a box with many articles arrived from the neighbourhood of Droitwich, and 1l. 8s. 9d, was received by the sale of articles.

May 25, 6s. 6d. came in.

May 27. Monday. On Saturday, after having supplied the need of that day, which was 5l. 15s., and now again little being left in my hands, a brother from Cork brought me a parcel which contained 6 pairs of childrens shoes, a pair of little boots, a pair of list slippers (all new), 2 books, 2 pincushions, a knitted watch pocket, and 102 thimbles. The same brother gave also 10s. 6d. and a book. In the evening a brother gave me 1l. — Yesterday was put into the chapel boxes 10s. with Eccles. ix. 10, and 2s. 6d. besides. By these donations, with what was left on Saturday, I am able to meet the demands of this day, being 2l. 17s.

May 31. By the produce of the sale of stockings, knitted by the Orphan-Boys, by some help which one of the labourers was able to give, by a donation, etc., we were supplied during the last three days. Now this morning, when again in much need, I received a note, which contained 5l. with Eccles. ix. 10. By means of this 5l. I was able to meet the expenses of today, which are 2l. 8s. 3d.

June 1. Yesterday there came in still further 2l.18s. 11d. by sale of articles, and today by needlework, done by the

Orphans, 1l. 13s. 9d. Thus I am able (including what remained of the 5l.) to supply the need of this day, which is 5l. 10s.—Still further came in 5s.

June 3. Monday. Yesterday came in 16s. 1 1/2d. This, with what was in hand from Saturday, met the demands of today.

June 4. This morning came in 3l. 2s. 4d. by the sale of a few trinkets and of some pieces of old silver. This was enough for this days need, and left something over, as only 1l. 16s. was required. This afternoon arrived a parcel from Westmoreland, containing 24 chemises, 2 shirts, 2 petticoats, a pinafore, 5 night caps, 7 pairs of stockings (all new), and 38 1/2 yards of print. Thus we are encouraged day after day, though for many days we have now been again very poor.

June 5. Last evening a brother gave me a dozen of modern silver tea-spoons, which, being this morning readily disposed of at a good price, supplied our need for today.

For several days I have now had day by day especial prayer with some of my fellow-labourers about the work, and particularly for pecuniary supplies; and surely we do not wait in vain upon the Lord. Before this day is over we have had another proof of it. This afternoon a parcel was brought by a brother from London, containing a silver cream jug, a pair of gilt earrings, a gold ring, 2 bracelets, and a muffineer. The same donor sent also a sovereign. The bearer brought also another donation of 2s. 6d. A lady also called this afternoon at the Infant-Orphan-House, to see the Institution, and gave 5s.

June 8. On the 6th came in 16s. 6d. and 3s. 6d.; and yesterday was received, by the sale of the silver cream jug and a few other little articles 4l. 0s. 9d., by the sale of stockings 5s., and by a donation 10s. Thus we had enough for today, though the need was 4l. 19s. 8d., as 4l. 15s. 9d. had come in yesterday, and a few shillings had been left before.

June 10. Monday. Though on Saturday all our necessities were comfortably supplied, yet I had then NOT ONE PENNY left. Our Heavenly Father, however, having given us grace to trust in Him, and not to be anxiously concerned about Monday, gave us, even late on Saturday evening, a proof of his loving tender care over us. The labourers met, as usual, on Saturday evening for prayer, and we continued in prayer from a little after seven till about nine oclock. After we had separated, a sister, who had been waiting at the Infant-Orphan-House, till our prayer was over, gave 4s., saying that she had intended to give it to me on the Lords-day morning, but had felt herself stirred up to bring it that evening.—Nothing came in yesterday. I met this morning with some of the labourers again for prayer, as I have now been doing daily for about a fortnight, and we again asked the Lord for help, with regard to the writing of the Report, that He would let His blessing rest upon it, bless the intended public meetings, when the account of the Lords dealings with us will be given, convert the children, give the needful grace and wisdom to us who are engaged in the work, give us means for the Day-Schools, means for ordering a quantity of oatmeal from Scotland, for colouring down the Orphan-houses, for the supply of the present need, etc. There was only the 4s. in hand for the need of today, which I had reason to believe would be about 2l. Now see the Lords help I just now, at eleven oclock, when the letter bag is brought for the money for todays need, I receive in it 2l. 7s. 3d., which had been taken by brother R. B. out of the boxes in the Orphan-Houses, and half-a-sovereign, which had been sent by a brother in Suffolk. Thus we have 3l. 1s. 3d., whilst only 1l. 15s. is needed today.

238

In the course of reading the Holy Scriptures in my family this morning, came the word: "Ask, and it shall be given you; seek, and ye shall find; knock, and it shall be opened unto you." (Matth. vii. 7.) I pleaded this word especially with the Lord, while I was again praying, after the family prayer was over, with some of the labourers; and surely He has proved afresh that he acts according to His word.

—Evening. The Lord sent still further help today. This afternoon a person called at the Infant-Orphan-House, and gave 7s., and two ladies met the teacher of the Infant-Orphan-House in the street, and gave her a paper, directed to me, which contained 10s. 2s. was also given by a person at Clifton.

June 12. By what had come in on the 10th we were supplied yesterday and also today, and I had three pence left, after I had sent off to the matrons of the four houses what they needed. I then gave myself to prayer with some of the labourers for the supplies of the present need, mentioning again before the Lord all the many things for which we need His help. About one hour after, I received 10s. for the Orphans from a brother of Guernsey, who has been staying a few days in Bristol.

June 13. Last evening came in still further, by the sale of articles, 2s. 3d.; and 6s. 4d. by the sale of some musk plants, which two sisters in the Lord rear and sell for the benefit of the Orphans; and this morning I received 7s. 11d., being six donations. Likewise two small silver coins were given me, and 1l. 15s. 3d. I received by the sale of articles.

June 14. There came in still further last evening 5s., and this morning by the boxes in the Orphan-houses 18s. 9d. This evening 1l. 10s. was sent with an Orphan, from Carne in Suffolk.

June 18. As only 13s. had come in on the 16th and 17th, we were now extremely poor; but the Lord looked upon our necessity, for 5l. was sent by a Christian lady at Scarborough, and a person from Manchester gave 1l.

June 22. Saturday evening. Only 1s. came in the day before yesterday, and 2s. 6d. was taken this morning out of the boxes in the Orphan-Houses.—This has been one of those weeks, in which I have prayed particularly much for means, and in which the Lord seemed little to regard my requests. But my soul, through grace, has been in perfect peace, being fully assured, that He in His own good time will again send larger supplies. In every way we are now very poor, and it seems desirable that we should have large sums to meet the present circumstances. After much prayer the Lord has closed the week with fresh proofs of His loving tender care over the work, which has been a great refreshment to my spirit. There came in this evening, between eight and nine oclock, by sale of stockings 9s., by sale of other articles 1l. 8s. 7d., by a donation from an Irish sister 5s., and a physician in Bristol kindly sent me 2l., and his little children 4s.—How can my soul sufficiently praise the Lord for His tender mercies and His readiness to bear the prayers of His servant! All these fresh deliverances in the hour of great need show most clearly, that it is only for the trial of our faith, for our profit, for the profit of others who may hear of it, and for the glory of the Lord, that He sometimes seems not to regard our petitions.

June 24, Monday. Yesterday came in by donations 14s. 8d., anonymously was put into the Chapel boxes 1s., add 3s. was given to ore as the produce of the sale of musk plants. Today two Orphans were brought from Bath; for though we are so poor, the work goes forward, and children are received as long as there is room. The person who brought them put two sovereigns into the boxes at the Orphan-Houses. Thus we have again, with what came in on Saturday evening, more than is needed for today and tomorrow.

June 25. Today I received from Scotland 10l., to be used as most needed, of which I took one-half for the Orphans, and the other half for the other objects. Thus, in our great need, the Lord supplies us from day to day, and hears our prayers, which we daily bring to Him, though there have not yet come in larger sums for oatmeal, salary of the labourers in the Orphan-Houses, colouring down the four houses, etc.; but the Lord in His own time will send means for these expenses also.

June 29. Day after day our great poverty continues; yet day after day the Lord helps us. This evening was received from the neighbourhood of Bideford 7s. 6d., a chess board, and a gold pin. There came in also by the sale of articles 1l. 8s. 3d., and by Reports 1s.

June 30. This evening I received 10l. between nine and ten oclock, at a time of the greatest poverty. A little boy likewise gave me 6d. this evening, and from a sister I received this morning 10s.

July 3. On the 1st came in 2s., and today, by the boxes in the Orphan-Houses, 2s. 10d., by sale of articles 1s. 9d., and from Suffolk was sent a donation of 2l. 10s.

July 7. It is now about six weeks since I have been daily entreating the Lord, both alone and with some of my fellow labourers, that He would be pleased to send us the supplies which we required, both to meet the ordinary and extraordinary expenses. Of late we have been also especially asking the Lord, that He would be pleased to send a rich supply before the public meetings, (which will commence, if the Lord will, on the 15th) in order that it may be seen that without public meetings, and without publishing fresh Reports, we are yet able, by faith and prayer, to draw down help from the living God. As to ourselves, through grace we should be able to lean upon the Lord, and expect help from Him, though not another Report were written, nor another public meeting held, at which the account about His dealings with us is given. We have given proof of this, in that when the year was up on May 10, 1843, no Report was published, and no meetings on the subject were held; and also when the second year had passed away, I still did not publish another account, because a weakness in one of my eyes seemed to point it out that the Lords time had not yet come, although by forcing the matter I might even then have written the Report. But whilst I do not write the Reports for the sake of obtaining money, nor give the account of the Lords dealings with us at the public meetings for the sake of influencing persons to help us with their means, nor do so for the sake of exposing our poverty; yet some persons might think so. Our prayer, therefore, had been particularly, that the Lord not only would be pleased to give us what we required day by day, but that He would also send in again largely, in order to show that He was willing to hear our prayers, and influence the minds of His children who have the means, to contribute considerably, though it was now more than two years since the last Report was published. Not that we were anxiously concerned even about this: for in the whole work we desire to stand with God, and not to depend upon the favourable or unfavourable judgment of the multitude; yet our souls longed, in pity to those who might seek an occasion, that even the shadow of ground might be cut off for persons to say:

"They cannot get any more money, and therefore they now publish another Report." My soul, therefore, had assurance that the Lord not only would supply our need up to the time when the accounts were closed and the public meetings would be held; but also that He would send in means more largely than He had done for some time past. And thus it was. When on Saturday evening, July 6th, more money was needed than there was in hand, I received about eight oclock a post-office order for 2l. from Jersey, of which half is for the Orphans and half for the other objects. There came in also at the same time 4s. 9d. by sale of articles. I received likewise at the same time a small paper box by post, containing four mourning rings (of fine stamped gold), 8 other gold rings, a gold seal, a gold locket, a pearl necklace, 2 brooches, a gold watch key, and a few other little things. This was a valuable donation, but doubly so under our circumstances. And now today A. B. sent 50l., of which I took one half for the Orphans, and the other half for the other funds. Besides the reasons just referred to, why this donation is so seasonable, I would only mention one more: The brother who kindly procures the oatmeal for us in Scotland, had written to say, that he had just now some which was very good, if we liked to have it. We could not say we needed none, for by the time it could be sent our meal would be gone: nothing therefore remained but to continue waiting on the Lord for means. And now, when we needed to send an answer, this 50l. came, so that we were able to order a ton of oatmeal. —1s. besides came in this day.

July 14. This is the last day before the accounts are closed, and this day also the Lord has sent in liberally. Being thus helped day by day up to the last moment of this period, we go on cheerfully to the next, leaning upon the Lord.

It is scarcely needful to state at the close of these details, with reference to the last two years and nine weeks, that, notwithstanding our having been often poor, and very poor, yet the children in the Orphan-Houses have always had the needful articles of clothing and nourishing food; indeed this is sufficiently proved by the healthy countenances of the children. Should any one question, that the children are provided with what they need, he may at any time have the proof of it, by seeing the children at their meals, inspecting their clothes, &c. But those who know what it is to walk in the fear of God, know also, that God would not help us, in answer to our prayers, if we hypocritically stated that the children were well provided with wholesome food, etc., and yet it were not true. Rather than keep the Orphans, whilst we were unable to provide for them, we would send them at once back to their relations.

On July 14, 1844, it was two years and nine weeks since the last public account about the Scriptural Knowledge Institution was given. In that last Report it was stated, that we desired to leave it to the Lords direction, as to the time when another should be published. When the year was expired, I saw no particular reason to lead me to think that I ought to serve the Church of Christ by publishing a fresh Narrative about the Orphan-Houses and the other objects of the Scriptural Knowledge Institution, neither did I see a leading of the Lord towards this service; and soon after, it pleased the Lord to call me to labour in Germany. Having returned in March 1844, it appeared to me desirable now to publish, at the close of the second year, which would be up on May 10, 1844, a fresh account: partly, because of the 5000 Reports, which had been printed, only a few copies were remaining; partly, because many believers expressed a great desire for some further account of the Lords dealings with us in the work; partly, because there was now an abundance of profitable matter ready to be communicated; and most of all, because I was longing to show by a public audited account, that the considerable sums, with which I had been entrusted, had been appropriated according to the intention of the donors. But much as I desired, for the above reasons, to have written the Report then, the weakness in one of my eyes already mentioned prevented my doing so, till at last, my eye being better, I was enabled to do so.

I now add a few particulars with reference to the operations of the Scriptural Knowledge Institution, for Home and Abroad, from May 10, 1842, to July 14, 1844. During this period also six Day-Schools for poor children were supported by the funds of this Institution. Besides this, the rent for the school-room of a seventh school, was paid during a great part of this period, and also occasional other assistance was given to this and two other schools. —The number of all the children that had schooling in the Day-Schools, through the medium of the Institution, from March 5, 1834, to July 14, 1844, amounts to 3319. The number of those in the six Day-Schools on July 14, 1844, was 338.

During this period likewise, one Sunday-School was supported by the funds of the Institution.

The number of adults that were instructed from Jan. 1841, to July 14, 1844, in the two adult schools of the Institution, amounts to 734 persons. The average attendance during the winter was from 50 to 70 persons, and in the summer from 20 to 40. The number on the list of adult scholars was on July 14, 1844, eighty persons. Books, writing materials, and instruction, are given entirely gratis to the adult scholars.

The number of Bibles and Testaments which were circulated from May 10, 1842, to July 14, 1844, is as follows: —237

Bibles were sold, and 284 Bibles were given away. 146 New Testaments were sold, and 162 New Testaments were given away.—From March 5, 1834, to July, 14, 1844, there were circulated 4,828 Bibles, and 3,357 New Testaments.

From May 10, 1842, to July 14, 1844, was laid out for missionary objects the sum of 234l. 8s. 6d., whereby assistance was rendered to the work of God in Jamaica, in Demerara, in Upper Canada, in the East Indies, in the Mauritius, and in Switzerland.

From May 10, 1842, to July 14, 1844, was laid out for the circulation of tracts the sum of 43l. 9s. 1 1/4d. During this period were circulated 39,473 tracts, and altogether were circulated, from Nov. 19, 1840, to July 14, 1844, 59,082 tracts.

From May 10, 1842, to July 14, 1844, there were received into the four Orphan-Houses, 39 Orphans, who, together with those who were in the houses on May 10, 1842, made up 125 in all. Of these: 1, One girl left the Institution against our will. Her aunt repeatedly applied to me to have her niece, who, having been more than eight years under our care, was now of use to her. I remonstrated with the aunt, and sought to show her the importance of leaving her niece with us for another twelvemonth, when she would be fit to be sent out to service; but all in vain. At last, knowing how exceedingly injurious her house would be for her niece, I told the aunt that I could not conscientiously dismiss the girl to go to her house; but the aunts influence induced the orphan to leave. May God, in tender mercy, visit the soul of this poor wanderer! Such cases are trying, very trying, but even concerning them faith contains a precious antidote. 2, Two of the children were removed by their friends, who by that time were able to provide for them. 3, One girl, who was received when grown up, we were obliged, after a long season of trial, to send back to her relations, in mercy to the other children. 4, Three girls were sent out to service, all three as believers. 5, Three Orphans died, one as an infant, and two in the faith. One had been more than two years in church fellowship, and had walked consistently. 6, Four boys were apprenticed, two of whom had been several years in church fellowship, before their apprenticeship.

There were on July 14, 1844, one hundred and twenty-one Orphans in the four houses. The number of the Orphans who were under our care from April 1836, to July 14, 1844, amounts to 183.

I notice further the following points in connexion with the Orphan-Houses.

1. Without any one having been personally applied to for any thing by me, the sum of 7748l. 16s. 4 3/4d. was given to me as the result of prayer to God, from Dec. 1835, to July, 14, 1844. 2. Besides this, also, many articles of clothing, furniture, provisions, etc., were given. 3. During these two years and two months we had very little sickness, comparatively in the four houses, though there was so much fever in Bristol. I mention this to the praise of the Lord, who mercifully preserved us.

The total of the income for the Orphan-Houses, from May 10, 1842, to July 14, 1844, was 2489l. 0s. 7 1/4d., leaving a balance of 1l. 11s. 11 3/4d. in hand on July 14, 1844.

—The total of the income for the other objects from May 10, 1842, to July 14, 1844, was 1164l. 18s. 4 1/4d., leaving a balance of 20l. 12s. 7d. in hand on July 14,1844.

I cannot omit mentioning that between. May 10, 1842, and July 14, 1844, there was admitted to communion one of the Sunday-School children, and one of the Day-School children. Likewise 6 more of the Orphans were received into church fellowship, so that up to July 14, 1844, altogether 29 of the Orphans had been admitted. In addition to this, between May 10, 1842, and July 14, 1844, one Orphan, before being received, died in the faith, and another, though but nine years of age, would have been received, had she not been just then removed by her relatives, who took her with them to America. But whilst we desire to receive these instances as precious encouragements from the Lord to continue our service, we cannot but believe, judging from the many prayers the Lord gives us for the dear children and adults under our care and instruction, that that which we see is but an earnest of a far larger harvest in the day of Christs appearing. —The greatest present visible blessing, which is resting upon the work, consists in what the Lord is pleased to do through the Narratives which are written and published respecting it; for a very considerable number, in various parts of the world, have through them either been converted, or, as believers, led on in the knowledge of God.

To avoid misunderstanding, it may be well to insert the following paragraph, which was written by my beloved brother and fellow labourer Henry Craik, and appended to the last Report.

"Hitherto, my name has been appended to the Report along with that of my beloved brother and fellow labourer George Müller; but, as the responsibility and management of the work devolve entirely upon him, it has seemed well to both of us, that, for the future, his signature should appear alone. —It is scarcely needful to add, that this alteration does not arise from any kind of disunion or even difference of judgment between us. I would especially recommend to the people of God, into whose hands this brief Narrative may fall, to read, examine and ponder the instructive facts and principles herein stated and illustrated; and I desire that the non-insertion of my name may not be understood as implying anything like a disapproval of the way in which the Scriptural Knowledge Institution has been conducted from the beginning. As the honour of being the instrument in this great and blessed work belongs to him, and, in no degree, to me, I feel a satisfaction in the omission of my name, lest, otherwise, I should even appear to glory in another mans labour.

HENRY CRAIK."

Thus far only, for the present at least, do I think it well to continue the accounts of the Lords dealings with me. But I cannot conclude this third part, without adding some hints on a few passages of the word of God, both because I have so very frequently found them little regarded by Christians, and also because I have proved their preciousness, in some measure, in my own experience; and therefore wish that all my fellow saints may share the blessing with me.

1. In Matthew vi 19-21, it is written: "Lay not up for yourselves treasures upon earth, where moth and rust doth corrupt, and where thieves break through and steal; but lay up for yourselves treasures in heaven, where neither moth nor rust doth corrupt, and where thieves do not break through nor steal: for where your treasure is, there will your heart be also."—Observe, dear Reader, the following points concerning this part of the divine testimony: 1, It is the Lord Jesus, our Lord and Master, who speaks this as the lawgiver of His people. He who has infinite wisdom and unfathomable love to us, who therefore both knows what is for our real welfare and happiness, and who cannot exact

from us any requirement inconsistent with that love which led Him to lay down His life for us. Remembering, then, who it is who speaks to us in these verses, let us consider them. 2, His counsel, His affectionate entreaty, and His commandment to us His disciples is: "Lay not up for yourselves treasures upon earth." The meaning obviously is, that the disciples of the Lord Jesus, being strangers and pilgrims on earth, i.e. neither belonging to the earth nor expecting to remain in it, should not seek to increase their earthly possessions, in whatever these possessions may consist. This is a word for poor believers as well as for rich believers; it has as much a reference to putting shillings into the savings banks as to putting thousands of pounds into the funds, or purchasing one house, or one farm after another.—It may be said, but does not every prudent and provident person seek to increase his means, that he may have a goodly portion to leave to his children, or to have something for old age, or for the time of sickness, etc.? My reply is, it is quite true that this is the custom of the world. It was thus in the days of our Lord, and Paul refers to this custom of the world when he says, "The children ought not to lay up for the parents, but the parents for the children." 2 Cor. xii. 14. But whilst thus it is in the world, and we have every reason to believe ever will be so among those that are of the world, and who therefore have their portion on earth, we disciples of the Lord Jesus, being born again, being the children of God not nominally, but really, being truly partakers of the divine nature, being in fellowship with the Father and the Son, and having in prospect "an inheritance incorruptible, and undefiled, and that fadeth not away" (1 Peter i. 4.), ought in every respect to act differently from the world, and so in this particular also. If we disciples of the Lord Jesus seek, like the people of the world, after an increase of our possessions, may not those who are of the world justly question whether we believe what we say, when we speak about our inheritance, our heavenly calling, our being the children of God, etc.? Often it must be a sad stumbling block to the unbeliever to see a professed believer in the Lord Jesus acting in this particular just like himself. Consider this, dear brethren in the Lord, should this remark apply to you.—I have more than once had the following passage quoted to me as a proof that parents ought to lay up money for their children, or husbands for their wives: "But if any provide not for his own, and especially for those of his own house (or kindred), he hath denied the faith, and is worse than an infidel." 1 Tim. v. 8. It is, however, concerning this verse, only needful, in childlike simplicity to read the connexion from verse 3 to 5, and it will be obvious that the meaning is this, that whilst the poor widows of the church are to be cared for by the church, yet if any such needy believing widow had children or grandchildren (not nephews), these children or grandchildren should provide for the widow, that the church might not be charged; but that, if a believers child or grandchild, in such a case did not do so, such a one did not act according to the obligations laid upon him by his holy faith, and was worse than an unbeliever. Not a word, then, is there in this passage to favour the laying up treasures upon earth for our children, or our wives. 3, Our Lord says concerning the earth, that it is a place "where moth and rust doth corrupt, and where thieves break through and steal." All that is of the earth, and in any way connected with it, is subject to corruption, to change, to dissolution. There is no reality, or substance, in any thing else but in heavenly things. Often the careful amassing of earthly possessions ends in losing them in a moment by fire, by robbery, by a change of mercantile concerns, by loss of work, etc.; but suppose all this were not the case, still, yet a little while, and thy soul shall be required of thee; or, yet a little while, and the Lord Jesus will return; and what profit shalt thou then have, dear reader, if

251

thou hast carefully sought to increase thy earthly possessions? My brother, if there were one particle of real benefit to be derived from it, would not He, whose love to us has been proved to the uttermost, have wished that you and I should have it? If, in the least degree, it could tend to the increase of our peace, or joy in the Holy Ghost, or heavenly-mindedness, He, who laid down His life for us, would have commanded us, to "LAY UP treasure upon earth." 4, Our Lord, however, does not merely bid us, not to lay up treasure upon earth; for if He had said no more, this His commandment might be abused, and persons might find in it an encouragement for their extravagant habits, for their love of pleasure, for their habit of spending every thing they have, or can obtain, upon themselves. It does not mean, then, as is the common phrase, that we should "live up to our income;" for, He adds: "But lay up for yourselves treasures in heaven." There is such a thing as laying up as truly in heaven as there is laying up on earth; if it were not so, our Lord would not have said so. Just as persons put one sum after another into the bank, and it is put down to their credit, and they may use the money afterwards: so truly the penny, the shilling, the pound, the hundred pounds, the ten thousand pounds, given for the Lords sake, and constrained by the love of Jesus, to poor brethren, or in any way spent in the work of God, He marks down in the book of remembrance, He considers as laid up in heaven. The money is not lost, it is laid up in the bank of heaven; yet so, that, whilst an earthly bank may break, or through earthly circumstances we may lose our earthly possessions, the money, which is thus secured in heaven, cannot be lost. But this is by no means the only difference. I notice a few more points. Treasures laid up on earth bring along with them many cares; treasures laid up in heaven never give care. Treasures laid up on earth never can afford spiritual joy; treasures laid up in heaven bring along with them

peace and joy in the Holy Ghost even now. Treasures laid
up on earth, in a dying hour cannot afford peace and
comfort, and when life is over, they are taken from us;
treasures laid up in heaven draw forth thanksgiving, that
we were permitted and counted worthy to serve the Lord
with the means with which He was pleased to intrust us as
stewards; and when this life is over we are not deprived of
what was laid up there, but when we go to heaven we go to
the place where our treasures are, and we shall find them
there. Often we hear it said when a person has died: he died
worth so much. But whatever be the phrases common in
the world, it is certain that a person may die worth fifty
thousand pounds sterling, as the world reckons, and yet
that individual may not possess, in the sight of God, one
thousand pounds sterling, because he was not rich towards
God, he did not lay up treasure in heaven. And so on the
other hand, we can suppose a man of God falling asleep in
Jesus, and his surviving widow finding scarcely enough left
behind him to suffice for the funeral, who was nevertheless
rich towards God; in the sight of God he may possess five
thousand pounds sterling, he may have laid up that sum in
heaven. Dear Reader, does your soul long to be rich towards
God, to lay up treasures in heaven? The world passes away
and the lust thereof! Yet a little while, and our stewardship
will be taken from us. At present we have the opportunity
of serving the Lord, with our time, our talents, our bodily
strength, our gifts, and also with our property; but shortly
this opportunity may cease. Oh! how shortly may it cease.
Before ever this is read by any one, I may have fallen asleep;
and the very next day after you have read this, dear Reader,
you may fall asleep, and therefore, whilst we have the
opportunity, let us serve the Lord. —I believe, and therefore I
speak. My own soul is so fully assured of the wisdom and
love of the Lord towards us His disciples as expressed in this
word, that by His grace I do most heartily set my seal to the

preciousness of the command, and I do from my inmost soul not only desire not to lay up treasures upon earth, but, believing as I do what the Lord says, I do desire to have grace to lay up treasures in heaven. And then, suppose after a little while you should fall asleep, some one may say, your wife and, child will be unprovided for, because you did not make a provision for them. My reply is, the Lord will take care of them. The Lord will abundantly provide for them, as He now abundantly provides for us. 5, The Lord lastly adds: "For where your treasure is, there will your heart be also." Where should the heart of the disciple of the Lord Jesus be, but in heaven? Our calling is a heavenly calling, our inheritance is a heavenly inheritance, and reserved for us in heaven; our citizenship is in heaven; but if we believers in the Lord Jesus lay up treasures on earth, the necessary result of it is, that our hearts will be upon earth; nay, the very fact of our doing so proves that they are there! Nor will it be otherwise, till there be a ceasing to lay up treasures upon earth. The believer who lays up treasures upon earth may, at first, not live openly in sin; he in a measure may yet bring some honour to the Lord in certain things; but the injurious tendencies of this habit will show themselves more and more, whilst the habit of laying up treasures in heaven would draw the heart more and more heavenward; would be continually strengthening his new, his divine nature, his spiritual faculties, because it would call his spiritual faculties into use, and thus they would be strengthened; and he would more and more, whilst yet in the body, have his heart in heaven, and set upon heavenly things; and thus the laying up treasures in heaven would bring along with it, even in this life, precious spiritual blessings as a reward of obedience to the commandment of our Lord.

II. The next passage, on which I desire to make a few remarks, is Matthew vi. 33. "But seek ye first the kingdom of God and His righteousness; and all these things shall be added unto you." After our Lord, in the previous verses, had been pointing His disciples "to the fowls of the air," and "the lilies of the field," in order that they should be without carefulness about the necessaries of life; He adds: "Therefore take no thought, (literally, be not anxious) saying, What shall we eat? or, What shall we drink? or, Wherewithal shall we be clothed? (For after all these things do the Gentiles seek;) for your heavenly Father knoweth that ye have need of all these things." Observe here particularly that we, the children of God, should be different from the nations of the earth, from those who have no Father in heaven, and who therefore make it their great business, their first anxious concern, what they shall eat, and what they shall drink, and wherewithal they shall be clothed. We, the children of God, should, as in every other respect, so in this particular also, be different from the world, and prove to the world that we believe that we have a Father in heaven, who knoweth that we have need of all these things. The fact that our Almighty Father, who is full of infinite love to us His children, (and who has proved to us His love in the gift of His only begotten Son, and His almighty power in raising him from the dead), knows that we have need of these things, should remove all anxiety from our minds. There is, however, one thing that we have to attend to, and which we ought to attend to, with reference to our temporal necessities, it is mentioned in our verse: "But seek ye first the kingdom of God and His righteousness." The great business which the disciple of the Lord Jesus has to be concerned about (for this word was spoken to disciples, to professed believers) is, to seek the kingdom of God, i.e. to seek, as I view it, after the external and internal prosperity of the church of Christ. If, according to our ability, and according to the opportunity which the Lord gives us, we seek to win souls for the Lord Jesus, that appears to me to be seeking the eternal prosperity of the kingdom of God; and if we, as members of the body of Christ, seek to benefit our fellow members in the body, helping them on in grace and truth, or caring for them in any way to their edification, that would be seeking the internal prosperity of the kingdom of God. But in connexion with this we have also "to seek His righteousness," which means, (as it was spoken to disciples, to those who have a Father in heaven, and not to those who were without), to seek to be more and more like God, to seek to be inwardly conformed to the mind of God. —If these two things are attended to, (and they imply also that we are not slothful in business), then do we come under that precious promise: "And all these things (that is food, raiment, or anything else that is needful for this present life), shall be added unto you." It is not for attending to these two things that we obtain the blessing, but in attending to them.

I now ask you, my dear Reader, a few questions in all love, because I do seek your welfare, and I do not wish to put these questions to you, without putting them first to my own heart. Do you make it your primary business, your first great concern to seek the kingdom of God and His righteousness? Are the things of God, the honour of His name, the welfare of His Church, the conversion of sinners, and the profit of your own soul, your chief aim? Or does your business, or your family, or your own temporal concerns, in some shape or other primarily occupy your attention? If the latter be the case, then, though you may have all the necessaries of life, yet could you be surprised if you had them not? Remember that the world passeth away, but that the things of God endure for ever.

I never knew a child of God who acted according to the above passage, in whose experience the Lord did not fulfil His word of promise "All these things shall be added unto you."

III. The third portion of the divine testimony, on which I desire to throw out a few hints, is in I John i. 3. "And truly our fellowship is with the Father, and with his Son Jesus Christ." Observe!, The words "fellowship," "communion," "coparticipation," and "partnership," mean the same. 2, The believer in the Lord Jesus does not only obtain forgiveness of all his sins (as he does through the shedding of the blood of Jesus, by faith in His name;) does not only become a righteous one before God (through the righteousness of the Lord Jesus, by faith in His name;) is not only begotten again, born of God, and partaker of the divine nature, and therefore a child of God, and an heir of God; but he is also in fellowship or partnership with God. Now, so far as it regards God, and our standing in the Lord Jesus, we have this blessing once for all; nor does it allow of either an increase or a decrease. Just as Gods love to us believers, His children, is unalterably the same (whatever may be the manifestations of that love:) and as His peace with us is the same, (however much our peace may be disturbed:) so it is also with regard to our being in fellowship or partnership with Him: it remains unalterably the same, so far as God is concerned. But then 3, there is an experimental fellowship, or partnership, with the Father and with His Son, which consists in this, that all which we possess in God, as being the partners or fellows of God, is brought down into our daily life, is enjoyed, experienced, and used. This experimental fellowship, or partnership, allows of an increase or a decrease, in the measure in which faith is in exercise, and in which we are entering into what we have received in the Lord Jesus. The measure in which we enjoy this experimental fellowship with the Father and with the Son is without limit; for without limit we may make use of our partnership with the Father and with the Son, and draw by prayer and faith out of the inexhaustible fulness which there is in God. —Let us now take a few instances in order to see the practical working of this experimental fellowship (or partnership) with the Father and with the Son. Suppose there are two believing parents who were not brought to the knowledge of the truth until some years after the Lord had given them several children. Their children were brought up in sinful, evil ways, whilst the parents did not know the Lord. Now the parents reap as they sowed. They suffer from having set an evil example before their children; for their children are unruly and behave most improperly. What is now to be done? Need such parents despair? No. The first thing they have to do is, to make confession of their sins to God, with regard to neglecting their children whilst they were themselves living in sin, and then to remember that they are in partnership with God, and therefore to be of good courage, though they are in themselves still utterly insufficient for the task of managing their children. They have in themselves neither the wisdom, nor the patience, nor the long-suffering, nor the gentleness, nor the meekness, nor the love, nor the decision and firmness, nor any thing else that may be needful in dealing with their children aright. But their heavenly Father has all this. The Lord Jesus possesses all this. And they are in partnership with the Father, and with the Son, and therefore they can obtain by prayer and faith all they need out of the fulness of God. I say by prayer and faith; for we have to make known our need to God in prayer, ask His help, and then we have to believe that He will give us what we need. Prayer alone is not enough. We may pray never so much, yet if we do not believe that God will give us what we need, we have no reason to expect that we shall receive what we have asked for. So then these parents would need to ask God to give them the needful wisdom, patience, long-suffering, gentleness, meekness, love, decision, firmness, and whatever else they may judge they need. They may in humble boldness remind their heavenly Father that His word assures them that they are in partnership with Him, and, as they themselves are lacking in these particulars, ask Him to be pleased to supply their need; and then they have to believe that God will do it, and they shall receive according to their need. — Another instance: suppose I am so situated in my business that day by day such difficulties arise, that I continually find that I take wrong steps, by reason of these great difficulties. How may the case be altered for the better? In myself I see no remedy for the difficulties. In looking at myself I can expect nothing but to make still further mistakes, and, therefore, trial upon trial seems to be before me. And yet I need not despair. The living God is my partner. I have not sufficient wisdom to meet these difficulties so as to be able to know what steps to take, but He is able to direct me. What I have, therefore, to do is this: in simplicity to spread my case before my heavenly Father and my Lord Jesus. The Father and the Son are my partners. I have to tell out my heart to God, and to ask Him, that, as He is my partner, and I have no wisdom in myself to meet all the many difficulties which continually occur in my business, He would be pleased to guide and direct me, and to supply me with the needful wisdom; and then I have to believe that God will do so, and go with good courage to my business, and expect help from Him in the next difficulty that may come before me. I have to look out for guidance, I have to expect counsel from the Lord; and, as assuredly as I do so, I shall have it, I shall find that I am not nominally, but really in partnership with the Father and with the Son. — Another instance: There are a father and mother with seven small children. Both parents are believers. The father works in a manufactory, but cannot earn more than ten shillings per week. The mother cannot earn any thing. These ten shillings are too little for the supply of nourishing and wholesome food for seven growing children and their parents, and for providing them with the other necessaries of life. What is to be done in such a case? Surely not to find fault with the manufacturer, who may not be able to afford more wages, and much less to murmur against God; but the parents have in simplicity to tell God, their partner, that the wages of ten shillings a week are not sufficient in England to provide nine persons with all they need, so as that their health be not injured. They have to remind God that He is not hard master, not an unkind being, but a most loving Father, who has abundantly proved the love of His heart in the gift of His only begotten Son. And they have in childlike simplicity to ask Him, that either He would order it so, that the manufacturer may be able to allow more wages; or that He (the Lord) would find them another place, where the father would be able to earn more; or that He would be pleased somehow or other, as it may seem good to Him, to supply them with more means. They have to ask the Lord, in childlike simplicity, again and again for it, if He does not answer their request at once; and they have to believe that God, their Father and partner, will give them the desire of their hearts. They have to expect an answer to their prayers; day by day they have to look out for it, and to repeat their request till God grants it. As assuredly as they believe that God will grant them their request, so assuredly it shall be granted. —Thus, suppose, I desired more power over my besetting sins; suppose, I desired more power against certain temptations; suppose I desired more wisdom, or grace, or any thing else that I may need in my service among the saints, or in my service towards the unconverted: what have I to do, but to make use of my being in fellowship with the

261

Father and with the Son? Just as, for instance, an old faithful clerk, who is this day taken into partnership by an immensely rich firm, though himself altogether without property, would not be discouraged by reason of a large payment having to be made by the firm within three days, though he himself has no money at all of his own, but would comfort himself with the immense riches possessed by those who so generously have just taken him into partnership: so should we, the children of God and servants of Jesus Christ, comfort ourselves by being in fellowship, or partnership, with the Father, and with the Son, though we have no power of our own against our besetting sins; though we cannot withstand temptations, which are before us, in our own strength; and though we have neither sufficient grace nor wisdom for our service among the saints, or towards the unconverted. All we have to do is, to draw upon our partner, the living God. By prayer and faith we may obtain all needful temporal and spiritual help and blessings. In all simplicity have we to tell out our heart before God, and then we have to believe that He will give to us according to our need. But if we do not believe that God will help us, could we be at peace? The clerk, taken into the firm as partner, believes that the firm will meet the payment though so large, and though in three days it is to be made, and it is this that keeps his heart quiet, though altogether poor himself. We have to believe that our infinitely rich partner, the living God, will help us in our need, and we shall not only be in peace, but we shall actually find that the help which we need will be granted to us. —Let not the consciousness of your entire unworthiness keep you, dear reader, from believing what God has said concerning you. If you are indeed a believer in the Lord Jesus, then this precious privilege, of being in partnership with the Father and the Son, is yours, though you and I are entirely unworthy of it. If the consciousness of our unworthiness were to keep us from believing what God has said concerning those who depend upon and trust in the Lord Jesus for salvation, then we should find that there is not one single blessing, with which we have been blessed in the Lord Jesus, from which, on account of our unworthiness, we could derive any settled comfort or peace.

IV. There is one other point which, in connexion with several portions of the word of God, which bear on the subject, I desire to bring before the believing reader, and it refers to the "scriptural way of overcoming the difficulties with which the believer now meets who is engaged in a business, trade, profession, or any earthly calling whatever, which arise from competition in business, too great a number of persons being occupied in the same calling, stagnation of trade, and the like." The children of God, who are strangers and pilgrims on earth, have at all times had difficulty in the world, for they are not at home but from home; nor should they, until the return of the Lord Jesus, expect it to be otherwise with them. But whilst this is true, it is also true that the Lord has provided us in all our difficulties with something in His own word to meet them. All difficulties may be overcome by acting according to the word of God. At this time I more especially desire to point out the means whereby the children of God who are engaged in any earthly calling may be able to overcome the difficulties, which arise from competition in business, too great a number of persons being occupied in the same calling, stagnation of trade and the like.

1, The first thing which the believer, who is in such difficulties, has to ask himself is, Am I in a calling in which I can abide with God? If our occupation be of that kind, that we cannot ask Gods blessing upon it, or that we should be ashamed to be found in it at the appearing of the Lord Jesus, or that it of necessity hinders our spiritual progress, then we must give it up, and be engaged in something else; but in few cases only this is needful. Far the greater part of the occupations in which believers are engaged are not of such a nature, as that they need to give them up in order to maintain a good conscience, and in order to be able to walk with God, though, perhaps, certain alterations may need to be made in the manner of conducting their trade, business, or profession. About those parts of our calling, which may need alteration, we shall receive instruction from the Lord, if we indeed desire it, and wait upon Him for it, and expect it from Him.

2, Now suppose the believer is in a calling in which he can abide with God, the next point to be settled is: "Why do I carry on this business, or why am I engaged in this trade or profession?" In most instances, so far as my experience goes, which I have gathered in my service among the saints during the last fifty-one years and a half, I believe the answer would be: "I am engaged in my earthly calling, that I may earn the means of obtaining the necessaries of life for myself and family." Here is the chief error from which almost all the rest of the errors, which are entertained by children of God, relative to their calling, spring. It is no right and Scriptural motive, to be engaged in a trade, or business, or profession, merely in order to earn the means for the obtaining of the necessaries of life for ourselves and family; but us should work, because it is the Lords will concerning us. This is plain from the following passages; I Thess. iv. 11, 12; II Thess. iii. 10-12; Eph. iv. 28. It is quite true that, in general, the Lord provides the necessaries of life by means of our ordinary calling; but that that is not THE REASON why we should work, is plain enough from the consideration, that if our possessing the necessaries of life depended upon our ability of working, we could never have freedom from anxiety, for we should always have to say to ourselves, and what shall I do when I am too old to work I or when by reason of sickness I am unable to earn my bread? But if on the other hand, we are engaged in our earthly calling, because it is the will of time Lord concerning us that we should work, and that thus labouring we may provide for our families and also be able to support the weak, the sick, the aged, and the needy, then we have good and scriptural reason to say to ourselves: should it please the Lord to lay me on a bed of sickness, or keep me otherwise by reason of infirmity or old age, or want of employment, from earning my bread by means of the labour of my hands, or my business, or my profession, He will yet provide for me. Because we who believe are servants of Jesus Christ, who has bought us with His own precious blood, and are not our own, and because this our precious Lord and Master has commanded us to work, therefore we work; and in doing so our Lord will provide for us; but whether in this way or any other way, He is sure to provide for us; for we labour in obedience to Him; and if even a just earthly master give wages to his servants, the Lord will surely see to it that we have our wages, if in obedience to Him we are engaged in our calling, and not for our own sake. How great the difference between acting according to the word of God, and according to our own natural desires, or the customs of the world, will be plain, I trust, by the following case. Suppose I were engaged in some useful trade. Suppose I had the certain human prospect, that within the next three months my labour would bring me in nothing, for certain reasons connected with the state of mercantile affairs. As a man of the world I should say, I shall not work at all, because my labour will not be paid; but as a Christian, who desires to act according to Gods Holy word, I ought to say: My trade is useful to society, and I will work notwithstanding all human prospects, because the Lord

Jesus has commanded me to labour; from Him and not from my trade I expect my wages. In addition to this the Christian ought also to say, Idleness is a dreadful snare of the devil, he has especial opportunity to get an advantage over the children of God when they are unoccupied; and, therefore, I will work though I have no human prospect of obtaining payment for my labour, but shall get only the cost price of the material, and shall have to give my work for nothing. Moreover the Christian ought to say, Though according to human probability I shall have to labour for nothing during the next three months, yet I will work, because the Lord may speedily alter the state of things, contrary to all human expectation; but whether He be pleased to do so or not, I labour because I am the Lords, bought by His precious blood, and He commands me to labour. —But there are motives still lower than to be engaged in our earthly calling merely that we may earn the means of obtaining the necessaries of life, why even Christians, true children of God, may be engaged in their calling, such as: to obtain a certain sum of money, and then to retire from business and to live upon the interest; or, to provide something for old age; or, to obtain a certain amount of property, without intending to give up business. If it be unscriptural to be engaged in our calling, merely, even for the sake of earning the means for procuring the necessaries of life for ourselves and family, how much more unbecoming that a child of God should be engaged in his calling for the sake of any of the last mentioned reasons. — This second point, then, Why do I carry on this business? Why am I engaged in this trade or profession? ought first to be settled in the fear of God and according to the revealed will of God; and if we cannot say in honesty of heart, I do carry on my business, I am engaged in my trade, or art, or profession, as a servant of Jesus Christ, whose I am, because He has bought me with His precious blood, and He has commanded me to work, and therefore I work: I say, if we cannot say this in honesty of heart, but must confess that we work on account of lower motives such as, that we may earn our bread, or on account of still lower motives, and such which are altogether unbecoming a child of God, who is not of the world but of God, such as, to obtain a certain sum of money in order to be able to live on the interest without having to work; or, to provide something for old age; or, to obtain a certain amount of property without intending to give up business: if these are our motives for being engaged in our calling, I say, can we be surprised that we meet with great difficulties in our business, and that the Lord in His abounding love to us, His erring children, does not allow us to succeed? But suppose this second point is scripturally settled, and we can honestly say that, because we are servants of Jesus Christ, we are occupied as we are— we have further to consider: 3, Whether we carry on our business, or are engaged in our trade, art, or profession as stewards of the Lord. To the child of God it ought not to be enough that he is in a calling in which he can abide with God, nor that he is engaged in his calling, because it is the will of his Lord and Master that he should work, but he should consider himself in his trade, business, art, or profession, only as the steward of the Lord with reference to his income. The child of God has been bought with the precious blood of the Lord Jesus, and is altogether His property, with all that he possesses, his bodily strength, his mental strength, his ability of every kind, his trade, business, art, or profession, his property, &c.; for it is written: "Ye are not your own; for ye are bought with a price." I Cor. vi. 19, 20. The proceeds of our calling are therefore not our own in the sense of using them as our natural heart wishes us to do, whether to spend them on the gratification of our pride, or our love of pleasure, or sensual indulgences, or to lay by the money for ourselves or

267

our children, or use it in any way as we naturally like; but we have to stand before our Lord and Master, whose stewards we are, to seek to ascertain His will, how He will have us use the proceeds of our calling. But is this indeed the spirit in which the children of God generally are engaged in their calling? It is but too well known that it is not the case! Can we then wonder at it, that even Gods own dear children should so often be found greatly in difficulty with regard to their calling, and be found so often complaining about stagnation or competition in trade, and the difficulties of the times, though there have been given to them such precious promises as: "Seek ye first the kingdom of God and His righteousness; and all these things shall be added unto you;" or, "Let your conversation (disposition or turn of mind) be without covetousness; and be content with such things as ye have: for He hath said, I will never leave thee, nor forsake thee." Heb. xiii. 5. Is it not obvious enough, that, when our Heavenly Father sees that we His children do or would use the proceeds of our calling, as our natural mind would desire, that He either cannot at all intrust us with means, or will be obliged to decrease them? No wise and really affectionate mother will permit her infant to play with a razor, or with fire, however much the child may desire to have them; and so the love and wisdom of our Heavenly Father will not, cannot, intrust us with pecuniary means, (except it be in the way of chastisement, or to show us finally their utter vanity,) if He sees that we do not desire to possess them as stewards for Him, in order that we may spend them as He may point out to us by His Holy Spirit, through His word.—In connexion with this subject, I give a few hints to the believing reader on three passages of the word of God. In I Cor. xvi. 2, we find it written to the brethren at Corinth, "Upon the first day of the week let every one of you lay by him in store, as God has prospered him." A contribution for the poor saints in Judea was to be made, and the brethren at Corinth were exhorted to put by every Lords day, according to the measure of success which the Lord had been pleased to grant them in their calling during the week. Now, ought not the saints in our day also to act according to this word! There is no passage in the word of God, why we should not do so, and it is altogether in accordance with our pilgrim character, not only once or twice, or four times a year to see how much we can afford to give to the poor saints, or to the work of God in any way, but to seek to settle it weekly. If, it be said, I cannot ascertain how much I have gained in the course of the week by my business, and therefore I cannot give accordingly; my reply is this, Seek, dear brethren, as much as possible to bring your business upon such a footing, as that you may be able, as nearly as possible, to settle how much you have earned in your calling in the course of the week; but suppose you should be unable to settle it exactly to the shilling or pound, yet you will know pretty well how it has been with you during the week, and therefore, according to your best knowledge, contribute on the coming Lords day towards the necessities of the poor saints, and towards the work of God, as He, after your having sought His guidance, may lead you. Perhaps you say, the weeks are so unlike; in one week I may earn three or even ten times as much as in another week, and if I give according to my earnings from my calling during a very good week, then how are such weeks, when I earn scarcely any thing, or how are the bad debts to be met? How shall I do when sickness befalls my family, or when other trials productive of expense come upon me, if I do not make provision for such seasons? My reply is, 1, I do not find in the whole New Testament one single passage in which either directly or indirectly exhortations are given to provide against deadness in business, bad debts and sickness, by laying up money. 2, Often the Lord is obliged to allow deadness in business, or

269

bad debts, or sickness in our family, or other trials, which increase our expenses, to befall us, because we do not, as His stewards, act according to stewardship, but as if we were owners of what we have, forgetting that the time has not yet come when we shall enter upon our possessions and He does so in order that, by these losses and expenses, our property which we have collected may be decreased, lest we should altogether set our hearts again upon earthly things, and forget God entirely. His love is so great, that He will not let His children quietly go their own way when they have forsaken Him; but if His loving admonitions by His Holy Spirit are disregarded, He is obliged in fatherly love to chastise them. A striking illustration of what I have said we have in the case of Israel nationally. The commandment to them was, to leave their land uncultivated in the seventh year, in order that it might rest; and the Lord promised to make up for this deficiency by His abundant blessing resting upon the sixth year. However, Israel acted not according to this commandment, no doubt saying in the unbelief of their hearts, as the Lord had foretold, "What shall we eat in the seventh year? Behold we shall not sow, nor gather in our increase." Leviticus xxv. But what did the Lord do? He was determined the land should have rest, and as the Israelites did not willingly give it, He sent them for seventy years into captivity, in order that thus the land might have rest. See Leviticus xxvi. 33-35. Beloved brethren in the Lord, let us take heed so to walk as that the Lord may not be obliged, by chastisement to take a part of our earthly possessions from us in the way of bad debts, sickness, decrease of business, or the like, because we would not own our position as stewards, but act as owners, and keep for ourselves the means with which the Lord had intrusted us, not for the gratification of our own carnal mind, but for the sake of using them in His service and to His praise. It might also be said by a brother whose earnings are small, should I also give according to my earnings? They are already so small, that my wife can only with the greatest difficulty manage to make them sufficient for the family. My reply is: Have you ever considered, my brother, that the very reason, why the Lord is obliged to let your earnings remain so small, may be the fact of your spending every thing upon yourselves, and that if He were to give you more, you would only use it to increase your own family comfort, instead of looking about to see who among the brethren are sick, or who have no work at all, that you might help them, or how you might assist the work of God at home and abroad? There is a great temptation for a brother whose earnings are small, to put off the responsibility of assisting the needy and sick saints, or helping on the work of God, and to lay it upon the few rich brethren and sisters with whom he is associated in fellowship, and thus rob his own soul!—It might be asked, How much shall I give of my income? The tenth part, or the fifth part, or the third part, or one-half, or more? My reply is, God lays down no rule, concerning this point. What we do we should do cheerfully and not of necessity. But if even Jacob with the first dawning of spiritual light (Genesis xxviii. 22) promised to God the tenth of all He should give to him, how much ought we believers in the Lord Jesus to do for Him; we, whose calling is a heavenly one, and who know distinctly that we are children of God, and joint heirs with the Lord Jesus! Yet do all the children of God give even the tenth part of what the Lord gives them?

That would be two shillings per week for the brother who earns 1l., and 4s. to him who earns 2l., and 2l. per week to him whose income is 20l. per week.

In connexion with I Cor. xvi. 2, I would mention two other portions: 1. "He which soweth sparingly shall reap also sparingly: and he that soweth bountifully, shall reap also bountifully." II Cor. ix. 6. It is certain that we children of God are so abundantly blessed in Jesus, by the grace of God, that we ought to need no stimulus to good works. The forgiveness of our sins, the having been made for ever the children of God, the having before us the Fathers house as our home: these blessings ought to be sufficient motives to constrain us in love and gratitude to serve God abundantly all the days of our life, and cheerfully also to give up, as He may call for it, that with which He has intrusted us of the things of this world. But whilst this is the case, the Lord nevertheless holds out to us in His Holy Word motives why we should serve Him, deny ourselves, use our property for Him, etc.; and the last mentioned passage is one of that kind. The verse is true, both with reference to the life that is now and that which is to come. If we have been sparingly using our property for Him, there will have been little treasure laid up in heaven, and therefore a small amount of capital will be found in the world to come, so far as it regards reaping. Again, we shall reap bountifully if we seek to be rich towards God, by abundantly using our means for Him, whether in ministering to the necessities of the poor saints, or using otherwise our pecuniary means for His work. Dear brethren, these things are realities! Shortly, very shortly, will come the reaping time, and then will be the question, whether we shall reap sparingly or bountifully. — But while this passage refers to the life hereafter, it also refers to the life that now is. Just as now the love of Christ constrains us to communicate of that with which the Lord intrusts us, so will be the present reaping, both with regard to spiritual and temporal things. Should there be found therefore in a brother the want of entering into his position as being merely a steward for the Lord in his calling, and should he give no heed to the admonitions of the Holy Ghost to communicate to those who are in need, or to help the work of God; then, can such a brother be surprised that he meets with great difficulties in his calling, and that he cannot get on? This is according to the Lords word. He is sowing sparingly, and he therefore reaps sparingly. But should the love of Christ constrain a brother, out of the earnings of his calling to sow bountifully, he will even in this life reap bountifully, both with regard to blessings in his soul and with regard to temporal things. Consider in connexion with this the following passage, which, though taken from the Book of Proverbs, is not of a Jewish character, but true concerning believers under the present dispensation also: "There is that scattereth, and yet increaseth; and there is that withholdeth more than is meet, but it tendeth to poverty. The liberal son shall be made fat: and he that watereth shall be watered also himself." Prov. xi. 24, 25. — In connexion with 1 Cor. xvi. 2, I would also direct my brethren in the Lord to the promise made in Luke vi. 38, "Give and it shall be given unto you: good measure, pressed down, and shaken together, and running over, shall men give into your bosom. For with the same measure that ye mete withal it shall be measured to you again." This refers evidently to the present dispensation, and evidently in its primary meaning to temporal things. Now let any one, constrained by the love of Jesus, act according to this passage; let him on the first day of the week communicate as the Lord has prospered him, and he will see that the Lord will act according to what is contained in this verse. If pride constrain us to give, if self-righteousness make us liberal, if natural feeling induce us to communicate, or if we give whilst we are in a state of insolvency, not possessing more perhaps than ten shillings in the pound were our creditors to come upon us; then we cannot expect to have this verse fulfilled in our experience: nor should we give at any time for the sake of receiving again from others, according to this verse; but if indeed the love of Christ constrain us to communicate according to the ability which the Lord gives

273

us, then we shall have this verse fulfilled in our experience, though this was not the motive that induced us to give. Somehow or other the Lord will abundantly repay us through the instrumentality of our fellow men what we are doing for His poor saints, or in any way for His work, and we shall find that in the end we are not losers, even with reference to temporal things, whilst we communicate liberally of the things of this life with which the Lord has intrusted us.—Here it might be remarked: but if it be so, that even in this life, and with regard to temporal things it is true, that "To him that gives shall be given, good measure, pressed down, and shaken together, and running over," and that "He which soweth bountifully shall reap also bountifully," then in the end the most liberal persons would be exceedingly rich. Concerning this remark we have to keep in mind, that the moment persons were to begin to give for the sake of receiving more back again from the Lord, through the instrumentality of their fellow men, than they have given; or the moment persons wished to alter their way, and no more go on sowing bountifully, but sparingly, in order to increase their possessions, whilst God is allowing them to reap bountifully, the river of Gods bounty toward them would no longer continue to flow. God had supplied them abundantly with means, because He saw them act as stewards for Him. He had intrusted them with a little which they used for Him, and He therefore intrusted them with more; and if they had continued to use the much also for Him, He would have still more abundantly used them as instruments to scatter abroad His bounties. The child of God must be willing to be a channel through which Gods bounties flow, both with regard to temporal and spiritual things. This channel is narrow and shallow at first, it may be; yet there is room for some of the waters of Gods bounty to pass through. And if we cheerfully yield ourselves as channels, for this purpose, then the channel becomes wider and deeper, and the waters of the bounty of God can pass through more abundantly. Without a figure it is thus: At first we may be only instrumental in communicating 5l. or 10l. or 20l. or 50l. or 100l. or 200l. per year, but afterwards double as much; and if we are still more faithful in our stewardship, after a year or two four times as much, afterwards perhaps eight times as much, at last perhaps twenty times or fifty times as much. We cannot limit the extent to which God may use us as instruments in communicating blessing, both temporal and spiritual, if we are willing to yield ourselves as instruments to the living God, and are content to be only instruments, and to give Him all the glory. But with regard to temporal things it will be thus, that if indeed we walk according to the mind of God in these things, whilst more and more we become instruments of blessing to others, we shall not seek to enrich ourselves, but be content when the last day of another year finds us still in the body, to possess no more than on the last day of the previous year, or even considerably less, whilst we have been, however, in the course of the year the instruments of communicating largely to others, through the means with which the Lord had intrusted us. As to my own soul, by the grace of God it would be a burden to me to find, that, however much my income in the course of a year might have been, I was increasing in earthly possession; for it would be a plain proof to me, that I had not been acting as steward for God, and had not been yielding myself as a channel for the waters of Gods bounty to pass through. I also cannot but bear my testimony here, that in whatever feeble measure God has enabled me to act according to these truths for the last fifty-one years and a half, I have found it to be profitable, most profitable to my own soul; and as to temporal things, I never was a loser in doing so, but I have most abundantly found the truth in II Cor. ix. 6, and Luke vi. 38, and Prov.

275

xi. 24, 25, verified in my own experience. I only have to
regret that I have acted so little according to what I have
now been stating; but my godly purpose is, by the help of
God, to spend the remainder of my days in practising these
truths more than ever, and I am sure, that, when I am
brought to the close of my earthly pilgrimage, either in
death, or by the appearing of our Lord Jesus, I shall not
have the least regret in having done so; and I know that
should I leave my dear child behind, the Lord will
abundantly provide for her, and prove that there has been a
better provision made for her than her father could have
made, if he had sought to insure his life or lay up money for
her.

Before leaving this part of the subject, I mention to the
believing reader, that I know instance upon instance, in
which what I have been saying has been verified, but I will
only mention the following:—I knew many years ago a
brother as the manager of a large manufactory. Whilst in
this capacity he was liberal, and giving away considerably
out of his rather considerable salary. The Lord repaid this to
him; for the principals of the establishment, well knowing
his value to their house of business, gave him now and then
whilst he thus was liberally using his means for the Lord,
very large presents in money. In process of time, however,
this brother thought it right to begin business on his own
account, in a very small way. He still continued to be liberal,
according to his means, and God prospered him, and
prospered him so, that now, whilst I am writing, his
manufactory is as large as the one which he formerly
managed, or even larger, though that was a very
considerable one. And sure I am, that, if this brother shall
be kept by God from setting his heart upon earthly things,
and from seeking more and more to increase his earthly
riches, but shall delight himself in being used as a steward

by God, cheerfully communicating to the need of Gods poor children, or to His work in other ways, and doing so not sparingly, but bountifully, the Lord will intrust him more and more with means; if otherwise, if he shut up his hands, seek his own, wish to obtain sufficient property that he may be able to live on his interest, then, what he has to expect is, that God will shut up His hands, he will meet with heavy losses, or there will be an alteration in his affairs for the worse, or the like.—I also mention two other cases, to show that the Lord increases our ability of communicating temporal blessings to others, if we distribute according to the means with which He has intrusted us, though we should not be in a trade or business, or profession.—I know a brother who many years ago saw it right not only to spend his interest for the Lord, but also the principal, as the Lord might point out to him opportunities. His desire was not, as indeed it ought never to be, to get rid of his money as fast as possible, yet he considered himself a steward for the Lord, and was therefore willing, as his Lord and Master might point it out to him, to spend his means. When this brother came to this determination, he possessed about twenty thousand pounds sterling. According to the light and grace, which the Lord had been pleased to give he afterwards acted, spending the money for the Lord, in larger or smaller sums, as opportunities were pointed out to him by the Lord. Thus the sum more and more decreased, whilst the brother steadily pursued his course, serving the Lord with his property, and spending his time and ability also for the Lord, in service of one kind or another among His children. At last the twenty thousand pounds were almost entirely spent, when at that very time the father of this brother died, whereby he came into the possession of an income of several thousand pounds a year. It gives joy to my heart to be able to add, that this brother still pursues his godly course, living in the most simple way, and giving away perhaps ten times as much as he spends on himself or family. Here you see, dear reader, that this brother, using faithfully for the Lord what he had been intrusted with at first, was made steward over more; for he has now more than one-third as much in a year coming in, as he at first possessed altogether. — I mention another instance: I know a brother to whom the Lord has given a liberal heart, and who bountifully gave of that over which the Lord had set him as steward. The Lord seeing this, intrusted him with still more, for through family circumstances he came into the possession of many thousand pounds, in addition to the considerable property he possessed before. I have the joy of being able to add also concerning this brother, that the Lord continues to give him grace to use his property as a steward for God, and that he has not been permitted to set his heart upon his riches, through the very considerable increase of his property, but that he continues to live as the steward of the Lord, and not as the owner of all this wealth. — And now, dear reader, when the brethren to whom I have been referring are brought to the close of their earthly pilgrimage, will they have one moments regret that they have used their property for the Lord? Will it be the least particle of uneasiness to their minds, or will their children be the worse for it? Oh no! The only regret they will have concerning this matter will be, that they did not serve the Lord still more abundantly with their property. Dear reader, let us each in our measure act in the same spirit. Money is really worth no more than as it is used according to the mind of the Lord; and life is worth no more than as it is spent in the service of the Lord.

Whilst the three mentioned points — 1, That our calling must be of that nature that we can abide in it with God; 2, That unto the Lord we should labour in our calling, as His servants, because He has bought us with His blood, and

278

because He will have us to labour; 3, That as stewards we should labour in our calling, because the earnings of our calling are the Lords and not our own, as He has bought us with His blood: I say, whilst these three points are particularly to be attended to in order that the Lords blessing may rest upon our calling, and we be prospering in it, there are, nevertheless, some other points to be attended to, which I mention in love to my brethren in the Lord, by whom they may be needed. 4, The next point is, that a believer in the Lord Jesus should do nothing in his calling, which is purely for the sake of attracting the world, such as for instance, fitting up his shop or rooms of business in the most costly manner, I do not in the least mean to say that his shop or rooms of business should not be clean, orderly, and of such a character as that there may be no positive hinderance to persons going there. All the needful conveniences that are expected may be there and ought to be there. But if any child of God seek to have the front of his shop, or the interior of his shop, or of his place of business fitted up in a most expensive way, simply for the sake of attracting attention, then let him be aware, that, just in so far as he is trusting in these things, he is not likely to succeed in his calling, because he puts the manner of sitting up the shop in the room of trust in the Lord. Such things the Lord may allow to succeed in the case of an unbeliever, but they will not prosper in the case of a child of God, except it be in the way of chastisement, just as the Lord gave to Israel in the wilderness the desire of their hearts, but sent leanness into their souls. Should any brother have fallen into this error, the first thing he has to do, when the Lord has instructed him concerning this point, is, to make confession of sin, and, as far as it can be done, to retrace his steps in this particular. If this cannot be done, then to cast himself upon the mercy of God in Christ Jesus. 5, Of the same character is: To seek to attract the attention of the world, by "boasting advertisements," such as "no one manufactures so good an article," "no one sells this article so cheap," "we sell the best article in the city," etc. Suppose these statements were quite correct, yet they are unbecoming for a child of God, who has the living God to care for him and to provide for him, and therefore needs not to make use of such boasting, whereby he may seek to ensure custom to himself and keep it from others. The law of love is, "Whatsoever ye would that men should do to you, do ye even so to them." Matt. vii. 12. Now what do I wish in this particular that others should do to me, but that they should not seek to keep away persons from dealing with me; but if I use such like expressions in my advertisements, as have been mentioned, what do they imply but, that I wish all people should come to me, and deal with me. If, however, already under the old covenant it was said, "Thou shalt not covet," how much more sinful and altogether unbecoming is it for us children of God, who are in fellowship with the Father and the Son, to make use of such means, in order to ensure to ourselves pecuniary advantages. But, however much the Lord may allow a man of the world to prosper in using such means, they are only hinderances to the child of God to getting on in his calling, because the Lord sees that they are substituted instead of trust in Himself; and should the Lord for a season allow His child apparently to be benefited by them, it will only be for his chastisement and connected with leanness in his soul. Therefore, my brethren in the Lord, I beseech you to put away all these things out of your calling, lest you should be hindering instead of furthering your real welfare. 6, Likewise of a similar character is the following point, which God may suffer to be a real hinderance to His children in their calling, it is, To seek the very best, (and therefore the most expensive) situations which can be had in a town or city. Now I do by no means intend to say, that in our trade, business, art, or profession, we should seek the most obscure, retired, out of the way place possible, and say, "God will provide, and I need not mind in what part of the town I carry on my calling." There are most assuredly certain things to be considered. The persons who are likely to buy the articles I sell, or employ me, are to be considered, and I have not to say, it matters nothing to me, whether I make them come a mile or two to my house, or to the most dirty and disagreeable part of the town; this would be the extreme in the other way. But whilst there is a certain consideration to be used with reference to those who may employ us in our calling, yet if the trust of the child of God respecting temporal prosperity is in the fact that he lives in the best situation, the Lord will surely disappoint him. He will have to pay a very high rent for the best situation, and yet not succeed, because his trust is in the best situation. He is substituting it for dependence upon the living God for customers. He is robbing his soul not only in not taking the customers as from the hands of the Lord, but he is also obliging his heavenly Father, in the very love of His heart, to cause him to be disappointed, because he is not trusting in Him. If the child of God were saying and acting thus: the best situation would cost me 50l. a year more rent, than one which is not really inconvenient for my customers, nor in an improper neighbourhood, and the like, this 50l. I dedicate unto the Lord, to be paid in instalments for His work, or His poor saints, whenever the rent day comes, such a brother would find himself to be no loser, if this indeed were done in dependence upon the Lord, and constrained by the love of Jesus. But if the 50l. more is paid for rent, and yet the living God, in the very love of His heart, should be obliged to withhold prosperity from His child in His calling, because He sees that he is laying undue stress upon the situation of the house, then not only the 50l. extra rent per year is lost, but also that which the Lord is obliged to withhold from His child besides, in order to teach him the lesson; and thus year after year, by our own fault, we may have scarcely any thing to give for the work of God. 7, The next obstacle to prosperity in our calling which I now would mention is, That children of God often use such expressions as these with reference to their calling: "this is our busy time," or "this is our dead time," which implies that they do not day after day deal with God about their calling, but that they ascribe their having much or little to do to circumstances, or to times and seasons. That the people of the world should do so is not to be wondered at; but that the children of God should act thus, who in the most minute affairs of life should seek the help of God, and deal with God about them, is a matter of sorrow to the spiritual mind, and is altogether unbecoming saints. But what is the result. The Lord, according to the expectations of His children, allows them to be without employment, because they say, "this is our dead season." "He did not many mighty works there because of their unbelief," contains a truth which comes in here. But what is the right way of looking at the matter? It is this: the child of God should say, though generally about this time of the year there is little employment to be expected, looking at it naturally, yet as a want of employment is neither good for the outward nor inward man, and as I only desire employment to serve God in my business, to have to give to those who are in need, or help in other ways the work of God, I will now give myself to prayer for employment, for I can by prayer and faith, as a child of God, obtain blessings from my heavenly Father, though not in the ordinary course of things. If thus the child of God were to say and to act, he would soon have employment in his calling, except the Lord meant to use his time otherwise in His work, which He would point out to him. 8, A further reason, why God may be obliged to resist children of God in their business, may be this, that they with the greatest carefulness seek to obtain persons for their shop who are considered "good salesmen," i.e. persons who have such persuasive ways, as that they gain an advantage over the customers and induce them not only to buy articles for which they ask, whether suitable or not, but that they also induce them to buy articles which they did not at all intend to buy when they came to the shop. Concerning this I notice in the first place, that if the child of God puts his dependence upon the "good salesmen," let him not be surprised if his heavenly Father should be obliged to disappoint him, because He sees His child lean upon the arm of flesh, instead of trusting in the living God; and therefore the business does not succeed. Further, it is altogether wrong for a child of God to induce the customers, by means of such men or women who have a persuasive tongue, to purchase articles whether they suit or not, and whether they are needed or not. This is no less than defrauding persons in a subtle way, or leading them into the sin of purchasing beyond their means, or at least spending their money needlessly. However such sinful tricks may be allowed to prosper in the case of a man of the world, in the case of a child of God they will not prosper, except God allow them to do so in the way of chastisement, whilst leanness and wretchedness is brought into the soul. I knew a case of this kind where it was the whole bent of the mind of a professed believer to obtain such "good salesmen," and where even a Jew was kept outside the shop walking up and down to induce persons to come in and buy; and yet that same professed believer failed twice in his business. 9, Another evil with reference to business, and why children of God do not get on in their calling is, that they enter upon business often without any capital at all, or with too little. If a believer has no capital at all, or only a very small capital, in comparison with what his business requires, then, ought

283

he not to say this to himself: "If it were my heavenly Fathers will that I should enter upon business on my own account, then would He not somehow or other have intrusted me with the needful means? And since He has not, is it not a plain indication that, for the present, I should remain a journeyman, (or shopman, or clerk, as the case may be)?" In a variety of ways the means might come. For instance, a legacy might be left to him, or money might be given to him by a brother in the Lord for that very purpose, or a brother or sister might propose to the individual to lend him money, yet so that if he were unable to pay it again, they would not consider him their debtor, or in many other ways God might intrust him with means But if in some such way the Lord did not remove the hinderance, and the brother would still go into business, he would, through the bill system and other things connected with the want of capital, not only bring great distress into his mind, and subject himself to the possibility of at last being unable to pay his creditors, whereby dishonour would be brought upon the name of the Lord, but he likewise could not be surprised (as he went into business contrary to the will of God, since He pointed out to him that he was not to do so for want of means,) if he should find that he cannot get on, and that the blessing of God manifestly is wanting. In such a case as this, if it can be done, the retracing our steps is the best thing we can do; but often this cannot be done, as others are involved in the matter, and then we have to make acknowledgment of our sin, and seek Gods merciful help to bring us into a right position. 10, But suppose all these nine previous points were attended to, and we neglected to seek Gods blessing upon our calling, we need still not be surprised if we met with difficulty upon difficulty, and could not get on at all. It is not enough that we seek Gods help for that which manifestly is of a spiritual character; but we should seek His help and blessing by prayer and supplication for all our ordinary concerns in life, and if we neglect doing so, we shall surely suffer for the neglect. "Trust in the Lord with all thine heart; and lean not unto thine own understanding. In all thy ways acknowledge Him, and He shall direct thy paths." Prov. iii. 5, 6.

These few remarks I commend affectionately to the prayerful consideration of all brethren and sisters in the Lord with reference to their calling; for though they are written by one who never was in business himself, yet the truths therein set forth have been learned by him in the school of God, and he has had them abundantly confirmed through his pastoral labours during the last fifty-one years.

And now, farewell, beloved reader. — Very many times have I sought the Lords blessing before I began preparing this third part for the press, and very many times have I done so while writing it, and now I am most fully assured, that He will abundantly bless this part also, because of the abundance of supplication which He has wrought concerning it by His Spirit in my soul. I ask you also, dear reader, if you know the power of prayer, to unite with me in seeking the Lords blessing upon this book, and then we shall rejoice together in the answers to our prayers, if not here on earth, at least in the day of Christs appearing.

[In 1856 was published the Fourth Part of this Narrative, as a second volume.]

END OF THE THIRD PART

1. My Journal gives the names of the individuals, whom the Lord has used as instruments, in supplying our wants; but it has appeared well to me, for several reasons, not to

mention them in print.

2. One bill I had to meet for a brother, the other was for money which in the form of a bill I had sent to the Continent; but in both cases the money was in my hands, before the bills were given.

3. At the beginning the name was, The Scriptural Knowledge Society for Home and Abroad;" but as the Institution was never a Society in the common sense of the word, there being nothing like membership, voting, a committee, &c., it appeared afterwards better to alter the name as above stated, for the sake of avoiding mistakes. I mention, moreover, that in this eighth edition the Institution is spoken of in the way in which it is now existing, without further notice of the alterations which have been made since its establishment on March 5, 1834, as its original character is substantially the same.

4. Only two Orphans were received under such circumstances. Since 1841 we have had no child on such conditions, as we now consider, that, if a relative would be able and willing to pay the average expense for the support of a child, such an Orphan could not be considered destitute. During the summer of 1855, thee Orphans were applied for, and their relatives offered to pay 50l. a year for these children to the funds of the Institution. They were, however, not only not received, but their names were not even entered on the list of those who are waiting for admission, as they could not be considered destitute. Our object is not to obtain funds for the Institution, but to provide by means of it for truly destitute Orphans hence, though 50l. is more than the average expense for three Orphans in a year, we did not receive those three just referred to.

5. The Schoolmasters, as well as the clergymen, in Prussia, are connected with the State.

6. We continued for many months to break bread only at Bethesda, till at last, though it is a large chapel, the body of it was no longer large enough to accommodate all who were in communion with us, so that we were obliged to have the Lords supper in two places. [Note to the second edition.]

7. Since February, 1849, I hare been obliged to discontinue my walks in the fields entirely, on account of a weakness in my right foot.

8. This little charity business was commenced in connexion with the church assembling at Bethesda and Salem Chapels, Bristol, for the purpose of seeking to provide employment for the poor believers, especially the poor sisters, when they were without work.

9. The evening before my departure, I had invited a number of believers to tea, to spend some time together in prayer, reading the Holy Scriptures, and in intercourse on spiritual subjects.

10. These were the expenses in 1850 and 1851; but, on account of the high price of almost everything now, in 1856, the average expenses of one day are. 12l. or upwards, for the support of the Orphans.

11. Preaching Tours and Missionary Labours of George Müller (of
Bristol.) By Mrs. Mulller. 1883. London: J. Nisbet and Co., Berners
Street. Price 3s. 6d. To be had also at the Bible and Tract Warehouse; at the Scriptural Knowledge Institution for Home and

Abroad, No. 34, Park Street; and through all book-sellers.

12. This third volume is still in print. Published by W. Mack, 38, Park Street, Bristol.

13. The Funeral Sermon was afterwards preached and published, and is still in print.

www.ingramcontent.com/pod-product-compliance
Lightning Source LLC
Chambersburg PA
CBHW030618030726
47497CB00006B/1544